HEA

Norah
very v
quality of insistent readability which
has made her novels so widely read
and admired. Whether she is writing of
childhood, as in the title story, or of the
occult, as in THE BLACK CHRIST
OF ADLERWALD, Norah Lofts has
the reader's attention from start to
finish . . .

Also by Norah Lofts

JASSY
THE BRITTLE GLASS
A CALF FOR VENUS
QUEEN IN WAITING
SCENT OF CLOVES
THE LUTEPLAYER
BLESS THIS HOUSE
THE DEVIL IN CLEVELY
OUT OF THIS NETTLE
TO SEE A FINE LADY
THE ROAD TO REVELATION
HESTER ROON
MADSELIN
I MET A GYPSY
HERE WAS A MAN
BLOSSOM LIKE THE ROSE
WHITE HELL OF PITY
THE LOST QUEEN
HOW FAR TO BETHLEHEM
THE CONCUBINE
REQUIEM FOR IDOLS

The House Trilogy
THE TOWN HOUSE
THE HOUSE AT OLD VINE
THE HOUSE AT SUNSET

Norah Lofts writing as Peter Curtis
DEAD MARCH IN THREE KEYS
YOU'RE BEST ALONE
THE LITTLE WAX DOLL

and published by Corgi Books

Norah Lofts

Heaven In Your Hand
and other stories

CORGI BOOKS
A DIVISION OF TRANSWORLD PUBLISHERS LTD
A NATIONAL GENERAL COMPANY

HEAVEN IN YOUR HAND

A CORGI BOOK 0 552 09105 7

Originally published in Great Britain by
Michael Joseph Ltd.

PRINTING HISTORY
Michael Joseph edition published 1959
Corgi edition published 1972

This book is set in 10pt Plantin

Corgi Books are published by Transworld Publishers Ltd.,
Cavendish House, 57–59 Uxbridge Road, Ealing, London, W.5.
Made and printed in Great Britain by
Cox & Wyman Ltd., London, Reading and Fakenham

NOTE: The Australian price appearing on the back cover is the recommended retail price.

CONTENTS

HEAVEN IN YOUR HAND

MY mother had a pretty sister, Emily, who had made a very good marriage and lived in a grand big house about ten minutes' walk away from the one we occupied. My father had died young, leaving Mother with six of us, the eldest only twelve; and since this was long before the days of widows' pensions and children's allowances, we were – not to put too fine a point upon it – beggarly hard up. But the bond between my mother and my aunt was, in its way, pretty strong, and as a consequence I was frequently cast into the company of my cousin Dorothy and spent a good deal of my ninth and tenth years in bitter envy.

Dorothy, an only child, was just a month younger than I, and since life had already taught me to conceal my inner feelings, I was regarded as eminently suitable company for the pampered little girl. My younger sister – a far nicer character – was too young; my elder – a far more sensible child – was too old; my three brothers, seldom in agreement, were unanimous in their loathing of their cousin, but I seemed just to fit. I went to play and to have tea at the big house at least once a week, was asked to parties, was once taken for a whole bitter-sweet month to the seaside, and for years and years had no clothes save the expensive and occasionally unsuitable ones which Aunt Emily in her kindness handed on to me every time Dorothy, who had outgrown me, had a new outfit.

I chanced, by nature, to be neither grateful nor sycophantic and although nobody guessed the truth, the situation often rankled in me. In fact, I think that my very soul might have become warped but for something which happened on Dorothy's tenth birthday.

My own had been celebrated a month earlier. Mother, who was just then starting her tea-shop (which later prospered moderately) forgot all about it until the day. Reminded, she did provide a good tea, with cucumber sandwiches and cakes from the shop, and she promised me a new hair ribbon. I was the champion loser of hair ribbons in my generation and they were not always replaced with good humour. My little sister spent a long-hoarded penny on a form of confectionery known as aniseed balls, which anyone old enough to have sampled will remember with affection – they were forty a penny, believe it or not; and my brother Fred allowed me, as a signal honour, to ride for ten minutes on the bicycle which had recently been purchased, at staggering cost, to enable him to attend a school, six miles away, to which he had won a scholarship.

And that was my birthday.

Aunt Emily, if she had been at home, would doubtless have come down with something handsome, probably ten shillings which Mother would promptly have confiscated and devoted to the common cause of keeping us all fed and clothed; but Aunt Emily was away on a visit and had forgotten me too.

A month later I was invited to Dorothy's birthday party. It was a perfect June afternoon and I wore, I remember, a white *broiderie anglais* dress with blue ribbon threaded through the yoke and hem. I would much have preferred to go in my school clothes, for the white dress had been Dorothy's last year and I hated wearing her dresses in her company. However, Mother had washed and ironed the dress and my elder sister had threaded in the ribbon and I hadn't the heart to mention my ungracious preference.

The big house was full of flowers, and full of people – girls from Dorothy's school (which was not mine) and their mothers. The mothers wore smart, garden-party toilettes, the girls frilly party frocks. The tea was magnificent, masses and masses of strawberries, with sugar in silver shakers and thick yellow cream in silver jugs, sandwiches of every kind, ice cream on little glass plates and several indescribably elaborate cakes, including an enormous iced one with ten candles atop.

But what impressed me most was the number of the presents. Dorothy's playroom, where they were all laid out for inspection, looked like a shop. In my foolishness I had thought that Dorothy already possessed everything possible, but money and ingenuity had triumphed and presents had been found. Her mother had given her a little desk and chair for her room, they were painted blue and decorated with wreaths of flowers. Her father had contributed a new bicycle. Some foresighted friend had sent a pair of skates. There was a tennis racket. There was some writing paper with a big blue 'D' at the top of each page; there was a fountain pen, and of course many dolls and dolls' appurtenances. In all there were sixty presents. All new, expensive and covetable. Sixty of them!

I was a child, as greedy and shallow-minded, as ignorant of real values, as deeply prey to the lust of the eye as all children are. I looked round at the display and felt quite sick with envy and – I admit – self-pity. I felt so ill that I had to remind myself harshly that I had eaten an enormous tea and that it would do me good to run about in the garden. So I threw myself heartily into the games and soon felt better and achieved that state of joyous abandon which had gained me the reputation of being such good company– but the moment the games stopped I remembered all those presents and thought about my hair ribbon, which had not materialized, and the aniseed balls and the ride on the bike. I felt sick again. Envy may be one of the deadly sins, it is certainly a deadly physical pain.

The party drew to its end; a few fathers came and were taken off to have drinks in the study; mothers began to collect their daughters. I would gladly have taken myself and my puling misery away, but Aunt Emily had whispered that if I waited she would send home some of the birthday cake for what she always called 'The Others'. I couldn't deny them that treat. So I waited and presently Dorothy and I found ourselves alone together in the play-room.

She stood by the window and I went to have another painful look at the dolls. There was a moody silence and I knew that it was up to me – as usual – to dispel it. I had been asked to the party, I was wearing her dress, I was going home laden with cake. So I turned and said brightly:

'Well, has it been a happy birthday?'

'It was all right. Connie couldn't come.'

She sounded so miserable that I felt a little pang of pity. I also had my very special friends and attributing a similar placing of affection to Dorothy I could see that the whole day, all the presents, might well be ruined by the absence of the chosen one.

'I noticed that,' I said. 'Why couldn't she come?'

Dorothy began to twirl the end of her sash; she said, in a voice of surprising bitterness:

'She's gone to Italy!'

'To live?'

'No. For a *holiday*. Mustn't that be lovely? Oh, I do *long* to go to Italy, don't you?'

It was a matter I had never considered. Italy, to me, was a piece of land shaped like a leg, a leg for ever kicking a football which was Sicily. Our geography mistress had offered that idea as an aid to our memories. The idea of *visiting* a place on a map had never occurred to me, but asked whether I would like to do so, I could only say that I would.

'Well, Connie's there now. We're just going to Thorpeness, as usual.' She spoke with contempt of the place where we had had that happy holiday. I knew that I ought to say, 'What a shame!' or 'Thorpeness is nice,' or 'Couldn't you ask your parents to take you to Italy instead?' but my eyes had wandered back to the dolls and I couldn't even *pretend* to sympathize with their owner.

You see, I had once had a doll. Her name was Susan and I had adored her. But at least two years ago my little sister had borrowed and dropped her and smashed her pretty china face. I had cried and Mother, busy and worried had snapped at me, 'Fancy crying about a doll! A great girl of eight! You're too big for dolls anyway. Wash your face and run to Foster's and fetch the sausages.'

That was my Susan's epitaph.

I was looking at Dorothy's dolls and thinking my sour thoughts when Aunt Emily came dancing in carrying an enormous white cardboard box tied up with red ribbons. I have so often remembered her way of making charitable gesture with grace. I did not know, of course, but the disease which was in four years to kill her and which was responsible for much of her beauty, was already upon her. Her eyes were brighter than anybody's; she looked flushed and lovely. She put the box into my hands and kissed me. She smelt like a flower and the kiss was like a butterfly's passing. I felt better and when she asked, 'Have you enjoyed yourself, darling,' I was able to say, quite heartily, 'Yes thank you, it was a *lovely* party.' She smiled at me and went and took one of Dorothy's long glossy curls between her fingers.

'To think,' she said, 'my little girl is ten years old.' Dorothy jerked her head free. I stood and stared. I simply could not avoid comparisons. Two years ago I had been 'a great girl of eight', Dorothy, at ten, was 'my little girl'. I did understand about circumstances, being poor and always too busy and having six children and no husband. Nevertheless . . .

'I think I must go now,' I said.

Aunt Emily turned to me with a smile which changed to a look of dismay.

'But darling,' she said, 'you're ten, too. You had your birthday while I was away and I forgot! Oh, I am so sorry!'

She turned to Dorothy who still stood sulking in the window.

'Darling, you've got such masses of things. Really all day I've been wondering where we were going to put them. And we missed Ennie's birthday. Wouldn't you like to give her something now?'

My heart froze. The sick feeling came back, worse than ever. My face went hot and stiff. The savage independence which was going to be such a trouble to me later on in life laid hold of me.

'I don't want anything, Aunt Emily, thank you,' I said.

'Rubbish,' said my aunt, 'of course you must have something. Look at what she has. What does any little girl want with two dolls' houses, for instance. Ennie, would you like the old doll's house?'

And where, in our crowded home would I put it, even if Mother would believe that I had brought it for my little sister. I said, with what I hope was dignity:

'No thank you, Aunt Emily.'

'A doll then,' she persisted.

She had found my weakness. I did most dreadfully want a doll. Even pride could not make me deny that.

'I . . . would . . . like . . . a doll,' I said, dragging out the shameful confession.

'Darling,' cried Aunt Emily in a tone of delight, 'did you *hear* that? Ennie would like a doll. Which can you spare?'

Twiddling her sash, not turning her head, Dorothy said:

'Any of them. All of them.'

Aunt Emily looked a little disconcerted, but she was used to her daughter.

'There you are then,' she said to me, 'take your choice.'

And with that I must needs go proud again. It was damnable of me. She meant so well, she was so pretty and kind and I loved her. When she died I cried a good deal in secret at the memory of that one moment. For I looked round and deliberately, poisonously, chose the smallest doll there. It was a tiny china doll, no more than three inches long and naked save for a little skirt of raffia and a minute string of beads. It looked very humble lying between two large dolls, one dressed in gay peasant dress, one in bridal array.

'I'd like this one,' I said.

'But it's such a scrap, almost nothing,' Aunt Emily cried. 'Are you *sure*, darling. Dorothy doesn't mind which one you have. She doesn't *really* care for dolls at all. Have this one, Ennie, or this.' She touched the bride, and another one, fat and dimpled in baby clothes.

'I like little things,' I said, rather sternly. But I made no move to take it. Aunt Emily had to lift it and put it into my hand.

Immediately something happened inside me. As my fingers closed about the little doll's body I experienced that sense of rightness, of completeness, of complete belonging that comes only once or twice in a lifetime. A great flood of happiness broke over my heart, washing away all self-pity, all envy and malice. I knew in a flash that the choice I had made in blind anger was the right, the only one. Anything bigger would have been an embarrassment; the little doll could be carried in my pocket, go with me to school, be tucked under my pillow. No one need know about her; I need share her with no one. She was my doll, made, destined for me.

Perfectly, almost crazily happy, I walked home through the golden June evening, one hand carrying the box of cake, the other curved about the little doll. As I walked I indulged in vast, positively philosophical thoughts – the first of a lifetime. I saw Dorothy in a new light. With all she had, she was still hungry for more, sulkily longing for Italy, that leg of land kicking the ball that was Sicily; I had satisfaction here within my bent fingers. And I knew something, something which, after all these years, still seems to me as true and important as it did then.

Heaven isn't something 'that lies about us in our infancy' and then is lost; nor is it something to be attained by the exercise of impossible virtues. Heaven is something that you can hold in your hand.

GOING DOWNHILL TOGETHER

MRS. CLAYTON was probably the most envied woman in Waterbury. Quite young women said that they envied her figure, so slim, so upright, so altogether elegant; people who were a little unsure of their own, envied her her unquestioned social position and the gentle dignity with which she upheld it; those who had never seen her kitchen envied her her beautiful Georgian house; every matron in Waterbury envied her Sarah.

Sarah was a museum piece, a proper, professional domestic servant of a type once said to be common, now almost extinct. (Captivity has had a similar effect upon other breeds.) She was a woman of medium height, stocky, strong and active as a pony. Her broad, highly-coloured face always shone from the latest application of soap and water, her only-just-grizzled hair was brushed back severely and secured in a knob which no exertion could disturb. She owned four of what the Bible calls 'changes of raiment'. When she went shopping in the morning she wore, whatever the weather, an ancient brown Burberry and a shapeless blue felt hat; if she opened the door to you before lunch you might view, with an antiquarian's interest, a striped print dress, apron and starched cap; after lunch she donned the traditional black and white parlourmaid's garb, and her cap was streamered; on Sunday evening, when she attended Evensong in the Cathedral, she wore a long black coat of undateable cut and a small black hat of hard straw with a bunch of black and white daisies placed dead centre of its front.

Sarah was sixty-one, five years younger than her mistress. They had lived in the same house for forty years, Mrs. Clayton entering it as bride, carried over the doorstep, Sarah by the back door, carrying a wicker hold-all, at twenty-one already a trained housemaid, capable of cooking on the cook's rare holidays and of acting as parlourmaid should occasion arise. Since that time there had been two wars and a bloodless revolution, and now Sarah was the only full-time, trained, resident domestic help in the whole of Waterbury and for miles outside it. Small wonder that other women, struggling along with the intermittent, heavily-bribed, often arrogant help of displaced persons, cretins, and distressed gentlewomen should envy Mrs. Clayton.

Mrs. Clayton did not seem to be unduly aware of her luck. She did not even regard it as remarkable that since the outbreak of the Hitler War, Sarah had run the big, unmodernized house with no other help than that of an old woman in whose activities even the Ministry of Labour took no interest. Naturally everything had changed, one no longer entertained, half the house was shut up, and Sarah seemed perfectly happy and contented. She earned good wages too; very good wages because, with each depletion of staff Sarah had offered, for some slight increase of pay, to shoulder the work of the departing one. She now earned fifty shillings a week, and often when Mrs. Clayton handed over the sum, she thought what a very long time it was since she herself had had even half that amount to spend as pocket money in a single week.

Mrs. Clayton's financial story had been told all too often. Pass lightly over the dismal account of investments becoming worthless, of taxes rising, of dividends dwindling and the cost of living soaring. Until 1935, when her husband died, Mrs. Clayton had led a sheltered life; John had often grumbled, but never in a way that either worried or enlightened her; it had been a great shock to her, after his death, to learn how poor she was. She had faced the situation with courage, and, she would have said, with resource. Bit by bit, without a word to anyone, she had sold all her jewellery, reserving only the half hoop of diamonds which was her engagement ring and a string of pearls – John's wedding present. They were the only things she wore regularly. She was a little disappointed by the prices she obtained, but she had been able to go on paying bills for some years and to have a few absolutely essential repairs done to the roof.

Later on she had sold pieces of furniture. Most of it had been in the house for two hundred years – the Claytons were a conservative family – and there was a great demand for antiques. It was a little unfortunate that many of the best pieces were in her drawing-room, the place where she received her friends. She had been driven to tell a few lies. The Dutch marquetry bureau, for example, she said had been sent as a wedding present to a *very* favourite god-daughter; the delightful little Queen Anne writing table had been lent to an old friend who was starting a business in reproductions and needed models. A great deal of silver stuff and a very valuable Chelsea clock, with some matching figures, had been, she said, put away to save work. She had volunteered these explanations to her friends, and to Sarah, and her unruffled manner, her sweet voice and candid blue-eyed glance had concealed completely her inward consciousness of a lost integrity, of a mounting fear. What next? There is a limit to which even a treasure house can be looted.

It so happened that Mrs. Clayton had reached this limit when two things happened. The gas and the electricity bills arrived. The Government had lately taken control of these services and appeared to have doubled their charges. While Mrs. Clayton was staring in dismay at the sums demanded, Sarah came in.

'Can I speak to you a minute, ma'am?'

'Certainly, Sarah.'

'Old Agnes, you know she been ill and away this last fortnight.'

'Poor thing, yes. Is she worse?'

'They took her to the Workhouse.' The name was obsolete; everyone nowadays referred to the institution as St. Giles' Hospital, but Sarah never had any time for euphemisms.

'Oh dear, I am sorry. Perhaps one day, Sarah, you could find time to make her a little sponge cake, or something nice, and I'd take it up. They allow visitors, I suppose.'

Sarah ignored this irrelevance.

'The thing is, I can't get another woman. I knew by the look of her she was a doner, so I been asking round and there ain't another charwoman to be had. So what I was going to suggest was, I do her work for the same money. I'd do it proper, the house shouldn't suffer.'

'I'm quite sure of that, Sarah.' Mrs. Clayton's eye caught a glimpse of those two shocking, unprecedented bills and suddenly she felt that she could no longer bear this thing in secret. 'The truth is, Sarah, that I don't think I can afford to pay you any more. I seriously wonder whether I can afford you at all.'

The delicate pink of her envied complexion deepened as she spoke these terrible words, and it was with a slight effort that she brought her glance up to meet Sarah's. Later on she remembered the most curious look which, for a moment, rested on Sarah's face ... satisfaction? achievement? triumph? ... it was gone before it could be identified.

'You,' Sarah said, 'hard up, ma'am. Dear me, I am sorry to hear that.' The tone was exactly right, respectful, regretful, slightly shocked.

'Money,' said Mrs. Clayton, as though explaining to a child, 'has lost its value. An income perfectly adequate for my needs even twenty years ago is now no use at all.'

'Not with brussel sprouts ninepence a pound,' agreed Sarah, giving, by concrete example, proof that she understood. 'If you ask me, ma'am, your best way'd be to give up this great house and buy something small and cosy.'

'That wouldn't help,' said Mrs. Clayton, with a small smile and a shake of her head. 'Nobody wants to buy a house this size, except for offices, and very cheap. The smallest house would cost about three times as much as I should get for this. I know, Sarah; I have actually asked about it.'

'Well, we gotta do *something*,' Sarah said, and she stood for a moment, looking very thoughtful.

An absurd thought flashed into Mrs. Clayton's mind. This was where, in an old-fashioned novel, the good faithful servant would say that her wages didn't matter; that she had her little nest egg and that as long as she could stand on two feet she would be at her mistress's service.

And that was exactly what Sarah did say, though not in such flowery phrases.

She said, 'Don't you fret about my wages, ma'am. I've always been a saving woman. And my brother left me that little old cottage over in Church Lane. I let that, with all his stuff, just as it stood and that brings me two pounds a week. So if that suit you I'd be right happy to stay here and not take your money. *And* look after you and see you comfortable just the same.'

Mrs Clayton felt the tears stinging in her eyes.

'Oh Sarah, what a generous offer ... but I couldn't possibly ...'

'Now don't take it like that. If you ask me thass time we knew where we stand. Funny times these are, and you ain't the first to feel the rub. This ...' she looked around the room in which everything was shabby, or faded and yet elegant, 'is all the home I ever had. You and me ain't going to fall out over fifty bob a week when you need it and I don't, I should hope.'

Mrs. Clayton recovered a little.

'I would see that you didn't suffer by it, Sarah. It's a little difficult to explain because I don't suppose you know about capital and income. I have some money . . . I could sell some shares, but this is a bad time to do it, and then, when I'd spent the money I should be even worse off. I have gone into that. But if we made this . . . this arrangement, I would alter my will. Instead of having fifty shillings a week you'd have a lump sum when I was dead.'

Sarah, whose grasp of financial matters much excelled Mrs. Clayton's, preserved a carefully blank face.

'Don't you talk about dying,' she said. 'Thass unlucky. We don't want to think about dying, we got years ahead of us, all happy and cosy. You'll see. Now, if you'll excuse me, I left something on the stove . . .'

Back in the dark, cavernous kitchen she gloated over her bargain. She always had intended to retire at sixty, but there was the problem of finding accommodation, the fear of loneliness, and a genuine reluctance to leave Mrs. Clayton of whom she was very fond. That was all settled now; in a few words she had made a bargain . . . a good bargain.

In the drawing-room Mrs. Clayton, without gloating, knew relief. Fifty shillings a week would make a great deal of difference in her narrow budget. Now she could hold on to those Malayan Tin shares until they had regained at least part of their value. And tomorrow she would make her will; Sarah should have everything, even the ring and the pearls. John would understand . . .

It is always a little difficult to pinpoint the precise moment when decay in any human relationship sets in. The process is subtle, active for some time before it becomes visible. There was, for instance, the question of afternoon dress; Sarah, neat, profoundly respectable in her Sunday evening alpaca, with a locket and chain and a cameo brooch, could not be regarded as 'unsuitably dressed', but it was uncomfortably like having a stranger in the house. There was also the matter of shopping. Mrs. Clayton, once or twice a week, walked into the town centre, and always, beforehand, she went into the kitchen and said, 'I'm going out this morning, Sarah. Is there anything we need?' Sarah had done her own errands on the other mornings. But the morning came when she said, in answer to the routine question:

'I'd like my book changed.' She handed to Mrs. Clayton a book, young in years but old in experience; greasy hands had held it, wet cups had ringed its cover, its odour suggested that strange things had been used as book-markers.

'And I'd be obliged,' Sarah said, 'if you'd tell that girl I'm due for *Death in a Split Second*, I put my name down ever so long ago.'

Well aware that Sarah had made hundreds of visits to Boots' Library on her behalf Mrs. Clayton was ashamed of the reluctance with which she undertook this simple errand, and of the dislike she felt both for the title of the book she must speak, and for handling it when it was offered. In the not very distant past it had been in close contact with a parcel of fish and chips.

Such trivialities were, however, soon lost sight of in the more serious problem of the dining-room stove. It was one of the slow combustion types and it had, for a long time, been so regulated that its combustion was very slow indeed; it warmed a tiny area of the large room, just behind Mrs. Clayton's Hepplewhite chair, and that was all she asked of it. On a very cold evening, about ten days after Sarah and Mrs. Clayton had struck their bargain, the stove began belching out such thick black clouds of smoke that the dining-room became untenable.

'That need the sweep,' Sarah said. 'If you ask me he didn't half clean it last time he come. Best thing for you to do is come and eat your dinner in my room.'

At half past seven Mrs. Clayton made her way along the stone passage and into the room opposite the kitchen. It was very bright and cheerful and made her think of pictures on calendars, and also, for some reason, of 'The Cottar's Saturday Night'. A good fire burned in the high-hobbed, old fashioned grate, a tabby cat lay curled on the gay rug on the hearth. There was a potted plant on the window-sill and above it hung a canary in a cage. There was one comfortable chair and a wireless set – neither of them, Mrs. Clayton realized, with a pang of compunction – of her providing.

A small round table stood well within range of the fire; it was spread with a cloth, almost aggressively clean, checked in red and blue. In the centre was an ornament, a green girl, made of plastic, quite naked and leaning negligently over a pool of water in which a few Michaelmas daisies floated. The table was laid with two places and Sarah, entering with two plates of soup said:

'I thought you wouldn't mind me having mine at the same time.'

'But of course not. It's very kind of you to take pity on me,' Mrs. Clayton said.

There was something rather touching, she thought, in the way Sarah played the part of hostess, conscientiously making conversation. She showed a regrettable tendency to talk as she chewed, and she chewed with remarkable vigour. She lifted a gravy-dripping knife and pointed to the canary:

'Look at Dicky, all excited to have company. If you ask me he finds it a bit lonely here, with just me.'

'He's very sweet,' Mrs. Clayton said. 'With him and the cat you have quite a family, Sarah.'

'Well, barring my brother I never had none of my own, and we wasn't close, not till his last illness. In a manner of speaking I've always looked on *you* as my family, and I'm sure, when Master John died, I . . .'

'Oh, I know, Sarah . . .' Don't intrude, don't tread there, please. Even to her most intimate friend Mrs. Clayton had never spoken easily of her bereavements.

Sarah was willing to change the subject.

'Isn't this cosy?' she asked, glancing around the room.

'Very cosy,' Mrs. Clayton agreed. 'But Sarah, you shouldn't have bought yourself a chair. The house is full of chairs. If only you'd asked . . .'

'Never ask for anything you can get for yourself, thass my motto,' said Sarah bluntly. 'Now I'll make your coffee. I always have tea myself.'

There was a challenge there.

'Oh, no, Sarah. Please don't bother. I should enjoy a cup of tea for a change.'

'It's cheaper,' Sarah said. She cleared the table, brought in the tea and switched on the wireless.

'Best programme of the week, this is,' she said.

It was called 'Up the Pole' and consisted, as far as Mrs. Clayton could see, of utter inanities, varied by the most obvious of insults being exchanged. Now and again she managed to muster a smile in answer to Sarah's enthusiastic:

'Good, i'n't it?'

Sarah laughed a good deal. Mrs. Clayton had not realized that she was so easily amused, or, to be frank, quite so simple. It was impossible without seeming ungrateful and unappreciative to leave while the programme lasted, but eventually it ended and Mrs. Clayton rose, and like a guest, took her leave.

'Thank you very much, Sarah. That was very pleasant.'

'Warmer than the dining-room, anyway.'

Warmer too than the drawing-room, where, thanks to the length of 'Up the Pole' the fire had dwindled to a mere handful of ash. Mrs. Clayton went to bed.

The sweep was very elusive, and when caught, very busy and for a fortnight Mrs. Clayton took her meals with Sarah. Then the stove was back in service and for three delightful days she was free of the green nymph, the wireless and Sarah's conversation. On the fourth day Sarah mentioned that the anthracite which this stove burned had 'run out'.

'Lasts no time at all,' she said. 'And so dear too. Did you read it'd gone up again. All that expense just to heat that room for a couple of meals. Not to mention the work.'

Nobody could have ignored such a hint.

'Don't bother to re-order, Sarah. In future I'll take my meals in the drawing-room, on a tray.' It was strange that such a simple statement seemed to demand so much courage to make, and when made should have such a defiant flavour.

Sarah was very thorough. Once enlisted in the cause of retrenchment she never wavered.

'I done you a herring tonight. Tasty and cheap. I always did say that if herrings was ten shillings apiece everybody'd be after 'em like mad.'

Or:

'This here is leeks. I read somewhere they was poor man's asparagus, so I cooked 'em according.'

Or:

'I was lucky today and got some nice sprats.'

The trouble with all these nourishing and admittedly flavoursome dishes was the smell. Even when Mrs. Clayton had opened the windows and fanned with a newspaper and stirred up the pot-purri in the Dresden bowl, the drawing-room still reeked like a cheap eating house. More and more often in the evenings, Sarah, preoccupied with the wireless would forget to remove the tray, and sometimes it was there when Mrs. Clayton had a caller. Squalid!

In the end Mrs. Clayton capitulated and returned to Sarah's table. The canary, Sarah said, was delighted.

In the bleakest part of January, Sarah, who had never before ailed anything, fell ill with influenza. Mrs. Clayton, earnest, fumbling and inept prepared trays and hot water bottles and carried them to the second-floor room where Sarah had slept since the last cook left.

'It's be a sight easier for you,' Sarah said, 'if I was to move down. I'll take the risk of a setback; I can wrap myself up well and take the stairs easy. I don't like you to have so much climbing.'

'A very sensible suggestion,' Mrs. Clayton said, wondering why it had not occurred to her. There were four bedrooms on the first floor, but only one had the bed aired and ready for an unexpected guest, and that was the one next to Mrs. Clayton's own. Relief at having less stairs to climb was soon mitigated by the discovery that Sarah snored. She snored ferociously even after the catarrhal effects of influenza – for which Mrs. Clayton made allowance – had worn off. Yet nobody but a heartless churl could have suggested her removal; her delight in the new room was so great, and so frankly expressed. 'Fancy me, in the guest-room, my word I do feel grand! I keep thinking I'm dreaming and thass a fact.'

And so it went on into the Spring, with Sarah encroaching here a little, there a little and Mrs. Clayton making a futile stand followed by a concession. The influenza had left Sarah with a dread of catching cold, so through a snowy February and a windy March it was Mrs. Clayton who did the shopping; it had left her slightly deaf, too, so that as often as not it was Mrs. Clayton who heard, and answered the bell.

There came a cold April evening, full of a sad green light, with the birds singing in the rocking trees as though to keep up their spirits. Mrs. Clayton had stared at the naked nymph, listened to Sarah saying, 'Now if you ask me . . .' and 'I always did say . . .' she had drunk the strong brown tea and heard the opening insults of 'Up the Pole' and then, feeling battered and old and sad, she made her way to the drawing-room, poked up the smouldering fire and settled down with her book. A measure of peace returned to her. I still have this retreat, she thought; the drawing-room is still my own. I have much to be thankful for.

Presently the door opened and there was Sarah. She had the wireless in one hand, a piece of puce-coloured knitting in the other. The cat followed her.

'I've gone and let my fire out now,' she said in a self-derogatory way. 'Mean I was, I suppose. Thought there was enough to last while I washed up and it went and died on me. I thought you wouldn't mind Pussy and me having a warm up before we tucked in.'

What could one say?

'I brought the wireless. There's a good play just coming on. *Blood on the Doorstep* it's called, a thriller. I thought we'd listen and take our minds off our troubles.'

Somewhat ostentatiously Mrs. Clayton marked the place in her book and laid it aside. Then, with stubborn ingratitude she sat and thought about her particular trouble until Sarah switched off and rose.

'There now, wasn't that cosy?' she asked. 'Come on Pussy, *somebody's* got to put the bottles to bed, you know.'

Cosy, that was the key word. To be cosy, that was Sarah's aim; and there was no harm in it. Here they were, two old women, sharing a house and pooling their small resources; why not be cosy and share a fire? I just cannot, Mrs. Clayton thought to herself; there are very few people with whom I could live in that way and Sarah is, very definitely, not of their number. What is the alternative?

For a moment she considered selling the ring and the pearls and paying Sarah wages again, but she was sensible enough to see that that would never work; to suggest it would affront Sarah and gravely hurt her feelings. Sarah did not deserve to be hurt; she had done no harm; she had merely retired, in the nicest possible way and wanted to be cosy herself and keep Mrs. Clayton comfortable. On her own terms, in her own way. And she would always win because she was dogged, ruthless and thick-skinned. It would be, Mrs. Clayton saw suddenly, quite dangerously easy to hate Sarah. And that mustn't happen either.

Mrs. Clayton rose and went to the table which had taken the place of the little Queen Anne gem, slowly selected a sheet of writing paper and took up her pen. She would write to the Lady Superintendent of that house across the Square where one could furnish a room of one's own and take meals in the communal dining-room and be attended in case of illness. Mrs. Clayton knew it well, for several of her old friends had taken refuge there and she had paid them visits. Always she had returned from such visits with a feeling of thankfulness that she still had her own house, but that was no longer true; even her drawing-room was no longer her own, for Sarah never retreated, with her a single occasion established custom. The house and furniture could be sold; they would bring in something . . . She would give Sarah some substantial sum of money and she could go and be cosy and share her wireless with someone else. Thousands of lonely women would welcome her gladly . . .

Upstairs, having put the bottles to bed, Sarah lighted her gas-fire and sat down with her knees spread wide to catch the heat and her hands resting on them. Her face wore a look of sullen bewilderment. She'd done her best, hadn't she? She'd been tactful and patient and tried to make all the necessary changes gradual and painless. You couldn't go right up to a woman for whom you had worked for forty years and of whom you were *fond*, and say – Look here, I'm over sixty, I'm independent and I'm retired, and though I'm willing to keep you cosy and comfortable, I can't waste time and energy on nonsense. That is what should have been said in the first place, then maybe Mrs. Clayton would have understood; but it was too late now.

The sullen look on her face deepened as she remembered the way in which Mrs. Clayton had laid away her book, the patiently suffering expression she had worn all through that jolly good play. *Why* couldn't she muck in and be cosy? Here they were, two old women, with, between them, all they needed for comfort and it must all be spoilt because one of them was – yes, let's face it – a silly stuck-up old snob! Sarah saw suddenly that it would be dangerously easily to hate Mrs. Clayton. One more rebuff and temper would get the better of her and she'd find herself saying things – true things – that she'd regret later on. That mustn't be allowed to happen. There was an alternative.

She got up clumsily and fished out from under her bed the tin attaché case in which she kept her savings certificates, the deeds of her little cottage, her insurance card and her writing materials. I'll leave her, she thought. She can stay here and go on playing the lady all by herself and see how she gets on then! I'll get myself a place in that house across the Square, the place intended for elderly persons of moderate means. She was that, wasn't she? And so long as she could pay her way, she was as good as the next.

In the laborious, unaccustomed but elegant hand she had been taught at school, Sarah began to write, her tongue clamped firmly between her teeth . . .

Now isn't that sweet, and really rather pathetic, thought the Lady Superintendent – a democratic idealist – as she laid the two letters side by side. Mistress and maid for so many years and now planning to go downhill together. Kindly she determined that if it were possible she would give them adjoining rooms and seat them at the same table in the dining-room.

ALL THAT IS NECESSARY . . .

LADY FENSTANTON'S letter arrived when Mrs. Bascombe had given up all hope of receiving it: it was a full month since her ladyship had come to discuss the possibility of her aunt – Lady Blyborough – coming to live at The Haven. During that time Mrs. Bascombe had often wondered if she had set her charges too high. She had quoted a low price, but you never knew with the 'new poor'. She wished Lady Fenstanton had said so, frankly, because she would have been prepared to forgo all profit. Lady Blyborough's presence would confer such prestige on the place, refute so completely some of the rumours that were going around.

Now the letter had arrived. It began by apologizing for the delay – 'My aunt proved unexpectedly difficult,' and ended on a warm and friendly note – 'It will be the greatest comfort to me when I am so far away, to know that she is being properly cared for in such very pleasant surroundings.'

The ladies arrived on a blustery afternoon in early March. Lending her aunt an unobtrusive arm, Lady Fenstanton led her into the ground-floor bed sitting-room with the tall french windows opening on to the garden. It was, she reflected, even more pleasant than she had remembered and described it as being. The bed, and the wash-basin were in an alcove, curtained off. A really splendid fire burned in the grate, and on the gate-legged table stood a bowl of spring flowers, daffodils, tulips and anemones.

'It is nice, isn't it?' said Lady Fenstanton, withdrawing her arm. 'And the window looks south, so you'll get all the sun. The garden must be *very* sheltered: the daffodils are almost out. Look.'

Lady Blyborough made no attempt to look. Since her first stroke she had walked with a drag and a shuffle, since her second she had spoken indistinctly; now, saying something which sounded like 'alien corn, Caroline,' she moved towards the fire and lowered herself into the chair. Lady Fenstanton sighed. The last days had been very trying, but it was all settled now, and within half an hour she would be on her way, on the first stage of her journey to rejoin her husband in Rhodesia.

A trim maid, in the now unfamiliar black-and-white, brought in one suitcase and a small dressing-case. Closely following her came Mrs. Bascombe, carrying a tea-tray. To the maid she said softly:

'That will do, Stella. I'll help you with the rest later on.'

She set the tray on the table.

'Aunt Isobel, this is Mrs. Bascombe,' said Lady Fenstanton.

Lady Blyborough subjected her new keeper to a second's searching scrutiny, borne by Mrs. Bascombe with admirable composure, and then extended her hand. Mrs. Bascombe just touched the swollen, mauvish fingers and said:

'I'm very glad to see you, Lady Blyborough. I hope you'll be happy and comfortable here.'

'I'm sure she will,' said Lady Fenstanton after an awkward little pause during which it was plain that Lady Blyborough was not even *trying* to speak. Lady Blyborough gave her niece a cold glance. She detested being spoken for, as though she were a child or a lunatic, just because her voice was unreliable.

Mrs. Bascombe poured out two cups of tea, leaving the ladies to help themselves to milk or lemon, to sugar, and then said:

'My other maid has the afternoon off today, so I am rather busy. If you want me before you leave, Lady Fenstanton, just ring the bell. Otherwise I'll say Good-bye and I hope you'll have a pleasant journey.'

Lady Fenstanton endeavoured to lighten the next twenty minutes by remarking how nicely the tea was served. 'I think these cups are Worcester': 'It isn't everyone who understands that some people prefer lemon in tea': 'How nicely this bread and butter is cut': 'The cakes seem to be home-made.' Lady Blyborough, refusing to eat anything, drinking but one cup of tea, maintained a stubborn silence. Finally Lady Fenstanton said:

'You're really making it very difficult for me, Aunt Isobel. I just *couldn't* go away again leaving you in that great house alone with old Bessie. It was squalor. And she's older than you, it just wasn't *safe*.'

She had said all this many times before. This afternoon, most surprisingly, out of the sullen silence came the response for which she yearned. Grimacing horribly in her effort to articulate clearly, Lady Blyborough said:

'I'm grateful, Caroline . . . ante-room of the cemetery . . . but comfortable.'

'You mustn't say that! Once you're properly looked after, with regular meals and some comfort, you'll feel better and *be* better. I think you'll be very happy here. But if I'm wrong, if this place isn't what it seems, you let me know at once. I can always fly back.'

She glanced at her watch, collected her handbag and gloves. Lady Blyborough heaved herself to her feet and stood working her hands together. She succeeded in dragging from her puffy, flaccid finger the half hoop of superb diamonds which was her engagement ring. Each of its five stones was large enough to make an impressive solitaire, and Lady Fenstanton who had never, in her closest, least sentimental assessment of her aunt's resources, dreamed of reckoning it as an asset, was horrified to feel it being thrust on to one of her own fingers.

'Oh no, Aunt Isobel, you really mustn't! I wouldn't dream of taking it.'

'Safer with you,' said Lady Blyborough. 'Might die . . . never know.'

The words lent a poignancy to their leave-taking; neither was a sentimental woman and they were not deeply attached to one another, but as they said good-bye some genuine emotion brushed them.

Soon after Lady Fenstanton had gone Mrs. Bascombe came in with Stella and carried Lady Blyborough's trunk behind the curtain.

'Stella will unpack for you,' she said. 'I expect that you are tired after the journey. Would you like dinner in bed?'

Lady Blyborough took from her handbag one of those little pads, useful for shopping lists or taking telephone messages, upon which one can write and then, with a slight pull obliterate the words.

'Hate meals in bed except when ill' she wrote.

'Very well,' said Mrs. Bascombe, amiably. 'Dinner is at seven-fifteen. Lady Fenstanton said that you liked a little help at bedtime. When do you like to retire?'

'Ten-thirty,' wrote Lady Blyborough.

'And don't forget to ring if there's anything you want.'

What I want, thought Lady Blyborough, quite savagely, is to be back in my own house. Nobody who hasn't lived in one house for forty-nine years realizes what a wrench . . . And this is Thursday, the day when Bessie went into the village and collected the fish from the bus, and picked up all the news. I want to be back too before Caroline came to visit me. No! What I want is to be as I was before my stroke . . . No! God, no, farther back . . . before I was old, and ugly and alone . . .

Like the first symptoms of an illness she felt within her the onset of the self-pitying mood which, more than anything nowadays, she dreaded. She mustn't, she wouldn't turn into one of those senile old women always weeping over the past. She snatched up her book, opened it at random, and stared at the page.

II

Within a month, however, she was prepared to admit that Caroline had been right. Life at The Haven was extremely comfortable, and she was aware of a sense of well-being. Soon she was not even lonely, for although the other women who lived in the house seemed to keep their distance, Mrs. Bascombe was never too busy to have a little gossip. She had, to begin with, been very restrained; it was Lady Blyborough who had asked questions. She had noticed from her window, a woman, not at all old, prettily made up, her silver-gilt hair carefully curled and arranged, who walked in the garden a good deal, often alone, sometimes pushing a wheel-chair in which a tiny figure, muffled to the very eyes was huddled. One bright morning the chair went past the window when Mrs. Bascombe was putting fresh flowers in Lady Blyborough's room.

'Nice-looking,' said Lady Blyborough with a little jerk of the head. 'Who is she?'

'Mrs. Childers, and the one in the chair is Miss Brady. She is crippled with arthritis.' Mrs. Bascombe re-arranged a flower. 'But of the two Madge Childers is the more pitiable case.' She would have left it there, not wishing to seem a vulgar gossip and not knowing that age and an ever-narrowing orbit had forced Lady Blyborough to take interest in anything that offered.

'In what way?' Lady Blyborough asked. Mrs. Bascombe reflected that – although she had told Madge to keep well away from the new guest – you never knew when, or how the two might come into contact. She would get her word in first.

'To put it quite bluntly,' she said, 'she drinks. But she has reason for that. Her's is a very sad story.'

Lady Blyborough's face betrayed a lively interest. Encouraged, Mrs. Bascombe said:

'She was left a widow, very young, with one boy. She took a little boarding house in Brighton and by working twenty-four hours a day, made it pay, moved into a bigger place and slaved and schemed, and maybe was a bit lucky. Anyway, she ended with a really good, first-class hotel. She sent the boy to a public school, and then to Oxford; he was brilliant and did well. He's now something very important in the Foreign Office and he married . . .' Mrs. Bascombe looked Lady Blyborough straight in the eye, '. . . a lady. The tragedy is, Madge can't sound an aitch to save her life and he's ashamed of her. She sold out and thought she was going to live near him, and it really is heartbreaking to hear her talk about the grandchildren. Of course there *is* his side to it.'

'Great pity,' Lady Blyborough said. Why, she wondered, had nobody thought of a few elocution lessons?

When Mrs. Bascombe realized that Lady Blyborough was interested in the people around her, she talked about them. The two funny little creatures, dressed alike in very juvenile clothes were Miss Elsie and Miss Gwen Wade, victims of an egomaniac father who had ordered their lives and doled them out pennies and then left sixty-four thousand pounds in trust for them. They were harmless, but infantile and spent most of their time making dresses for one another. Every month somebody came to see that they were alive and well, and to pay Mrs. Bascombe. To be taken into the town and treated to ice-cream, or a cinema sent them into the seventh heaven.

Also living in the house, Lady Blyborough learned, was a Miss Griffiths who was blind and a Mrs. Paget. Mrs. Bascombe smiled, wryly, tolerantly, as she named her.

'She really is a case,' she said. 'Clever as they come, never at a loss for a quotation, but so forgetful. And the stories she tells. Even now, sometimes, she can fool me, and I'm used to her. It's a queer household,' said Mrs. Bascombe, as though realizing it for the first time. 'It isn't what I set out for at all, you know. I wanted a proper nursing home. I'd nursed my mother for years and then, when she died, I used to go out to nurse people, not too ill, people who just wanted looking after. One of my patients, such a dear old man, left me a legacy and I bought this place. It was all right during the war; officers' wives used to come here and have their babies . . . I had a board out then, The Haven Nursing Home. Later on they became fussy and particular, and because I wasn't qualified I had to take the board down and call this a guest house. But I stuck to people who were . . .' she realized that she was speaking to one of her guests, '. . . not very well, because I do like looking after people.'

'Do it very well,' said Lady Blyborough.

Mrs. Bascombe laughed.

'Not according to Mrs. Paget! Miss Griffiths has a grudge against me too. She used to have this room, but she is blind, I can't see that the view meant anything to her. So I moved her and there was a rumpus. Still, it's all in a day's work.'

She gave one of her half-humorous, resigned shrugs and Lady Blyborough thought again how wrong, despite the byword, first impressions can be. She had disliked Mrs. Bascombe on sight and was now coming to admire her; always so busy and cheerful, so sensible – and so kind.

III

Mrs. Bascombe drove a big, rather shabby car and usually before she set out for the morning's shopping, asked Lady Blyborough if she would like to accompany her. As time went on Lady Blyborough accepted the invitation less frequently; Mrs. Bascombe seemed to have a great many acquaintances and was rather free with her introductions; Lady Blyborough, never certain of her voice, found this embarrassing. One morning in April, in the middle of a spell of beautiful weather, having refused the offer of a ride she said:

'What I should like to do is sit in the garden for a while.'

'But of course! Why didn't I think of that?' said Mrs. Bascombe. She settled her in a sunny corner, where the bulk of the house shielded her from what wind there was. Near at hand was a bed of pink tulips, raising their heads above a haze of forget-me-nots, behind them was a stretch of smooth lawn, then a laurel hedge, and beyond it the tops of the orchard trees; the pears were in full white shining bloom, the apples in rosy bud. Presently a cuckoo began to call. Lady Blyborough looked at the flowers, listened to the urgent, aching cry and began to think of other springs. Hastily she opened her book and began to read.

She was startled when somebody, rounding the corner of the house quickly, almost walked into her. It was Mrs. Childers.

'Oh I am sorry, me lady,' she said. 'Wasn't expecting anybody here. But it's a morning to bring anybody out, ain't it?' Her voice was coarse and throaty, but warm and friendly. Lady Blyborough tried to speak, emitted a croak, found her pad and wrote:

'Lovely morning! Voice unreliable.'

'I know,' said Mrs. Childers sympathetically. 'We was warned not to intrude ourselves on you. Madge Childers is me name.'

She held out a thin hand with knotted fingers, a hand which had worked hard in its day; before Lady Blyborough could touch it it was hastily withdrawn.

'Sorry,' Mrs. Childers said, 'filthy! I been helping Mrs. Paget 'unt 'er ring and 'er room could do with a turn out and no mistake. Nothing but fluff under the bed. Still, they like to be 'umoured.' She gave a wide, tolerant smile. Lady Blyborough noticed that the face, so pretty at a distance was still attractive at close range, but there were discoloured pouches under the eyes, and something about the eyes themselves, an unsteadiness, an almost slippery look. She tried her voice again and the words came:

'Mrs. Paget . . . forgetful?'

Mrs. Childers laughed.

'I'll say she is. The trouble is you never know where you are with 'er. Yesterday, today and tomorrer, all one. Like this ring. Star sapphire or something some big-wig give 'er mother, out in India. I must admit I never did see it, and Flo – Mrs. Bascombe that is – swear she never 'ad it 'ere. Maybe you 'eard the rumpus last night. No? Well, you are on the quiet side of the 'ouse. And I went out as soon as they started. I've done meself a bit of good a time or two over Mrs. P. She told me once she was paying fifteen guineas a week and like a mug I told Flo I thought that was a bit much for what she was getting, and Flo said she pay thirty shillings. And when I told Mrs. P *that* she laughed like a drain and said, "That's right. Thirty pieces of silver. Union rate for betrayal!" So now I don't bother much. All the same . . .'

Her blue gaze met Lady Blyborough's, darkened and slipped away.

'Very sad to lose one's memory,' said Lady Blyborough.

'And be old, with nobody to care what 'appens to you. Of course there's always public institutions. I sometimes think . . .'

She broke off; her eyes flickered wildly; tiny drops of moisture popped out on her upper lip. At the same instant Lady Blyborough could smell the rather highly-scented powder used by Mrs. Bascombe. She reached out and took Mrs. Childer's hand, saying as distinctly and loudly as possible:

'If you would. So kind,' and heaving on the hand began to pull herself up.

'It is turning a little chilly, that's the worst of this time of year,' said Mrs. Bascombe, coming up behind Lady Blyborough. 'Thank you, Madge, dear. Look, let me, I'm more used . . . You take those through to the kitchen for me, will you?' She slipped her arm under Lady Blyborough's, and handed Mrs. Childers some parcels with which she hurried off as though making an escape.

Very curious, thought Lady Blyborough. Christian name terms, and one so frightened . . . And why did *I* instantly begin pretending that I had asked Mrs. Childers to help me?

'I thought poor Madge was busy with a treasure hunt,' said Mrs. Bascombe, helping Lady Blyborough, in just the right way, back into her room. 'Did she not tell you about the Maharajah's ring that belonged to Mrs. Paget's mother?'

Lady Blyborough assumed her interested, inquiring look.

'Mrs. Paget's father was something rather grand in India, and there may well have been such a ring. But I should think it was sold years ago – mind the step – Mrs. Paget has been very poor for a long time. Nobody here has ever seen it; not even Madge can say that; but she'll encourage the old silly and hunt around. I honestly believe that if you went up to her and said your head grew out from under your arm, she'd say, Yes, she could see it did and how painful it must be for you. That is how she is. And now that has reminded me of something I *did* want to ask you, Lady Blyborough. You were wearing a ring when you arrived I noticed. If you want it, or any other treasure put away safely, I have a little safe . . .'

'Gave it to my niece, keepsake,' said Lady Blyborough. 'Nothing of value left.'

'Oh well,' said Mrs. Bascombe cheerfully, 'I often think things like that are just a responsibility.'

IV

Next morning Lady Blyborough made Mrs. Paget's acquaintance. It was again warm and sunny and she was sitting out, and reading when a clear voice said:

'Good morning. I hope I didn't startle you. It's the fault of these ridiculous slippers. They've taken my shoes away now.'

Lady Blyborough looked up and saw a remarkable figure; a very tall, extremely thin old woman with a mass of wild white hair insecurely pinned into an Edwardian coiffure. She wore a black and white striped blouse with all its buttons missing, pinned at the neck with a large safety pin. Her long skirt sagged about her hip-bones from the frail support of a single hook. The most noticeable thing about her, however, was an enormous bruise which began under one cheekbone and ran up under the white hair.

'I live here,' Mrs. Paget went on before Lady Blyborough had found her voice. 'My name is Paget. I expect I have been told yours but I'm very forgetful nowadays.'

'How do you do, Mrs. Paget. I'm Lady Blyborough.'

'You've got laryngitis,' said Mrs. Paget. 'I used to know a very good cure for that. You put it in a jug with some boiling water and make a tent with a towel. It had a Catholic-sounding name . . . monks . . . nuns . . . No, just be patient with me, I shall remember.'

'Friars' Balsam. No good to me. Voice gone.'

'Then I fail to see how you *manage*. I'm very fluent and I can make myself heard and I have great difficulty at times in holding my own. Look at this!' She lifted a long thin, beautifully shaped hand and touched the bruise. Before Lady Blyborough could say a word she rushed on:

'Never have I been so insulted. To say that I had dropped it into the lavatory, of all places. I never wore it, it was far too big, even for my thumb. I *know* where it is. Dozens of times she has asked me to allow her to put it in her safe. "Ha," I say, "with Miss Poley's ear-rings?" You see, I'm not entirely forgetful. I don't know your name, but I do remember Miss Poley. Her wrist was broken. I suppose I should think myself fortunate to escape with a bruise, though I have the solidity of the cheekbone to thank for *that*. "Cheek" is used to express a certain invulnerability, is it not?'

'How did you . . . bruise your face?'

'I? Why should I bang my head against a wall? I admit that I lost my temper – over the lavatory suggestion, you know. And it was like the Duke of Norfolk's remark about Mary Tudor. You recall it?'

Lady Blyborough shook her head.

'Henry the Eighth wished her to sign away her rights and she refused, and the Duke said, "If she were my daughter I would bang her head against a wall till it was as soft as a baked apple." I always thought that an apt simile. Now it has happened to me. Have you the time?'

'Twelve o'clock.'

'Dear me. And I am so hungry. Cod again, I expect. I'll tell you something though. *Somebody* here has delicious food. On a tray. I saw it, and learned to my horror that one's mouth can water, literally. I drooled like a dog. Of course Mrs. Bascombe always says I am gluttonous. They say "Speak of the Devil" don't they?' She spoke without lowering her voice. 'Here she comes, with a look that bodes me *no* good.' It was curiously like the situation on the previous morning, but Mrs Paget was not frightened. Across the top of Lady Blyborough's head she said arrogantly:

'Now don't tell me that I disgrace your establishment! I am wearing my slippers because my shoes have vanished.'

Mrs. Bascombe rounded Lady Blyborough's chair. She looked over-heated and tired; she was laden with parcels and in one hand carried a pair of stout black shoes tied together by their laces.

'Wrinch was good enough to mend these while I went to the shops,' she said, holding them out. 'Also I did give you four buttons for that blouse you know. Anyway, you have your grey one. Go and put that on. I hate to see you going about like that.' She spoke patiently, a little wearily, like a mother to a troublesome child at the end of the day.

'My mother bids me bind my hair, so I'll bid you good day,' said Mrs. Paget. She took the shoes, without thanks, and moved with dignity towards the house. Mrs. Bascombe looked after her for a moment.

'One day she'll have an accident. Did you see her face? She fell in the bathroom and nobody could think why, it has a rubber floor, no mats to trip over. Then I thought to look at her shoes and the soles were just flapping. I told her I'd try to get them mended this morning, but she says they've vanished. Into my elastic safe, I suppose, with the Maharajah's ring and all the other treasures!'

Almost against her will Lady Blyborough found herself becoming mentally involved with these conflicting stories, one so melodramatic, the other so mundane. She thought about them, searching for clues, for nuances, as though she were reading one of her favourite detective stories. One woman was lying; one was dangerously inventive, one dangerously plausible. Highly interesting, better even than old Bessie's village gossip.

V

The weather broke. Drenching rain alternated with sunny intervals. One morning, in a fair spell Lady Blyborough saw Mrs. Paget and the blind woman hurry across the garden and into the orchard. Mrs. Paget was dressed as before, except that she had a wide black hat pinned on top of her hair; Miss Griffiths wore a long camel-hair dressing-gown. Soon after they had vanished behind the laurel hedge it began to rain heavily; Lady Blyborough watched for their return and when she did not see them, concluded that there was some other path between the orchard and the house.

That evening, when Mrs. Bascombe came to help her to bed, she said:

'Isn't this weather dreary? I'm going to try to cheer things up and have a tea-party tomorrow. I've asked a nice little neighbour – Mrs. Crane; she lives just along the road, that house with the lovely rockery. Will you join us, Lady Blyborough? I'm going to open the big lounge.'

'No good. Can't talk.'

'Oh, you can. Do come. Actually it's a party *for* something, but I'm keeping that as a surprise.'

'Very well . . . glad to accept . . . understood . . . can't talk much.'

At four o'clock on the following afternoon Mrs. Bascombe came to Lady Blyborough's room accompanied by a very young, very pretty woman whose extreme ill-ease of manner contrasted sharply with the sophistication of her appearance. Mrs. Bascombe introduced her and said:

'Would you mind going along to the lounge together? I want to fetch Miss Brady. Nobody else seems capable of manoeuvring her chair indoors without scratching the paint.'

As soon as she had gone Mrs. Crane, with the air of one about to take a very high dive into very cold water, said:

'Lady Blyborough, are you comfortable here?'

'Extremely so.'

'You mustn't mind me asking. I haven't much time. My husband . . . all nonsense, he said, leave it alone . . . Mrs. Bascombe, is she *kind* to you?'

'Very kind.'

'And to the others?'

Such a difficult question.

'So far as I know.' What evidence was there to the contrary?

'Would you . . . take my arm . . . Lady Blyborough?'

She could feel, within the sleeve of the beautifully cut suit, the uncontrollable vibration. A shy girl, she thought, compelling herself to ask awkward questions, to investigate something she would much sooner leave alone.

They moved towards the door of the large, seldom-used drawing-room, where they met Miss Brady in her chair. Stripped of her mufflings she was seen to be a boyish-looking little old woman, with close cropped hair and a face as lively as a monkey's.

Inside the room Mrs. Childers sat on one side of the fire, Mrs. Paget on the other. She was almost unrecognizable, her newly washed hair piled high and securely pinned, her grey blouse neatly tucked into her mended skirt-band. The Wade girls, identical in tartan dresses with white, school-girlish collars sat together on a sofa.

Mrs. Bascombe swung the chair so that Miss Brady's place was on Lady Blyborough's right hand, and then went to stand behind a table, spread with a fine lace-edged cloth and laden with the materials for a truly festive tea. She had begun a little speech of introduction when Mrs. Paget leaned forward and said in her loud voice:

'Sandwiches! Four, five sorts of sandwiches. And cake! It looks like a birthday.'

The Wades giggled; Mrs. Bascombe smiled; Mrs. Childers turned her head and stared into the fire. Nobody claimed the birthday. Miss Brady, leaning stiffly in her chair asked Lady

Blyborough whether she cared for wireless. 'I have an excellent set, sent me by my brother. You'd always be very welcome to come and listen.' She was – for anyone in Lady Blyborough's condition – an easy companion, very garrulous and undemanding. She seemed to have a number of devoted friends and relatives, all of whom sent her beautiful presents; some of which she never received, 'the post isn't what it was, you know,' and she spoke highly of the efforts Mrs. Bascombe made to trace things that were lost. 'In fact she is wonderful about all my correspondence. Four or five letters she writes for me every week. I can only just make a scrawl nowadays.' Lady Blyborough saw that Mrs. Crane, who had been placed on Miss Brady's other side was listening and losing something of her strained look. Mrs. Bascombe poured the tea, Stella brought round the cups, the milk and lemon, the sugar; Mrs. Childers, moving lke an automaton and not speaking at all, rose and passed sandwiches.

Presently Mrs. Paget said:

'Birthdays always remind me of Venice.'

'Of Venice, Mrs. Paget, why?' asked Mrs. Bascombe.

'Elizabeth Barrett Browning died there. And she was the one who wrote about the birthday of her heart. That, you see, I can remember with the utmost clarity – even the reflection of the sun from the water upon the ceiling of the room where she died. But I have already forgotten whose birthday this cake celebrates.' She looked around the room, her gaze travelling from face to face. 'I give up,' she said.

Mrs. Bascombe also looked around the room, gathering attention. Then she said:

'It's yours, you know. So you must cut the cake.'

Mrs. Paget dropped a half-eaten sandwich and jumped to her feet.

'This is not my birthday. I was born in November; November the . . .' confidence deserted her. She said crossly, 'There are too many things to remember in November, Armistice Day and Gunpowder Plot. *And* my birthday.'

'Well, I can't show you your birth certificate because if you remember you threw it away after you'd claimed your Post-War Credits,' said Mrs. Bascombe equably, 'but I do know that every other year your birthday has been on the twelfth of May. However, it doesn't matter. You needn't cut the cake if you don't wish to.'

Mrs. Paget stood irresolute, then strode to the table and snatched up the knife.

'It says in the Bible – "Answer a fool according to his folly, lest he be angry and hate thee." I certainly *don't* wish any more hatred.'

She began to hack the cake into untidy, uneven portions. Mrs. Bascombe placed a piece on a plate and said to Stella:

'Run up and see if Miss Griffiths is awake. Take this, in case.'

'Is Miss Griffiths ill?' Lady Blyborough inquired of Miss Brady.

'Oh yes. Did you not know?' Miss Brady lowered her voice. 'Mrs. Paget is to blame. She took her a walk yesterday, in her dressing-gown, if you please. They came back drenched. Mrs. Bascombe was afraid of pneumonia, but she's only exhausted. Wasn't it naughty?'

'They came to my house,' said Mrs. Crane, who had again been listening. 'They looked as though they had been in the river. I wrapped them in blankets and gave them . . .'

Stella had returned and murmured something to Mrs. Bascombe.

'Mrs. Crane. Your other protégé is still asleep. Would you like to just peep at her?'

Again with that air of forcing herself to do something she would rather not, the girl said:

'Oh, yes, I would.'

Leading the way from the room Mrs. Bascombe paused by Miss Brady's chair and said:

'Don't worry. I shall be back to wheel you in for your precious serial.'

'You never forget anything, do you dear?' said Miss Brady dotingly. 'It's the Children's Hour, really,' she went on, turning back to Lady Blyborough. 'But it's so exciting. I do enjoy it.'

'Now *where*' demanded Mrs. Paget, 'have I seen that pretty little face before? I don't see so many. And this one is in some odd way connected with a very beautiful Persian carpet. I'd have asked, but people are always so offended if you don't remember them.'

'Crane. Her name is Crane,' said Lady Blyborough.

'Means nothing to me,' said Mrs. Paget. She looked at the cake. 'My birthday! As though I should forget my own birthday! How all things do conspire against me.' She began to cry.

‘ ’Ere, ’ere,’ said Mrs. Childers, jumping up and putting an arm around her. ‘What’s a birthday more or less? Look, you’ve ’ad a good tea and you’re all dressed up. I’ll take you to the pitchers.’

‘Can we come too? Oh, please,’ cried the Wades.

‘I don’t see why not.’

As they trooped out Miss Brady looked at her watch.

‘Stella, paint or no paint, you’ll have to wheel me back. Lady Blyborough, you’re sure you wouldn’t care to join me? Well, any time . . .’

The door was left open, and Lady Blyborough heard Mrs. Bascombe and Mrs. Crane descend the stairs. As they walked across the hall the girl said, ‘No I must get back. And Mrs. Bascombe, I do apologize again for yesterday . . . I think you’re . . . you’re simply marvellous . . .’

VI

Lady Blyborough always read in bed. On the evening of the tea-party she had just closed her book and was awkwardly reaching for the light switch when her door opened. From the other side of the curtain Mrs. Childers said:

‘ ’S’only me.’ The door closed again, very cautiously and Mrs. Childers came through the opening between the curtains.

‘I wouldn’t ’ave waked you. But I see your light and thought now was my chance.’

Her hair was in curlers and her face was curiously mottled, reddish-purple and greyish-white. The mingled odours of Chanel scent and whisky came with her into the alcove. She pulled forward a stool and sat down, planting her hands on her knees and staring at Lady Blyborough with owlish, drunken intensity.

‘You . . . wanted . . . something?’

‘Too true I do. I’m desprit really. And I dunno nothing about you. You may be a ’ard-’earted old snob, like Flo says. But I gotta risk it. You see, she set such store by you, Lady and all that. She’d listen to you. Me, I say a word and back I go into a drunks’ home. See?’

‘What is this all about?’

‘I’ll make it clear and short. Yestiddy Mrs. Paget and Miss Griffiths run away. Miss Griffiths got a grievance. She lent Mrs. Bascombe all ’er savings when the nursing home went flop; now she say she's being done and 'd be far better off in a public institution, and in 'er place I'd feel the same. So she got Mrs. P. to smuggle 'er out and they were caught in the rain, and that pretty little noodle that was 'ere to tea today, took 'em in and they pitched 'er a tale. She was for taking 'em to the perlice, but 'er 'usband brought 'em back 'ere . . .'

Mrs. Childers leaned farther forward and spoke with greater intensity.

'You see yourself 'ow that ended. She is asked to tea, old Paget is made to look so daft she don't know 'er own birthday, and Miss Griffiths, full of dope, is in the best bed with a bunch of lily-of-the-valley for company.'

Mrs. Childers' mottled face broke up, it seemed uncertain whether she would laugh or cry. She worked her hands together and swallowed hard several times.

'Now they're gonna 'ave 'Ell. Flo in a temper is the very devil, and 'olding it in time she put Mrs. Crane off the scent ain't improved it any. The minnit we got in from the pitchers she took 'old of poor old Paget and shook 'er till 'er teeth fell out and broke. Poor old dear, she did cry. " 'Ow'm I gonna eat?" she says; and Flo says, "You won't want no teeth to eat what you'll get 'ere in future." Me lady, this is God's truth I'm telling you. I was there, I saw and 'eard . . .'

She found her handkerchief and blew her nose violently.

'I never was one to stand by and see a kid or a animal ill treated, but if I fall out with Flo where do I go? I tried 'otels; sooner or later I go on a bender, and 'otels don't like that. I tried 'omes, they don't do me no good. But I can't just stand and watch . . . she's a woman in the prime of life and they're both such poor old things, like kids really, and 'armless. Would you just say to 'er to go easy on 'em. She'd listen to you.'

I must keep very calm, Lady Blyborough told herself. The doctor warned me against excitement. She braced herself to speak clearly and at greater length than usual.

'Very difficult position. Apart from . . . what you say . . . no evidence. Can't mention you. Very difficult.'

'You see old Paget's face all bruised. You could say Mrs. Crane told you about the running away, and say they didn't mean no 'arm. Casual like, just to show you was on their side and took interest.'

'Could do that. Very kind to me . . . Miss Brady . . . Wades.'

'Kind to me, too, come to that. For why? Money. Root of all evil they say. Miss Brady, she's robbed right, left and centre, but she don't care, she don't notice so long as she get 'er letters writ and 'er wireless. The Wades is a gold mine; know what they pay? Fifteen guineas a week each, and if they get a sixpenny ice-cream they dance in the streets. You're good value too. But Miss Griffiths just 'anded over 'er cash for bed and board the rest of 'er days; and there was a lot of jiggery-pokery with old Paget's affairs too. Die tomorrer they can and good riddance.'

'Very terrible . . . accusations. Mrs. Childers . . . wonder if you . . . realize what . . . you are saying.'

'Oh, I'm drunk, if that's what you mean. Drunk as a fiddler's bitch. But I ain't a liar. And I'm scared. You see, this ain't the worst of it. There was a Miss Poley 'ere . . .' She broke off and shuddered. 'Why bring 'er up? It's that poor old pair I'm asking you to 'elp.'

The slippery, evasive look had gone from her eyes; they faced Lady Blyborough's squarely, urgently beseeching.

Such a pity, Lady Blyborough thought, just when I was settled and comfortable and getting better, to be involved in all this. Nothing worse for one's blood pressure than not to know what to believe, what to say, what to think. I must keep calm.

'I'll do what I can,' she said at last.

'I thought you would. I ain't often wrong about people. Fr'instance, if tomorrer you said you'd like to see Miss Griffiths, that'd sound natural, 'er being ill. She's locked in, this minnit, but Flo'd get 'er out if you asked. And *you* could say you'd like a word or two with Mrs. Paget; you talk the same way, after all. She'd get 'er teeth done then. That's all I'm asking.'

'Very well,' Lady Blyborough said.

Mrs. Childers stood up.

'I didn't want to worry you. But you was the only one I could think to turn to.'

'That's all right,' Lady Blyborough said. 'Not worried. Good night.'

'Thanks a lot. Good night,' said Mrs. Childers, and stole away.

VII

There was nothing to be done tonight; tomorrow's action – if any – must be dictated by the turn of events, so it was useless to lie there in the dark and worry. But half an hour passed. Then she realized, crossly, that before she could sleep it would be necessary for her to go across to the bathroom. It was one of the marked advantages of her room that she could make the journey unaided. Just outside her door was a stone Jacobean chest, beyond it the end of the banister rail, beyond that again a sturdy chair, and then the door. She could hand herself along from one to another. The light switch, however, was across by the front door; so she took a torch.

She was on her way back, the bathroom door just behind her, her hand reaching out for the support of the chair, when it happened. First a scuffling sound on the dark upstairs landing, then the light there switched on. Lady Blyborough could see, advancing towards the head of the stairs, Mrs. Paget in her nightdress, her hair streaming, and Miss Griffiths, a blanket over her shoulders and a long, official-looking envelope clutched to her breast. Then the door of the bedroom nearest the stair head opened and there was Mrs. Bascombe, wearing a cyclamen-coloured robe and holding a cigarette.

It was like a theatre, when the lights go up; and as in a theatre, sight was followed by sound. Mrs. Paget gave a loud cry. Then there was a din, out of which only certain isolated sentences emerged. Miss Griffiths said, 'This is illegal detention,' Mrs. Paget shouted, 'Take your hands off me!' Mrs. Bascombe was shouting, roughly. The three figures merged into a writhing Laocoön.

Mrs. Paget, much the frailest of the three, was thrown clear first; she fell away from the head of the stairs, hit the landing wall and crumpled down on to her hands and knees; but she was up in a moment and had seized Mrs. Bascombe from the rear.

'Run, Griffy, run. I'll hold her,' she shouted.

The blind woman, her hand on the wall, pulled free of Mrs. Bascombe's grasp and took a step nearer the stairs. Mrs. Bascombe threw Mrs. Paget backwards once more.

From the lower hall Lady Blyborough tried to call, 'Mind the stairs!' but though she mouthed the words no sound came.

She saw Mrs. Bascombe take Miss Griffiths by the shoulder, and thought, 'Saved.' But Mrs. Bascombe pushed. The blind woman screamed as she hurtled forward. Her feet never touched the stairs at all; her body made an arc above them and then landed, head first, with an ominous crack, on the tiled floor of the hall.

On the landing Mrs. Bascombe was shaking Mrs. Paget and crying, 'You wicked woman! Look what you've done!' Lady Blyborough saw then that Mrs. Childers was there on the landing, white-faced and screaming.

The whole scene had taken far less than a minute. In that time all the power had drained out of Lady Blyborough's 'good' leg, leaving it as limp and heavy as the other. The chair upon which her hand had just closed, was not sufficient support; she felt her knees buckle as she settled down, just outside the bathroom door into the ridiculous position of a pin-cushion doll, her legs folded under her, her dressing-gown spread out all round.

Holding Mrs. Paget by one shoulder, Mrs. Bascombe reached out and gave Mrs. Childers a smack on the face.

'Stop that noise, Madge. Hysteria won't help. Go and call Stella.'

Mrs. Childers moved away out of sight. Quite calmly Mrs. Bascombe opened her own bedroom door, pushed Mrs. Paget inside, slammed the door and locked it. Alone for a moment she found the cigarette that she had dropped in the struggle and stamped on it. From somewhere along the landing the Wades were calling, and she called back to them:

'It's all right. Something fell. Nothing to worry about.'

Then, and only then, did she switch on, from above, the light of the lower hall. Unhurriedly she descended the stairs and stooped over what lay on the floor, making a thorough and knowledgeable examination. She straightened herself as Mrs. Childers came dragging, reluctant, sick-faced, down the stairs.

'Get yourself a drink, Madge and go back to bed. There's nothing you can do.'

Just behind Mrs. Childers Stella appeared, buttoning a pink cardigan over yellow pyjamas.

'Ring Doctor Talbot, Stella. Two-six-five. Tell him it's an accident and he must come at once.'

Stella skirted the foot of stairs and saw Lady Blyborough. She let out a sharp cry.

'What now!' said Mrs. Bascombe, whirling round. 'Oh, poor Lady Blyborough. What happened? Did you fall? Are you hurt?'

Speech, movement, alike impossible. I sit here like a stone Buddha, she thought to herself; and she thought, It's another stroke, of course . . .

'Stella hurry!' cried Mrs. Bascombe. 'Say it's urgent. Madge, you *can* help, now. Let me just see . . .' The expert, knowledgeable hands, murderer's hands, investigated the possibility of injury to Lady Blyborough's legs. 'Nothing broken. I'll lift her, you take her feet. That's right.'

Stella came to help with the lifting on to the bed.

'He said he'd only just come in, so he'd be here in less than five minutes. What happened? I didn't hear anything till somebody screamed.'

'Mrs. Paget pushed Miss Griffiths and she fell downstairs. I'm afraid Lady Blyborough *saw*. A terrible shock . . . Stay by the door, Stella, and bring Dr. Talbot straight in *here*.'

VIII

There was a timeless interval. There were pills and warm drinks and hot water bottles. She slept, woke to half-consciousness, slept again. Sometimes, just on the fringe of her mind there was anxiety, the third stroke? Utter helplessness from now on? Worse than death. But before the full horror of the thought could take possession there was the pill, the warm drink, and oblivion again.

Then there was a morning when she woke to full consciousness, moved one limb and then another and knew that the worst had not happened. She turned her head and looked at her bedside table. Someone had wound her little clock, so that it was waiting to welcome her. It showed the hour to be half past ten.

High heels clicked on the tiles of the hall and Mrs. Childers came into the room – the curtains were open now.

' 'Ullo,' she said, 'you're awake. You're better. Oh, I am glad. Seeing you lay there like a log was the last straw. I did blame meself for bothering you.'

My voice, she thought; I haven't tried my voice yet.

She said, 'Good morning, Mrs. Childers,' and the sound came, certainly no worse than before. I am no worse than before. Dear God, I do thank you!

Mrs. Childers was, as usual, beautifully dressed, carefully made up, but she looked ill. She had lost weight and in her shrunken face the pouches under her eyes were more prominent.

'Is there anything you fancy?' she asked. 'Anything at all?'

'Like to go . . . to the bathroom.'

'Now that's one thing you can't do. No exertion, the doctor said. If you don't fancy my ministrations – though I'm 'andy – I'll get Stella.'

'I am . . . going to . . . the bathroom. Glad of your . . . arm. Otherwise going . . . alone.'

Their eyes met in a brief battle of wills. Lady Blyborough's very straight and steady, Mrs. Childer's slippery.

'All right, if it's like that. No excitement; he said that too. Here we go.'

She was more sinewy and strong than Lady Blyborough had expected; gentle-handed too. But the short journey seemed long and was conducted in a breath-sparing silence, for the shock, or the time in bed – how long? – had resulted in great feebleness. Once back in bed, however, Lady Blyborough refused to be laid down.

'Prop me . . . up. Lot to . . . talk about. What day is this?

'Thursday. There now. You ain't supposed to talk *at all*. Nothing to do with me. Doctor's orders; complete rest and quiet. If you want anything you just ask, but no talking.'

'Has there been . . . inquest?'

Mrs. Childer's eyes flickered like a frightened foal's.

' 'S'on this morning; eleven o'clock. Flo's down there now. And she left me look after you and not to talk.'

'Where is Mrs. Paget?' asked Lady Blyborough relentlessly.

'She's all right. You don't 'ave to fret about 'er. Nor about nothing. You just gotta lay and get yourself well.'

'Mrs. Childers . . .' Despite the croakiness of the impaired voice the words came out with an authority which Mrs. Childers recognized. 'Stop this . . . pretence. Upsets me . . . far more . . . not to know. Where is Mrs. Paget?'

'They took 'er away. Beckersfield Asylum'

'Saying that . . . she pushed . . . Miss Griffiths?'

Mrs. Childers gave a miserable nod. Turning away she went to where she had thrown down her handbag before helping Lady Blyborough out of bed. She opened it and took out a half-bottle of whisky. Wrenching off its seal and fumbling with its cap, she said:

'This is your fault. I just 'ad a snifter for breakfast and I promised Flo I wouldn't touch a drop time I was minding you. But you went and brought it all up, and I can't bear it. Not sober, I can't.'

She tipped the flat bottle to her mouth and took a long pull, drew a breath, drank again and wiped her mouth on a dainty, lace-edged handkerchief, highly scented.

'I shall feel better when that's taken,' she said, speaking as though of a vaccination. 'If you must know, the thought of old Paget is what is getting me down. Miss Griffiths, she's dead. I don't know your view on *that*, but to my mind the dead are past hurting and past helping. But the minute I put my 'ead on my pillow I see poor old Paget, what wouldn't 'urt a fly, really, locked up with chaps that carve up little girls and women that bash their babies . . .'

'That's just it. Needn't happen . . . if we say . . . what we know . . . What is the truth.'

'And what good'd that do? I ask you. I could go down there and say I didn't see poor old Paget do no pushing. 'Oo'd take my word against 'ers? And suppose they did, first thing they'd say, "*'Oo* did, then?" Where'd that get us?'

'I saw . . . everything,' Lady Blyborough said. 'I could . . . confirm . . . what you said . . . Mrs. Paget . . . quite innocent.'

A look of real terror swept over Mrs. Childer's face.

' 'Old on,' she cried. 'I only said I never saw no pushing 'S'matter of fact I did say that to Flo, and she said I didn't get there in time. I dunno what *you* saw, but she'd 'ave the answer to that, too. She's smart. And whatever else 'appened or didn't happen, we know one thing would, we'd be out on our ears. I dunno if *you* know any place where'd you be as comfortable and well looked after. If you do, you're lucky. I don't. And there's another thing, too. My boy wouldn't want me getting mixed up in no scandal. And scandal is what this'd be. *News of the World* stuff. Why, they might go digging up Miss Poley! We gotta forget it. You 'ave a pill and a nice cuppa Ovaltine and go to sleep. I got my own medicine. Pulled me through worse than this . . .'

She took another drink.

Kind-hearted, fundamentally a good woman, Lady Blyborough reflected but frightened, weak, unstable. Such people were easily persuaded, always at the mercy of the nearest strong character. Am I, Lady Blyborough wondered, here, close at hand, strong enough to compete with the absent Mrs. Bascombe? There must be no question about it. I *have* to be, she told herself. She thought – and it was for the first time in exactly this way – of the old family from which she sprang, of the stone Crusader in the church, of the soldiers and administrators ... And the Blyboroughs, too, she remembered, brave men and just ...

'Mrs. Childers,' she said, 'this is ... miscarriage of ... justice. We know ... we have a duty. You must ... help me dress. Call a ... taxi. You need ... not come ... Do it alone. No need ... for your boy ... to know.'

'But I ain't going to help you to chuck yourself out of a comfortable 'ome. You've always 'ad things easy. You don't know the world. I do. I 'ad my lesson about not interfering, years ago. I 'ad a 'otel, as maybe you know, and there was a lady, proper top-notcher, used to send her two kids and a nanny, every summer, six weeks straight and no expense spared. Cruel bitch that nanny was; no slum kids ever 'ad it worse than little Lord Plum-Pudding and 'is sister, and after I'd 'ad them twice I up and wrote to their Ma. What 'appened? She kept the nanny and they went somewhere else to stay. I seen 'em, on the beach. And what is more, two more of my best families, friends of 'ers, you see, never come near me again. I'd done them no good and myself a lot of 'arm. It'd be the same now. There ain't no justice in this world and we might as well face it.'

Lady Blyborough thought about the weakness of her legs. No exertion, no excitement; that third stroke lying in ambush.

'Go by myself,' she said.

'No you don't. I shan't let you. I was left to mind you and little as I'd fancy it, if you move off that bed, I'll shove you back. Out of your mind, see? 'Ad to be restrained.'

The whisky was taking effect now; she would soon be out of reach of reason or persuasion. Lady Blyborough made one last effort, remembering that it was Mrs. Childers who had first hinted at things being wrong. She rooted about and found her pad.

'Mrs. Childers ... too long to say ... look.' She wrote, keeping it small to get it in. 'A wise man said that, read it,' she held it out.

Screwing her eyes Mrs. Childers read the words aloud:

'All that is necessary for the complete triumph of evil is that good men should do nothing. That's right. That's absobloodylutely right. But I ain't a good man; I'm a rotten dipso. You're good, I thought that the minute I laid eyes on you, but you ain't a man either, you're just a poor old crock. We need Flo, and Flo need poor old Paget. Simple accident just wouldn't do this time, not so soon after the other . . . Once, when my boy was a tiddler I used to read him tales. Brer Rabbit, you ever come across that? "Lay low and say nuffin." That's what you and me must do.'

There was a silence.

'You'll thank me in the end,' Mrs. Childers said earnestly. 'This is for your good. And mine.'

'Then we must . . . take our medicine. Pill for me . . . whisky for you.'

'Now you're talking,' said Mrs. Childers. She moved, with the experienced drinker's caution to the gate-legged table, where, on a tray, stood a thermos jug, one of the Worcester cups, and a box of pills.

'All that is nesh . . . necessary for complete triumph of evil is good men do nothing,' she repeated. 'No good men about. All die young. Very peculiar thing. Good men, die young. Ever notice that? Never mind. Little pill, little drink. We get by. All be the same in hundred years. Swallow it down.'

She handed Lady Blyborough the pill and set the cup on the bedside tale and then went back to her bottle.

' 'Nother dead man. Good old friend, dead. All good men dead.' She set the bottle down as Lady Blyborough went through the pretence of pill-swallowing. The Ovaltine she drank; she would need all the strength she could muster. Mrs Childers sat down in the comfortable arm chair.

'You go to sleep. Me too. Had a lot of bad nights.'

The little clock ticked away. Ten minutes to eleven. The next five were elastic, endless. Presently Lady Blyborough risked a cautious movement. Mrs. Childers did not stir. All that is necessary for the triumph of justice, Lady Blyborough thought wryly, is that the waverers should fall asleep. Mrs. Childers seemed to have done so; her head had fallen sideways against the wing of the chair; her mouth was slightly open.

Lady Blyborough eased on her slippers, wrestled silently with her dressing-gown. If she were challenged before she reached the bathroom door she would give that as her destination. And from there to the telephone was only a few steps. No fiddling with the telephone directory, she thought. Just pick it up, give her name and address and ask for the police.

As she moved towards the door she remembered, with great clarity, Mrs. Childers remark about knowing another place where she would be so comfortable and well looked after. She knew no such place. It probably did not exist.

She reached the hall, and there turned her head and looked back into the room where she had been, and might have continued to be, so comfortable.

Then she went on.

FORTY YEARS ON

JOHN BULLYER and I met for the first time in 1956 when we were both in our early sixties, but it is true to say that he did more to shape my life than any other person, and is largely responsible for the diffidence which has, I know, been a handicap to me, though I am told that I conceal it very well.

John Bullyer came into my life when my Uncle George, who lived close by us, married, rather late in life, a most delightful woman who thus became my Aunt Carrie and quite my favourite relative. In those days wholesale indulgence of the young had not yet come into full fashion, and a pretty aunt always free with caresses, sweets, words of praise and excuses for misdoings was something of a rarity and greatly to be treasured. For me she had but one drawback; she was also aunt to John Bullyer, the son of her sister who lived in Gloucestershire. She invariably referred to him as 'Little-John-my-other-nephew' all in one word, and she referred to him far too often.

Later in my life I could see her motive; she came to us as a stranger; my mother was a relative by marriage, a near neighbour and a potential friend; we children were common ground, a safe topic for those early, difficult conversations over the teacups.

From Aunt Carrie's point of view it was fortunate, from mine, disastrous, that John Bullyer and I were of comparable age, practically twins, in fact, having been born within four days of one another. Probably hundreds of comparisons were made before I became aware of them, the first that I remember with any clarity was made soon after I began school where I had lain on the floor and wailed that I wanted to go home. Shortly after that my mother reported in a voice that was to become all too familiar, that Little-John-Aunt-Carrie's-other-nephew had started school on the same day and taken to it like a duck to water.

And so it went on. Incredible boy, he knew his nine-times

table while I was still hopelessly bogged in the fours; he was dealing expertly with fractions what time I wrestled unsuccessfully with tens and units. I began to dread Aunt Carrie's erstwhile most welcome visits. She was still just as pretty and gay, still as sweet-smelling, still ready to take part in any childish game, to be enthusiastic about any pursuit, certain to produce chocolate or sixpence from her reticule; but, as soon as she had gone, Mother was sure to say the dread words:

'Aunt Carrie was telling me that John Bullyer ...'

The comparisons were, without exception, to my detriment. The wretched boy never set foot upon a football field without scoring a goal; never took bat in hand without making some notable number of runs. I was hopeless at games; at football I fell in the mud, and caught a cold which became bronchial; at cricket I made ducks, dropped easy catches and was afflicted with nose-bleeding. I became so conscious of my inferiority that even when I overheard my parents speak of John Bullyer as 'The Child Wonder' I never even suspected the irony; I took it literally and believed that they regarded him with the same awe and envy as I did.

To me it seemed sinister that Mother always passed on, with pitiable pride, any small achievement of mine. Once, at my prep. school, I had a story in the magazine and Mother was momentarily jubilant.

'I must have another copy of that,' she said, 'so that Aunt Carrie can send it for John Bullyer's mother to see.' What a boomerang that proved! By return of post came the news that John had won a scholarship.

To anyone now on the bright side of forty it will seem strange that we boys never met, but in those days Gloucestershire was as far removed, in travelling time, from Suffolk, as New York is today, and my father was a man who preferred his own bed to any other. Aunt Carrie kept saying, 'Really, you boys should know one another, I'm sure you'd be such friends,' and once or twice she tried to arrange that John should stay with her in the holidays. Mercifully for me something always prevented him from doing so.

I did have, however, one horribly narrow escape. An elderly couple, distant relatives of my father's, were celebrating their Golden Wedding. They lived in London, reasonably accessible, and they issued such a pressing, sentimentally-worded invitation that even Father was bound to accept. As soon as he had done so Aunt Carrie came over in a state of high excitement. Wasn't the world a small place, the Bullyer family and Father's old relatives had once been near neighbours and all three Bullyers had been bidden to the feast.

I saw my mother look at me, not, I admit, with any lessening of affection, but with a strange, anxious appraisement. When Aunt Carrie had gone Mother said to me:

'You sit there huddled over a book until your back is bent like a bow. Go out and get some air.' I stood up, obediently, and she added, 'Oh, I wish the sun would shine; you look so much better with a little tan.' I realized from that that she and I visualized John Bullyer in the same way, tall, big for his age, straight as a ram-rod, with a handsome brown face and hair like the man pictured on Father's bottle of hair tonic.

Walking made no perceptible difference to my posture and the sun remained disobliging, so Mother, like the practical believer in self-help that she was, tried another tack:

'You'll need a new suit at Easter anyway, you might as well have it now. *And* I'm going to find a different barber. I *cannot* believe that that piece of hair would stick up like that if it were properly cut.'

It was plain to me that I was repulsive to look at as well as being a clown at games and a booby at arithmetic.

On the evening before we were to make our early morning start for London, Mother came into my room and made me try on the new suit. I could see, by the expression on her face that it worked no miracle. Nor, alas, had the new barber. But Mother did not take defeat easily; looks weren't everything, my manners, at least, should pass muster! So while I glumly divested myself of the wasted suit, she gave me a few final instructions. I kept saying, 'Yes, Mother' and 'No, Mother,' and 'I'll remember Mother,' and gritted my teeth together until my jaws ached.

'Have you anything in your mouth *now*?' she demanded.

'No, Mother.'

'Well, hurry into bed and get a good night's sleep.' (Everything looks better in the morning!) She kissed me, fondly, but at the same time she stroked down the obstinate tuft of hair. I felt exactly like a very ugly dog of low pedigree which some doting owner has entered for a show.

I did not sleep well; I had, in fact, the worst night I had ever known. Although I had ceased gritting my teeth my jaws still ached. The pain spread up into my head, back into my ears, down into my throat. With the covers over me I broke into a hot sweat, when I pushed them off deadly chills shook me. In addition to my physical woes I had mental agonies, including that first sad loss of simple faith; I had prayed, as never before, that something might occur to prevent this meeting. The smallest excuse would have served; Father was already regretting his acceptance, he would have seized gladly at any chance to retract it.

I saw the dawn that morning, watched my window grow grey, heard the first bird chorus. After several centuries had dragged by I heard the strident alarm go off in my parent's room and thankfully rose from my bed of torment. I felt little, if any better when I was on my feet. I washed more thoroughly than usual, hopefully plunging the whole of my stuffy-feeling head into the cold water; then I dressed and in honour of the occasion, went to the looking glass to arrange my tie. For a moment, I swear, I thought that nervousness had affected my eyesight; the face that looked back at me was a dreadful caricature of my own, only just recognizable. My ears, ordinarily so prominent, were hidden by the bulge of my jaws and I seemed to have no neck.

Horrified I reeled into my parent's room; Mother was settling a beribboned corset-cover over her bosom and Father was gloomily stropping his razor.

'Do *you* think I look funny this morning?' I blurted.

They both turned. Mother screamed. Father said:

'I wouldn't say *funny*. You look damned peculiar.'

It was mumps. It left me very open-minded about prayer.

Aunt Carrie thought it a great pity that John and I could not go to the same public school; I was spared that by the intransigence of our respective fathers. Harrow, in its charity, accepted my unpromising self; John took his talents to Winchester.

Time went on; so did the comparisons. By word of mouth during the holidays, by phrases that leaped out of letters during term time I was kept up to date with John's prowess and progress. Thus goaded I began at last to look round for something that I *could* do, something at which I could excel. When I found it I worked with a savage intensity, minding nothing else; let this be mine, John Bullyer could have all the rest.

I was, however, still a Grub Street hack, counting it a good week in which I made five pounds, when John attained some glittering appointment in India. That ability to master the nine times table had proved no flash-in-the-pan; he had developed into some kind of financial wizard and was now being 'lent' to the Maharajah of a native state whose exchequer was in a deplorable tangle. There was a paragraph in the daily papers about it.

Aunt Carrie took the cutting to show to my mother. I was glad later that she had that pleasure, for that was her last visit, her last report. She was dead before her other nephew reached his destination. The line which had for so many years vibrated between Gloucestershire and Suffolk was lifeless and dumb.

Three or four times during the next forty years I saw mention of John Bullyer in the press. His was not the kind of career to attract much publicity but those rare paragraphs charted a steady success which culminated in a knighthood when he retired in 1956. On that occasion there was a half column about him; it said that his last job, the handling of some currency crisis in a young South American Republic, had forestalled a revolution. When asked, in an interview, what he intended to do with his leisure Sir John replied 'I hope to take up golf; I have never had time to take it seriously.' I pictured him again, lean and tanned, with a head of well kept grey hair, getting his handicap down in record time. I was sorry that Aunt Carrie could not cut out that half column, sorry too that there was no photograph; I could have looked at it almost unflinching, I thought. I was, by that time, not unsuccessful in my own line.

Late that year, in November, I was in my club, sipping a glass of sherry before dinner. A rather deprecating cough at my elbow made me look round. I saw a short stout man, a round dumpling of a man, glitteringly bald, with a little snub nose that looked too small to support the framework of his heavy glasses. They were of that peculiarly thick kind which reduce the eyes to pin-points. Diffidently, with more than a suggestion of a stammer, he spoke my name and I somewhat grudgingly admitted my identity. Since I attained some measure of fame I have on occasion been accosted by strangers and no matter how flatteringly they speak I am always horribly embarrassed.

'You d-don't know m-me,' said the little man. 'My name's

John B-Bullyer. We once sh-shared an aunt, C-Caroline Lacey.'

I leaped up and shook hands, expressing my pleasure at meeting him at last, and then we settled down to drink sherry together. His stammer, like my shyness, soon wore off.

'I used to hear so *much* about you,' he said with a grin. 'Then I learned that you were a member here and I could not resist asking someone to point you out to me. Though, if you'd looked the least bit as I always imagined I don't think I'd have d-dared to approach you. You see . . . I grew up with the idea that you were at least eight feet tall, tremendously handsome and more talented than da Vinci.' His grin broadened – and I knew why! 'Really,' he said, 'the letters Aunt Carrie used to write about you and the way my mother used to read them out. You were the b-bug-bear of my life.'

'They were nothing,' I said, 'to the letters *your* mother used to write about *you*. I was told every time you got a sum right. I always thought of you as nine feet high, better looking than Robert Taylor and more versatile than Churchill. So they played the game both ways, did they?'

We laughed.

'But it was worse for me,' he said. 'I've always been undersized, and I always had these,' he touched his glasses. 'And there were you, tall and handsome, with *such* nice manners. And so clever too. I had to do something; and all I could ever do was sums, and jolly well kill myself at games in an effort to be popular. I might almost say,' he said, with something like resentment, 'that because of you I've been doing sums all my life!'

'Substitute spinning yarns for doing sums and you have exactly my story,' I said.

We looked at one another. Then it probably dawned on us both that the place in which we sat is not the haunt of men who have been failures in life, and that, boys being what they are, an occasional prod in the rear is no such bad thing. Together we lifted our glasses, and though neither of us spoke, I know that we drank to the memory of Aunt Carrie.

RAPUNZEL, RAPUNZEL, BIND UP YOUR HAIR!

A MONTH or two before my twelfth birthday I had measles – an affliction rather more seriously regarded in those days than it is now – and afterwards I was sent into the country, to my grandparents' farm to recuperate. Summer in that particular place always seemed, and for that matter still seems, to me to be as near to Heaven as anything can be on this earth. My grandparents were extremely indulgent, the weather was glorious and I was beside myself with happiness. Perhaps children can become intoxicated, lifted out of themselves by joy, just as adults are by alcohol. That is the only reason that I can offer for a performance so out-of-keeping with my ordinarily diffident and timid behaviour.

Amongst the men who worked for my grandfather was a man named Padgett. All the male Padgetts, for generations, had tended these same acres with one exception. A boy named Bob, at the age of seventeen, had quarrelled with his father and run away to Canada. That had happened twenty years or so earlier, but he was the first-born, and Mrs. Padgett still grieved for him. In the summer of my visit she had become ill and expressed a wish to see Bob once more; and Bob, now able to afford the trip, came home. He was still not on good terms with his father, who resented his having left home, and his apparent prosperity, and furthermore, held it against him that as soon as he was home Mrs. Padgett 'settled in for to die,' as he put it. It was not, in fact, too far-fetched a statement, for as soon as Bob was home Mrs. Padgett did fade gently away. Bob tended to leave the cottage when his father entered it, and walking through the lanes and woods we often fell in with each other. He had interesting things to tell me about life in a distant land, I was an avid listener, and we were soon fast friends.

The third person in our little triangular story was known to me as Cousin Ada, although our relationship was nothing like as close as the name implies; her mother was my grandmother's cousin. She was a widow, left in comfortable circumstances, with three daughters of whom Cousin Ada was the youngest and either the most intelligent – so that she realized the horrors of her fate, or the most sensitive – so that she suffered from it. Cousin Maud and Cousin Kate appeared to bear up well under a régime of martinet discipline, deliberately inflicted physical discomfort, complete lack of privacy, and mental bullying. Mrs. Storman, known to me as Aunt Janet, was a terrible old woman indeed.

Cousin Ada took refuge in ill-health which gained her some mitigations of the régime; she had a fire in her bedroom occasionally, was allowed warm water for washing, was excused from the 'good brisk walks' and sometimes, even, from church-going.

The Stormans lived in a small town, about four miles from the farm, and although my grandparents disapproved of and laughed about Aunt Janet's autocratic behaviour and my grandfather steadfastly refused to eat what he called her 'workhouse food,' yet she was family, and always, on market day, my grandmother paid a short visit and drank a cup of tea in the big, gloomy house. I went with her only once during that holiday, when I was regaled with a piece of very dry ginger cake which, even *there* tasted peculiar. I turned it over and discovered a healthy growth of blue mould. Such was Aunt Janet's personality, however, that I made no complaint; nor did I leave the cake. I broke off small pieces and swallowed them as though they were pills. Aunt Janet said that she did not like to see growing girls 'pingling' over their food, did I take enough exercise, had my grandmother tried the bracing up effect of a cold bath every morning? Throughout the visit Cousin Ada reclined upon a sofa with a knitted rug over her legs; Cousin Kate and Cousin Maud sat bolt upright on parlour chairs, save when they hurried off on errands. None of them said anything except 'yes' and 'no' in answer to a direct question.

I told my grandfather about the blue mould and he said, 'More fool you to eat it! You should have screamed and dropped the plate.'

When I had been at the farm for a fortnight Dr. Wright, a dear old man, came out from the town to judge how my health was progressing. That took him no time at all, and as I was dismissed from the room with a compliment upon my rosy cheeks I heard my grandmother mention Cousin Ada.

Dr. Wright must have been far ahead of his time, and he was, perhaps, a little indiscreet, for he told my grandmother that all that ailed Cousin Ada was her mother. Her insomnia, her lack of appetite, her nerves, even her fainting fits were all the result of being too strictly dominated.

My grandmother reported this to my grandfather at the supper table that evening adding:

'I'd ask her *here*, but I hardly know what excuse to give. I could hardly say change of air.'

'You couldn't say that if you lived at Brighton,' said my grandfather, carving an enormous joint of cold silverside. 'You'd only get one of those poor girls out of the house for something unpleasant.'

My grandmother mused for a moment; then, with a mischievous grin which accorded ill with her dignified appearance, said:

'Then I know. Enny,' she looked at me, 'I don't mean this. But I could say I found you rather a burden, that I wanted somebody to take you off my hands a bit.'

'You'll get Maud and Kate, handcuffed together,' said my grandfather.

'But I shall ask for Ada. After all she's the youngest, most likely to be company for the child.'

'Oh *Gran*!' I said.

'You'll be told that poor dear Ada is too delicate,' said my grandfather.

'Not if I make it sound tedious enough. Easy, but tedious. I shall say I want Enny kept up with her school lessons, and her piano practice, and to be read to.'

'Read to a great girl of twelve?'

'After measles there is always danger of eye-strain,' said my grandmother triumphantly.

'Oh *Gran*,' I said again.

'It needn't make any difference to you, Enny. You're just the excuse. I hope it will work.'

It worked. Next market day my grandparents brought Cousin Ada, her shawls and scarves, her bottles of tonic, her boxes of pills. Aunt Janet had thrown herself whole-heartedly into the scheme, and she had sent, for me, one of those old-fashioned copy books, each page headed by a maxim or proverb to be copied six times on the lines below. 'Ill gotten gains never prosper.' 'Bad wishes always come to roost.' 'The wicked fleeth when no man pursueth.' Where had she found something so completely in accord with her taste? She had sent me, also, 'Czerny's First Exercises for the Piano,' and two books; *The Daisy Chain* and *Jessica's First Prayer*. I have taken no trouble to describe Aunt Janet, but I think that she emerges fairly clearly in her offerings.

My fears that my holiday would be ruined proved to be ill-founded. In the genial atmosphere of the farm Cousin Ada perked up in no time at all. She became, in fact, unrecognizable. She didn't have a fainting fit, or a nose-bleed; she didn't miss a meal or suffer from insomnia once during the next three weeks. She aided rather than handicapped me in all my activities.

I reciprocated.

I do not intend to give one of those sickening, coy, 'child's eye' accounts of a budding love affair. There was Bob Padgett, unoccupied, hanging about waiting until his mother died; there were Cousin Ada and I making the most of the glorious summer weather and her new freedom. We would meet and they would talk, and if I grew bored I would drift away and follow my own pursuits, seldom out of earshot and never out of sight. A better-chaperoned courtship was never conducted, of that I am sure.

There was a trace of deception about it. After about our third meeting with Bob, Cousin Ada, with a blazing blush, said to me as we returned to supper:

'Enny, perhaps we shouldn't mention meeting Bob again.'

'Whyever not?'

'Well . . .' She hesitated and blushed even redder. 'I think they'd think it was rather funny, being so friendly with one of the workmen.'

'But Bob isn't. He's quite different. He's a farmer too. He and his partner have a farm a lot bigger than this one. And he's aiming, he says to buy his partner out.'

'Yes,' said Cousin Ada. 'He told me that, too. And it may be true. All the same . . . I'd rather you didn't mention it.'

'All right,' I said.

I took it for granted that they would fall in love. It was a state in which I took only an academic interest. Had I been but a year or two older I should have fallen in love with Bob myself. He had such kind, merry blue eyes, and such lovely red hair, not just ginger like the other Padgetts'; and getting away had given him something, a jauntiness, an independence, a way of speaking. I was no fool, I couldn't have imagined Cousin Ada marrying any of Bob's brothers, living in a small thatched cottage, getting water from the well on the green and getting up at six every morning to make a breakfast. But I could see her, in Canada, ruling a farmhouse just as my grandmother ruled hers. It would, I thought, be a wonderful thing for her; she'd escape from that gloomy house, from that dreadful old mother; she'd grow prettier and prettier as she grew happier. They'd live happily ever after.

Mrs. Padgett died and was buried. We all went to the funeral. In the jostle outside the churchyard gate afterwards I saw Bob and Cousin Ada exchange two or three words, no more. But that evening, after supper, Cousin Ada said to me, 'Shall we just walk as far as the kingfisher's nest.' We walked towards the river, and Bob joined us. I went off to watch for the bright blue bird and they talked, longer, more earnestly than usual. It was getting dusk when we turned towards the house.

At the place where we ordinarily parted company they seemed to have forgotten caution, so I nipped Cousin Ada's arm and grimaced a warning. She said:

'It's all right, darling. Bob and I are going to get married. He's coming up to the house to tell Uncle Richard.'

It all seemed so natural, so unmomentous that when we reached the farm I went into the pantry, poured myself a glass of milk and found a plate of oat-cakes and went off to bed, never dreaming of the scene taking place below.

The truth was, of course, that Cousin Ada had been absolutely right in her assessment of my grandparents' attitude towards 'workmen.' They belonged to a generation which acknowledged rigid class distinctions. To give them their due they would have been just as much shocked if Cousin Ada had walked in and announced that she intended to marry Sir Francis Sheladine from the Hall. 'Quite unsuitable,' my grandmother would have said. As she said it now.

I think that, as well as being shocked, they were a little frightened. Aunt Janet's formidable reputation had not been built upon nothing. She would attack them savagely; and they were bound to admit to some guilt. This extraordinary thing had happened while Ada was under their roof, in their care. And if they were shocked, what would the mother's feelings be? It is symbolic that amongst the things my grandmother said was this:

'If you will promise, my dear, to abandon this hare-brained scheme, I promise never to mention it to your mother.'

Cousin Ada, full of good food and oxygen – for the first time in her life, full too of self-importance and the afflatus of love, refused to promise any such thing.

'Bob and I are going to be married,' she said.

'Then you must go home tomorrow, Ada, and tell your mother and make your arrangements from there. Your Uncle Richard and I cannot have any responsibility now. We are sorry for you, but you have been very silly.'

Cousin Ada then began to cry.

'Couldn't I stay here? Please. I'll write and tell Mother and I know that when she hears she won't *want* me back. It's only for just a few days. Bob's going to get a special licence and we're leaving for Canada as soon as we are married.'

The mention of special licences completed the rout. No respectable people were married without the asking of banns, the gathering of relatives, wedding breakfasts, white veils and orange blossom. However, my grandparents, though old-fashioned, were kind-hearted. They agreed that Cousin Ada should stay at the farm; she must write a letter which would be taken, by hand, into the town first thing in the morning.

Cousin Ada, to whom love had made the whole world new, obviously believed that her mother was included in the metamorphosis. She wrote the letter and then, with no sign of apprehension, settled down to give me my morning 'lessons.' My grandparents did not delude themselves. My grandmother donned her second best dress, her gold chain and cameo brooch – her social armour; and my grandfather did not go more than a hundred yards from the house all the morning.

Ada and I were busy with Czerny's sixth exercise when Aunt Janet arrived in the vehicle known as the station cab, a motorcar which the enterprising owner of a livery stables had just introduced to the town. Its noisy approach warned the defending forces and my grandfather joined my grandmother upon the front doorstep. I stopped playing. Cousin Ada stood up.

Aunt Janet, speaking no word, charged into the house and into the parlour. She took Cousin Ada by the arm and shook her as though she had been a four-year-old caught raiding a jam pot. Every bit of colour, of flesh, of spirit that the poor girl had acquired during her brief holiday, fell away; she collapsed completely, and would, I think, have fallen, but for her mother's grip on her arm.

Hustling her towards the door Aunt Janet came again face to face with my grandmother who again tried to speak.

She got as far as, 'We're sorry, Cousin Janet but I'm sure . . .'

Cousin Janet thrust her aside.

My grandfather, misliking this treatment of his wife said in a more blustering voice:

'Look here, Janet . . .'

She pushed him away too, and was out of the house and into the station cab before anyone could speak again. Once inside it she shouted:

'I shall write and tell you what I think of *you*!'

The letter arrived by next morning's post and was treated, I thought, with more gravity than it deserved. True, my grandfather did say, 'Well, if she never speaks to us again it will be no great loss.' But he did not say it lightly and my grandmother said:

'She is my cousin; and living so close it will be very awkward. There's bound to be *talk*.'

They said, of course, 'Poor Ada.' They were sorry for her, but in all the wrong way; sorry that she had been silly, and that she had incurred her mother's rage. They did not pity her on account of the broken love affair, for that had never seemed real to them, just a bit of silliness which should never have happened.

I was the one whose heart was wrenched with pity for Ada, and for Bob. I was romantic by nature, and an addict of *Grimm's Fairy Tales*. Within a few hours I was seeing Cousin Ada as Rapunzel, Bob Padgett as the Prince, and Aunt Janet as the wicked old witch.

Bob lived up to the role assigned him. He borrowed a bicycle and rode into town, mounted the steps of that gloomy house and actually achieved an interview with Aunt Janet. Cleverer than my grandparents, she made no mention of social differences but took her stand on the unassailable ground of Cousin Ada's health. She actually made Bob wait in her blood-red and dark brown parlour while Cousin Maud went to fetch an ally – Dr. Wright.

The kindest thing I can say about *him* is that he must have been extremely ignorant about conditions in Canada; or else, like everyone else, he was less bold in Aunt Janet's presence than out of it. He gave her his whole-hearted support; a delicate young lady like Miss Ada would never survive the cold, the privations, the terrible thunderstorms; that was, if she ever reached her destination, which was doubtful. One bout of seasickness would probably finish off a girl so frail . . .

Bob reported this to me, the only sympathetic hearer within reach.

'I kept trying to tell them that she'd have a damn sight more comfortable home than she has now; but they wouldn't listen. They carried on as if I was aiming to murder her.'

'Did they let you see her?'

'No. I asked. But they reckoned it'd be too much of an upset. And if I wrote her a letter she wouldn't get it. I don't even know how she's bearing up, poor little dear.'

I thought that there, at least, I could be of help. I was considered capable of driving a very old, staid, fat pony attached to a small buggy, and I suggested to my grandmother that perhaps it would be right for me to drive into town taking the things which Cousin Ada had left. My grandmother welcomed this idea.

'You are in no way to blame for anything; I don't see why you should be unwelcome. You could find out how poor Ada is.'

I packed very cunningly, taking only duplicates of Ada's garments, but scrupulously including everything Aunt Janet had sent for my benefit. My grandmother sent a peace-offering; a plump young fowl, a pound of butter, a pint of cream and some choice Victoria plums.

Aunt Janet received me civilly, but grimly; I was, after all, from the enemy camp. My grandmother's offering she rejected, though I could see that it hurt her to do so.

'You may say,' she said sternly, 'that a breach of trust is not to be mended by a mess of pottage.'

Still, I had gained an entry and now set myself out to charm her. In my smoothest, smuggest manner I thanked her for the things she had provided for my edification, yes, even for *Jessica's First Prayer* I thanked her. I could see all her opinions about me undergoing a rapid revision. I was plainly a nice child, being spoiled by wrong-handling, a child out of whom she could have made something good, another Maud, Kate, Ada.

'You may keep all the books,' she said.

I thanked her again, fulsomely. Then I squeezed out a tear. Cousin Ada, I said, had been so kind to me, and I hadn't had a chance to say good-bye to her.

I could see, as plainly as though it had been written in that copy-book, that later on a fresh reproach would be heaped upon poor Ada's head – 'Look how your wicked behaviour upset that innocent child!'

'You may take up her belongings. Don't stay for more than a moment. Her room is first on the right.'

Even on this warm summer day there was a deadly chill in that house, the chill that comes from having the sunlight excluded, the floors and furniture too well polished. Cousin Ada's room was a tomb, faintly scented with Eau de Cologne.

She looked terrible; she must have cried ever since she left the farm; her face was puffy and almost transparent; even her fair bright hair looked dark and flat and damp. She began to cry anew at the sight of me. I daren't even wait for the crying to stop.

'Are you still in love with Bob?' I demanded brusquely.

'I always shall be, always,' she snuffled. 'Tell him that, please dear. Please tell him that, from me.'

'Would you run away and marry him?'

'How could I? I'm watched every minute.'

'Never mind that. Would you?'

'Of course I would, but . . .'

'Enny!' came Aunt Janet's sergent-major's voice up the stairs. 'I said a minute!'

'Coming,' I cried. 'Cousin Ada, could you get well enough to go on with my piano lessons?'

I began to back towards the door, keeping my eye on her. She looked confused and dubious, but she did give a little nod. I went demurely downstairs.

'Aunt Janet,' I said, to the watcher in the hall, 'I am going to miss my piano lessons. I was getting on so nicely on that new book. I wanted to give my mother a surprise when I go home. Do you think if I came in sometimes Cousin Ada would feel well enough to teach me some more?'

'I should have to ask Dr. Wright about that.'

'Will you, please, Aunt Janet?'

'I will.'

'When?'

'He will look in this afternoon, I expect.'

'Then I'll come tomorrow and find out. Oh, I do *hope*,' I said, clasping my hands, 'that he will say yes.'

'Don't forget my message,' she said. 'Can you remember it, word for word?'

I repeated it and took my leave. All the way home I gorged myself on the rejected Victoria plums which, on the earlier journey, had been a great temptation to me.

Dr. Wright said he thought that any interest would be of benefit to poor Miss Ada in this crisis. So I resumed my piano lessons. And nobody not nailed to the floor would have stayed in the parlour while I made my way through Czerny's seventh and eighth exercises, so Cousin Ada and I had plenty of opportunity to perfect one end of the plan.

At the other I had far more trouble.

'But that's eloping,' Bob said. 'I wasn't reckoning on anything like that! Like people in the Sunday papers.'

'You'll be on your way to Canada by the next Sunday, so why should you fret?'

'Why must there be all this hole-and-corner business? Why can't it be done decent like? There must be some other way.'

'All right, you find it,' I said.

He tried. He went to see my grandfather, showed him a snapshot of his house, told him the name of his bank and invited an investigation into his solvency, begging him to use his influence on Aunt Janet. I'm afraid that my grandfather did not see a handsome, pushing young man with a future ahead of him, he just saw a Padgett and a renegade Padgett at that. He said – which was true – that he had no influence on Mrs. Storman, and – which was unkind – that even if he had he would hesitate to use it.

'And your Gran stood there all the while, straight as a ramrod and not a word either way.'

'Well, I told you so,' I said with asperity. 'You'll have to do it my way nor not at all.'

'I went to the house again, yesterday,' he said, miserably. 'The old woman slipped the chain on the door and talked to me through the crack. She said if I went there again she'd call the police.'

'And *that,*' I said nastily, 'is the woman you're going to leave Cousin Ada with for the rest of her life, while you go off back to Canada and marry somebody else, I suppose.'

'Not on your life,' he said. 'Even your way'd be better than that.'

I resented that 'even'; so I said firmly:

'Well, I'm going to have a lesson this afternoon and I shall arrange one more for Tuesday morning at half past ten. I'll pick you up – if you come, at Button's Green and drop you just outside the town. The best train to London goes at ten to eleven.'

He said – and if he had been a woman he would have been half crying, 'They won't let me do the thing straight, like I wanted to, so I'll have to do it crooked. That's all their fault!'

I had my penultimate lesson and my last talk with Ada, and arranged to come for my last lesson on the Tuesday. That time I took with me the items of clothing which I had reserved – enough to last Cousin Ada to Canada, I thought. I picked Bob up at the place appointed, dropped him and the luggage and drove on to the witch's castle, where, entering, I was careful to leave the door just ajar.

Aunt Janet, Maud and Kate were in the kitchen, the mother supervising, the daughters making, a batch of plum jam. Cousin Ada waited for me in the parlour. I sat down, placed my hands heavily on the keys and said:

'He's at the station getting the tickets. Off you go!'

Since that morning I have been kissed many times, never, I swear with more fervour. She kissed me and was gone. I banged my way through all the exercises with which I had nodding acquaintance. I played *The Bluebells of Scotland* and *The Bells of Aberdovy*. The great ugly black marble clock on the draped mantelpiece ticked away and presently, most grudgingly, struck eleven. I went back to exercise one.

At ten minutes past eleven – late, because of the jam-making, Maud brought in the refreshments which were one of the penalties of the morning lesson. For Ada there was a sponge finger and a glass of milk, for me a slice of ginger cake and some sour, watery lemonade.

'Where's Ada?' she asked.

'Gone to the lavatory,' I said.

I poured my lemonade into the aspidistra, put the ginger cake in my pocket – the pony which I had left hitched to the lamp-post would eat anything. I played exercises two and three. I drank the milk and ate the sponge finger – that would fool them, I thought. Then I went to the kitchen door and said, just as usual:

'Good-bye, Aunt Janet, thank you very much. Good-bye, Cousin Maud, good-bye Cousin Kate.'

There was, of course, an inquiry. I stuck to my story. Two minutes before Maud brought in the elevenses, Cousin Ada had excused herself and left me. I had eaten my cake, drunk my lemonade and finished my exercises and just come home.

Incidentally Cousin Ada, in making her bid for freedom, all unwittingly struck the shackles from her sisters, too; for Aunt Janet's fury resulted in a slight stroke which changed her from a formidable tyrant to a rather pitiable dependant. And serve her right!

On the following Christmas Cousin Ada sent me a very beautiful and expensive muff-and-tippet set of sable. But gratitude, like everything else, is expendable. There were Christmas cards and then they ceased.

Forty-two years – so long a time when they lie ahead, so short a time to look back upon, went by. My grandparents had no grandson, and the farm was left to me. I did not inherit any Padgetts, the more's the pity. Those forty-two years included the Kaiser's War and the Hitler War and two of Bob's brothers are remembered on one side of our village war memorial, three of his nephews on the other. A surviving nephew is the borough surveyor in the town where Aunt Janet lived.

One morning, quite recently, I opened my door in answer to that note in the dogs' barking which says 'stranger', and, with a sense of time slipping backwards, beheld Bob Padgett. There were the same kind, merry blue eyes, the red hair; but this boy was younger than the Bob I had known and dressed in modern, colourful fashion.

He told me his name, and I told him mine.

'Ah,' he said, 'that makes it easier. My Grandma said to ask at the farm first.' He then told me his errand; he was over here on a trip and had come to look up his grandparents' families. 'My Grandma,' he said, 'is one of those folks you do what she says even when you're five thousand miles out of reach. She's a Tartar.'

'Your Padgett Grandmother – Ada?'

'That's the one,' he said, with a grin in which amusement and admiration and ruefulness all had a part.

I asked the boy into the kitchen, where I was bottling plums. I should, I felt have been making jam, that would have rounded the story off properly. I tried to imagine Cousin Ada, frail, ailing, drooping lily, in the role of Tartar, and failed. What I could call to mind, with astonishing clarity after all these years, was the figure of Aunt Janet.

I made some coffee, and over it asked, and answered questions. It seemed impossible to keep away, for long, from Grandma Padgett.

'Of course we get a lot of laughs out of her,' he said. 'But to live with, oh boy!' He cast up his eyes. 'Poor old Grandpa, she put him through hoops.'

'In what way?'

'Oh, drop your shoes before you come in the house; no smoking in the parlour; no back answers. You know the kind of thing.'

I clutched my 'happy ever after' dream by the last fluttering rag.

'I know,' I said. 'But maybe for all that they've been happy. Some men like masterful wives.'

'Well, I dunno,' the boy said; he wrinkled his young forehead and pursed his mouth, thoughtfully. 'I should say not. I judge that by the only bit of advice I ever had from him. You see, by the time I was old enough to pay him any mind she'd got him so he didn't feel qualified to hand out any advice. But one day he did say a piece to me.'

'And what was that?'

'He said to me – "Son, whatever you do, don't make a runaway match. There's two things against it," he said. "One if the girl has to run, she's running from something that's likely to break out in her, later on. And two, if you run off with a girl she'll think you're so darn set on her, she'll know she's got you by the short hairs!" '

'And he was speaking from experience?'

'It sounded that way.'

'How sad,' I said. Poor Bob Padgett, with his kind merry eyes, paying all through life for my mistake. I'd been so busy with my thoughts about Rapunzel and the Prince and the wicked old witch that I had overlooked one important thing. Rapunzel was *not* the old witch's daughter . . .

PORTRAIT OF A MOTHER

WHEN I was a young man, newly qualified and desperately in need of what employers call experience, I took a job in a small West Indian island. Four dull but pleasant years there, spent in the routine pursuit of my profession appeared to work much to my advantage. Even today someone occasionally refers to my valuable West Indian experience and it amuses me to think that the only thing I experienced in St. Agnes which I might not equally well have experienced in Surbiton, was in no way connected with my job.

I lived, during those four years, in a charming small bungalow, surrounded by a lush garden, halfway up a hill that overlooked the town and the harbour. The bungalow 'went' with the job and a housekeeper named Rosanna Watkins appeared to 'go' with the bungalow. Now in her middle forties, she had served, most efficiently, a number of my predecessors. She was very handsome, and, so far as one could judge from her looks, of pure Negro blood – a rarer thing in the islands than is commonly supposed. She had great dignity of manner and spoke ordinary English in an ordinary way. I did not realize that this is also apparently uncommon until I made a circle of acquaintances and learned how often somebody else's cook or gardener gave vent to some utterance which, properly relayed, could set a dinner table in a roar of laughter. Rosanna never provided me with any such social ammunition. Indeed, only once did she ever say anything to me that my own mother might not have said, and that I have, until now, kept to myself.

In those days I was somewhat shy, and Rosanna was not the type to make uninvited communications, so the little I learned about her at first was told to me by other people. She was a widow and had a son named Thomas for whom she was very – some people thought over – ambitious. At quite an early age she had sent him out of the island to a boarding-school, and he was now taking a medical course in London. Hearing this I did for a moment wonder about the money; by English standards Rosanna's wages were very small and I knew how expensive living in London could be, how lengthy medical training. But that was no affair of mine. Thomas might have won scholarships; his father might have left money; there were half a dozen explanations. Later on, when Rosanna and I were on more confidential terms, she explained, during one of our long talks about Thomas, where the money had come from. An early predecessor of mine, Rosanna's first employer, had left her a thousand pounds in his will.

'And that,' she said, 'with what I earned and saved, got Thomas out of the Islands and gave him a chance to *be* something.'

It was a large legacy, and perhaps the trite, unworthy suspicion which slid uninvited into my mind showed on my face.

'I'd earned every penny of it, sir,' said Rosanna, giving me a straight look from her fine dark eyes. 'Mr. Barker was taken with his first stroke on the ship coming here, and he was, the whole of his time, till he died, helpless as a baby and a lot heavier.'

'But he was here, and at work, for six years,' I said in astonishment. I had heard a good deal about Barker, his efficiency and cleverness had established a kind of legend in the island. Not one reference to him had even hinted at infirmity.

'Ah,' Rosanna said, 'he was clever, you never thought about his being so crippled. It was as though all the strength had gone out of his legs into his brains. He was a nice gentleman, too. The best I ever worked for.'

Later on I remembered how sincerely, and with what lack of emotion, she paid Mr. Barker that tribute.

Eventually I was sufficiently admitted to Rosanna's confidence to be shown the photograph which always stood beside her bed, and to share the letters which arrived with commendable punctuality every Thursday by airmail. The photograph was an enlargement of a Polyfoto taken in an Oxford Street store, and showed a very handsome, intelligent face with that smooth finished look which I have noticed before in those whose parents have closely resembled one another. Most of our uglinesses are the result of unfortunate combinations of features. Of the letters' contents Rosanna always offered me any reference to the English weather and to Thomas's out-of-college activities. I had taken my own degree so recently, and so painfully that once or twice it occurred to me that for a student Thomas Watkins led a very full and peripatetic life. There were mentions of a visit to Stratford-on-Avon, to a walking tour in Cornwall; he patronized the Ballet and the theatre; he watched cricket at Lord's and tennis at Wimbledon. These diversions would not have been possible to me in my student days, but then I had not been very clever and I had not been studying medicine. Besides, as everyone knows, educational systems become more elastic every year. So I never commented, but contented myself by describing to Rosanna any place or event mentioned by Thomas and even half-familiar to myself. As I did so a dreamy, satisfied look would come over her face. It was plain that she shared her son's experiences and was, in a very real sense, fulfilled by them.

In two ways – only one of which concerned me – Rosanna differed from most of her kind. The one that mattered to me was the way she cooked. St. Agnes had originally been settled by the Spaniards and their method of cooking, to my taste over-oily and over-flavoured, had outlasted the Spanish occupation by two centuries. Rosanna cooked in the English fashion which suited my somewhat queasy stomach. Her other departure from type was that she was not a Methodist. Wesley's influence was also strong in the islands and I can say without reserve that in St. Agnes every really decent, industrious native attended the chapel which stood downhill of the bungalow. The sound of hymn-singing and sometimes of a more than ordinarily vehement exhortation would come drifting up to us. It struck me as strange that Rosanna, such obvious Methodist material, should not be a member of the community.

Time went along and the examination which should decide whether Thomas might call himself Dr. Watkins or not, drew near. Rosanna and I sometimes spoke of the future immediately beyond this ordeal. She was extremely sensible about it. She did not hope that he would return to St. Agnes.

'It'd be nice for me to be able to see him and look after him, but there's no future for him here; it's too small and he'd be lonely. And I don't want him to stay in London, either; one more decent educated black man wouldn't count there. It's on the bigger islands where his sort are badly needed. Still, it's his life and he must choose for himself.'

Never, at any time, did she mention the possibility of his

failure. I don't think it ever occurred to her. On the eve of the examinations she sent him a costly cable of loving good wishes, and then we settled down to wait.

Like everything else in a climate where the early morning hours are most conducive of energy, the letter delivery began betimes, and the postman, never over-laden, always reached the bungalow before breakfast, usually while I was in my bath. He rode a bicycle and heralded his approach by the merry ringing of the bell. I heard him one morning and did not attach any significance to the sound; it was a cable we were awaiting, not a letter. To me the cable had seemed a little slow in coming, but then any waiting is tedious and I was unfamiliar with the procedure of medical examiners.

On this morning I went down to the verandah where I took my breakfast, and found the table unprepared. The folded cloth lay beside a tray of crockery and cutlery, just as Rosanna had left them when the postman arrived. I waited a little, and then I realized that no pleasant breakfast smells, and no sound came from the kitchen. It was with a pang of foreboding that I walked along to the door and looked in.

Rosanna sat at the white-scrubbed table, her large capable hands folded and weighing down a sheet of paper which bore a few lines of writing. An ordinary white envelope, lacking the gay airmail edge, lay torn and gaping on the floor. I saw so much; then I saw Rosanna's face, more mortally stricken, I thought, than anything but news of sudden death could warrant. The dark velvety bloom of her skin had bleached to a colour hard to name, a dead, dirty, pinkish-grey, a little like that of the surplus plums which an over-laden tree discards early in the season. Every feature drooped and sagged, and as she stared straight ahead of her the white line of eyeball showed below the iris.

I said, as gently as possible, 'Rosanna.' Without moving she said:

'He failed.'

Relief ran through me. 'Is that all! Rosanna, I thought he was dead. Good heavens, what's one failure? He can try again. I knew a man who failed three times and then passed . . .'

'This is different,' she said. 'This is the judgment of God. On me. I looked to be punished, but I never dreamed He'd take it out on Thomas.' She spoke in a flat dead voice until she came to the name; then her voice broke. 'Oh my poor, poor boy! My poor Thomas, working so hard and now it's all wasted.' She put her head down on her hands and sobbed, not noisily, but very bitterly.

'This is silly,' I said, putting my hand on her heaving shoulder. 'I'll tell you something, Rosanna. I don't think Thomas *has* worked so hard. He's been going around far too much and having too good a time. This will be a lesson to him; he'll grind away at his books and pass next time with flying colours. You'll see.'

'No,' she sobbed. 'No. It's true what the Bible says. The sins are visited on the children and God is not mocked. Oh, but it's hard to be punished this way, to see him suffer. I sold my soul to get Thomas his chance. You'd think that'd be enough . . .'

This looked as though it was going to turn into hysteria; I must avert that. With an affected briskness I said:

'Look, Rosanna, this is all very well. I'm sorry you've been disappointed, but I want my breakfast. How about making some coffee?'

'I'm finished,' she said.

'You'll feel better if you buck up and get back to work.' This time there was genuine impatience in my voice. 'One simple little setback and you're behaving as if it was the end of the world. What about *me*?' I demanded. 'Am I to starve, or make my own breakfast?'

She just went on crying. I turned from her and began my somewhat fumble-fisted preparations. When the coffee was made I poured a cup and set it on the table.

'You drink that, Rosanna,' I said. 'You'll feel better soon.'

She did not lift her head.

'You mean well. But you don't understand. No matter how hard Thomas worked, he'd fail. I did a great sin to get Thomas started, and this is the end of it. God knew I didn't care what happened to me, but I had to be punished some way.'

I thought she might feel better if she talked about it; also I was not entirely free from curiosity. I poured another cup of coffee and sat down at the opposite side of the table.

'What sin did you do, Rosanna?'

'I killed Mr. Barker.'

That, I knew, was sheer nonsense. Barker had actually died in the office of a cerebral haemorrhage: the manner of his death was part of the legend and either an exhortation to, or a warning against, over-devotion to duty. I gently reminded Rosanna of how and where and why Mr. Barker had died.

'That's all they know,' she said.

'Why should you blame yourself?'

Staring straight ahead, she told me. To this day there are moments when the scent of freshly-made coffee can bring to my memory the sound of Rosanna's tear-soaked contralto voice making its sad confession.

This was the gist of her tale—

When she began to keep house for Mr. Barker she was already a widow and Thomas was four years old, 'the honey-sweetest little boy you ever saw,' Mr. Barker had been incapacitated by his first stroke, aboard ship, and had to be helped into and out of his clothes, into and out of the car that took him to the office. One day, under an impulse of gratitude he had promised to remember Rosanna in his will. By that time Rosanna was looking round and wondering what there was for Thomas except to be a dock labourer, like his father. The promise gave her hope, for Mr. Barker was a sick man. But the years went by. (Any parent will testify how fast they go, the early years of a child's life.) Thomas was clever, had learned all the little local school could teach him. He became twelve. 'They age early in the islands, boys do, and he was beginning to run around with a lot that took no account of schooling and such. I knew it'd soon be too late.' So Rosanna – then a member of the Methodist chapel, took leave to point out to God the salient features of the situation, and prayed that Mr. Barker might soon be relieved of his troublesome body and taken to Heaven with all its joys. And – these were her very words, 'God did His best, I will say that.' The best was not good enough. Mr. Barker had another stroke which left his face a little twisted. So then Rosanna 'tried the other thing'. There was a woman, a Voodoo practitioner who lived up in the hills. Rosanna visited her and told her what she wanted. The woman asked for a cutting of Mr. Barker's hair and fingernails; she also asked for a sum of money – a full month's wages. All these Rosanna supplied and within twenty-four hours Mr. Barker was dead. 'I knew what I was doing. I knew I couldn't go to chapel again; nor hope for Heaven when I died; but to me that looked well worth while, to get Thomas his chance. But I can see now that wasn't enough. What you take on yourself can't count as punishment. Punishment has to *hurt* and God knew just how to hurt me worst.'

I had – I am glad to say – enough sense to receive this confession with gravity.

'I know just how you feel,' I said, 'but I assure you, you have no reason to blame yourself. Mr. Barker would have died without any help from you. I'll talk to you about it this evening. I'm half an hour late already.'

When I returned she was still sitting where I had left her, the cup of coffee untouched and scummed beside her. That she had moved – though not on my account, for my bed was still unmade – was proved by the fact that she had written to Thomas. It was a bulky letter and the address was smudged. I guessed that it contained her self-denouncement.

'Shall I post this for you? I have some letters of my own.'

She nodded. I took the letter and locked it away until such time as she came to her senses. I pretended to go to the post and came back prepared to reason with her. I had, by that time, heard a little about the variety of old magical cults and superstitious practices covered by the word Voodoo. The whole thing stemmed back to the beliefs in the African witch-doctors which the slaves had brought with them. It had gone underground in the islands and though few people lent it any credence, some fanciful and highly dramatic stories were current. My own scepticism was so deep and so certain that Rosanna's story shocked me no more than if she had told me that she had ridden through the air on a broomstick. I was sure that I had only to talk to her to convince her.

So I went light-heartedly into the kitchen and began to open tins and make a meal for us both. I talked as I worked, as reasonably and persuasively as I could. She sat and stared at the wall. Now and again I said, 'Are you *listening* to me, Rosanna?' and she nodded her head, but it was plain enough that nothing I said meant anything at all. She ignored the plate of food that I offered her. I began by feeling sorry for her, but within an hour I had learned that pity is extremely volatile; mine had evaporated completely and I longed to shout at her, shake, slap her.

In the end I left her and went to make my bed. I slept badly and dreamed that Rosanna brought me a cup of coffee, heavily scummed, with bits of hair and finger-nails resting on the scum.

When I went into the kitchen in the morning, she was still sitting where I had left her and her appearance gave me a fright. In twenty-four hours she had shrunk. Her handsome, full-fleshed face and good solid body had taken on the flabby, failing look of a half-deflated balloon. I took her by the arm and said:

'Rosanna, you must come and lie down.' It was like guiding a somnambulist back to bed. I covered her with her quilt of intricate patchwork and returned to the kitchen, made coffee, boiled eggs.

I took her her breakfast and said things like 'making bad worse,' and 'pulling yourself together' and 'making an effort for Thomas's sake.' None of them reached their mark.

I was busy in the office that day and it would have suited me to have lunched in the town, but I was anxious and went home. There was no change, except that Rosanna seemed a little more shrivelled, a little farther out of reach. After lunch I went straight to the doctor's office; I told him that my housekeeper, Rosanna Watkins had had a disappointment and was taking it badly, no physical ailment that I could see, just a withdrawal from life.

'Was it her boy? Well, he's been her one concern. Her mainspring, I should say. I'll come and see her if you like, but there's nothing I can do.'

'There *must* be.'

'There isn't. I've known similar cases. It isn't a theory in favour with whites but it is a fact, Negroes are much more mind over matter than we are. That is why they can survive physical hardships to an incredible extent and then lie down and die because someone ill wishes them.'

'You aren't implying that Rosanna is going to die!'

'She may – if she's set her mind to it. And there's nothing that I or anyone else can do about it. There's another fact. As a race, you know, they have shown themselves to be extremely resistant to any kind of psychiatry. Odd, isn't it? To be at once so susceptible and so impervious . . .'

He was interested, but in a detached, impersonal way, proper, no doubt to his profession. But I – I realized it suddenly – was very fond of Rosanna.

'I've thought of something that might rouse her,' I said. 'If it doesn't work I should be obliged if you'd come up and see her.'

'I'll do that,' he said and gave me a glance, interested, detached, impersonal, noting, I do not doubt, that I was young and making a great fuss about a small thing.

I looked in at the office and said I should not be back again that day; then I drove home. I went first into my bedroom, and then into the kitchen where I heated a glass of milk, sugared it well and added some whisky. This I carried to Rosanna's bedside.

'Now,' I said, 'you drink this. That is an order. If you don't I shall pour it down your throat.'

She looked at me with her dead eyes. I lifted her head, held the glass to her mouth, pushing the edge of it roughly between her lips and tipped it. She gasped and gulped and a good deal of the liquid spilled, but a good deal more went down her throat. When I set the glass down I took up the photograph of Thomas.

'Rosanna,' I said, 'I am going to *prove* to you that this is all nonsense; that you had nothing to do with Mr. Barker's death. I want you to go and find that Voodoo woman and give her this . . .' I put down in the space Thomas's photograph had stood, a piece of paper containing some nail clippings and a bit of my flaming ginger hair. I laid some money beside it. 'You are to buy for *me* Rosanna, exactly the same spell that you bought for Mr. Barker.'

For the first time something showed in her eyes. And it was fear.

'Oh no, sir. I couldn't do that. That'd be *two*. You don't know what you're asking.'

'I'm asking you to have a spell put on me. And nothing will happen. Then perhaps you'll realize that what you did had nothing at all to do with Mr. Barker's death.'

She began to whimper.

'Oh Lord, sir. Leave it alone. Leave me be. The harm's done now. I can't have two on my conscience.'

'Will you do it?'

'No, sir. What I did, I did for Thomas. Nothing'd make me do it again.'

'Then I shall go to that woman and take this photograph and buy a spell for Thomas.'

That brought her up to a sitting position on the bed.

'You wouldn't,' she cried. 'Oh, sir, you couldn't do that! Not *Thomas*!'

'Oh, couldn't I? He's an idle young scamp and I have him to thank for a very uncomfortable time. I'll buy him the best spell ever, I'll have his hair and his legs and his liver.'

'But you don't believe in spells,' she said in a pitiable attempt to reason me out of it.

'Of course I don't. I believe in them so little that I'll buy one for Thomas with no more thought than I'd give to buying a postage stamp.'

She was on her feet now, her hand pressed to her mouth.

'That's true. It'd be a joke to you. You don't know what you're handling.'

I thought I was handling an obstinate, superstitious woman, and doing it rather well.

'You make up your mind. It's me or Thomas.'

'Then you don't leave me any choice. Thomas never had anything to do with it. You pushed in, sir. This time you're to blame. You're forcing this on me. You remember that!'

Some quality in her voice sent a little chill wriggling between my shoulder-blades, but I said stoutly:

'That's right, Rosanna. I'm forcing you to do it. Off you go. And ask her for a quick-working one, because I'm very tired of the whole business.'

She gave me the sort of look which an unusually sensitive bystander in the days of public executions might have turned upon one of those callous rogues who joked upon the scaffold. She was a pitiable figure; she was still wearing the dress and apron in which she had received the letter and her usually meticulous coiffure was in sad disarray, but there was a kind of dignity about her still.

'I'm begging you not to force this on me, sir.'

'Go along,' I said.

She took up the paper and the money and moving slowly made for the door. I watched her walk between the pink and white flowers of the ginger bushes, and then, taking Thomas's photograph with me, went into the sitting-room and wrote some over-due letters.

Dusk fell and presently I was hungry. I went into the kitchen and opened another tin, cursing Thomas Watkins as I did so. Since manufacturers are touchy about their reputations I will not mention the name on the tin's label, nor its contents, but it was a brand of repute and the food, I swear, in perfect condition. While it heated I made some toast, burning it as usual. I drank a bottle of my favourite beer. I wrote two more letters, read a book for a while and then went to bed, leaving the door unlocked because Rosanna had not returned.

I am no stranger to a mild form of indigestion which assails me occasionally after a dinner-party, or an excess of shell-fish, or strawberries, any dish containing twice-cooked meat leads to trouble and I have to be a little careful about cucumber, radishes and pickles. The pain which woke me in the middle of the night was familiar, though unjustified, I thought. One simple, Spartan dish, partly composed of burnt toast, akin to the charcoal which is a remedy for acid stomachs. However, there it was; I woke with indigestion, switched on the light, noted that it was half past one, and padded to the bathroom where I prudently kept a supply of a tried and efficacious cure. I gulped it down and went back to bed, telling myself that the anxiety of the last two days was to blame. I had suffered in this way before on the eve of examinations or interviews. The pain grew worse and at two o'clock I repeated the dose, less hopefully; apparently nervous indigestion was less easily cured; relaxation was necessary. I went back to bed and endeavoured to relax.

The pain grew worse. Distraction, I thought, and put on the light and attempted to read. The most engrossing literary work is, alas, wasted on a person in whose stomach a wild cat, with several extra feet, all armed with red hot claws, is imprisoned and trying to tear its way out. Presently my heart took objection to its unpleasant neighbour and began to bang, as offended neighbours will, upon the communicating wall. My lungs then became involved and soon I could only breathe in short, noisy little gasps. I became very hot, broke into a profuse perspiration, and turned very cold. Agonizing cramps in my legs added to the misery. Somewhere I had read about the sweats and cramps of death . . . but nobody ever died of simple indigestion. Indigestion was an old joke. People went rushing off to doctors saying they had angina or coronary thrombosis, were given bi-carbonate of soda and a new lease of life. Those neat little tables, showing at a glance the causes of death in each year didn't even *have* a column labelled 'Indigestion'.

I thought all these comforting and sustaining thoughts; and had my mind been better practised in governing my matter, they would, doubtless, have assuaged my pains; as it was they did little to help and in the end deserted me entirely. I reached the point where I was willing to admit, against all evidence, that some people did die of indigestion and that I was about to be of their number. I passed on to the stage where I was prepared to welcome death, whatever the reason. I spared a sentimental thought for my parents, bereft of their son in their old age, for my wife, as yet unchosen, for my children, unborn. From time to time I groaned.

Just after four o'clock even that wild-cat grew weary; each slashing stroke was weaker than its predecessor. My heart left off banging, my lungs expanded, the cramp eased away. Finally I slept.

Until Thomas's failure disturbed our routine Rosanna woke me every morning at a quarter to seven with a tray of tea. My sub-conscious mind had become, as they say, conditioned; and on the morning after my ordeal, the opening of my bedroom door at half past eight, woke me as usual, though I had slept so little. Rosanna stood in the doorway, looking towards the bed with that mingling of horror and interest with which some people regard street accidents. The pinky-grey hue of her face was more marked than ever, her cheeks and eye-sockets hollowed. In her dishevelled hair drops of water and bits of leaf and flower petals were caught.

I said, more brightly than my condition warranted:

'Good morning, Rosanna. A bit late, aren't you?'

She gave a sort of yelp, flung herself into the room and fell on her knees by the bed, crying and thanking God and blessing me with great fervour. She would have gone on for an hour had I not pointed out that we were late and that I wanted a proper breakfast.

On the following Sunday Rosanna resumed her chapel going; and in due course Thomas passed his examination. In only one respect am I dissatisfied with my brush with the occult. I should like to test the effect of that particular tinned food, sometime when my mind is at ease, but I have never been able to do so. The thought of it, its name, the glimpse of its label in a shop window or in an advertisement afflicts me with an inexplicable nausea.

THE BLACK CHRIST OF ADLERWALD

MARTHA BELLAMY is one of those unfortunate people whose enthusiasm defeats its own purpose. Heaven alone knows how many good books, films and plays I have shied away from because she has recommended them to me over-eagerly.

'You simply must read it,' she says; or, 'You really mustn't miss it.' Her eyes glitter, her teeth flash and a perverse antagonism takes me in grip. This is particularly maddening because she is not unintelligent or without taste.

I met her at a party on the eve of my Austrian holiday and she inquired my destination. As soon as I named it she said vehemently:

'Oh, then you'll go quite near Adlerwald. You simply must stop there and see Franz Bruckner's house and the Black Christ.' She spoke the last three words in an everybody-knows-about-it way, as though mentioning the Taj Mahal or the Statue of Liberty.

'And what's that?' I asked nastily. 'A pub?'

She looked at me dubiously for a moment and I wondered whether she had, at last, sensed the effect she had upon me. But the doubt passed.

'Oh, you are funny,' she said gaily, 'No, it's a . . .' Before she could proceed with a delightful task of imparting information, someone mercifully laid a hand on her arm and spoke a distracting word. Over her shoulder she said to me, 'I've got a book about it. I'll send it to you.'

She never forgets anything – that is one reason why she is such a bore – and in due time along came the book, marked at the relevant page. It was one of those worthy, flat, educate-yourself-in-one-gulp volumes and it was called *Famous Painters of the Nineteenth Century*. I should have laid it aside, unread, but for the certainty that next time we met Martha would subject me to a viva-voice on the subject and fill in any gap in my knowledge.

The writer had devoted only a short passage to Franz Bruckner. I read that he was born in Adlerwald in 1820 and died there in 1851. He had studied in Vienna, Italy and Paris, achieved an enormous popularity with pictures of little worth, ceased to paint in 1847, disappeared into Africa, returned four years later with a superb picture now known as The Black Christ of Adlerwald and shortly after died insane. Following this stark biography there was a patronizing assessment of his work. If he had lived to exploit to the full his new and mature style, he would doubtless have achieved permanent fame; as it was, it was on the strength of this one wonderful picture that he was 'entitled to mention in this modest little volume'. And that was that.

Martha's geography was good. One morning, driving along an over-crowded, over-placarded road I saw a signpost which said that Adlerwald lay twenty kilometres away. The narrow road, little more than a track, ran up and lost itself between flower-covered slopes; it looked peaceful and pretty. Upon impulse I turned out of the streaming traffic and found myself in a different world. Gone were the invitations to drink this or that beverage, to eat this or that kind of ice-cream, to try this or that brand of permanent wave. On either side of the road the steep flowery meadows climbed up to meet the dark pine forest, and in twenty kilometres I passed nothing save an ox-drawn wagon piled high with fragrant hay.

Adlerwald rose up out of the fields. There was none of that depressing no-man's-land where the huts and the new houses encroach upon the country and the country strikes back with nettles and brambles. The uncut hay, the green heads of young corn brushed against the walls of the first houses, the dirt road became a cobbled street and in the matter of moments I was in the centre of the town.

It was a typical, small Austrian town, quite unspoilt. In its centre was a square with a fountain and a drinking trough in the middle of it. Along one side ran the rather Eastern-looking arcade with small shops set back in the shade, and flourishing window boxes of daisies, geraniums and begonias decorating the windows above. Another side was occupied by an ancient church surrounded by great mulberry trees, so old that their branches had iron supports. There was a smithy, and a café, and a little knot of stalls, gay with fruit and vegetables and flowers. The rest of the Square was made up of houses, some of grey stone, some of dark timber and pale plaster. It was quite delightful, and having stopped the car I spent some moments taking pictures.

Camera in hand I amused myself by trying to identify Franz Bruckner's house. I fixed on one rather larger than the rest, and very well kept. It was the only one whose paint had been renewed in the last decade. Six steps, set parallel to the house front, led up to a little platform from which the door opened, and at the outer edge of each step, and on the platform were pots spilling over with flowers.

I was right. Over the door a small plaque said:

FRANZ BRUCKNER

1820 1851

Thinking how pleased Martha would be if she could see me, I set about mounting the steps, as I did so the door at the top creaked open and a small man came out. He walked straight forward, without glancing to the left, where the steps were, and he vigorously shook a duster. Bits of grey fluff settled on my clothes, dust fell into my eyes. I made a wordless sound of protest and he swung round.

'Oh sir,' he said, 'I am very extremely sorry. Please accept my apologies.'

'That's all right,' I said. 'Do I look *so* English?'

'It was the car,' he said. 'I was looking towards it when I performed this careless action. To myself I was thinking that soon I should have an English visitor to see the picture and to myself I was being congratulated that the house is now clean. If you will enter, I will, with your permission, brush off the dust.'

He found and plied a brush while I stood, looking about me. The hall was stone-flagged and held three pieces of furniture; an enormous, heavily carved old chest, one of those angry-looking Victorian stands upon which hung a caped ulster, a long dark overcoat with a velvet collar, a stove-pipe hat and an age-yellowed panama, and between the two an iron flower-pot holder capable of taking a dozen plants. At the moment it was empty and the pot plants stood just outside an open door at the back of the hall; the sunshine sparkled on their freshly watered flowers and foliage. This evidence of housewifely activity, together with the handiness of the clothes-brush, the garments on the stand, the scent of furniture polish gave the place a homely, occupied air, oddly at variance with another and more undefinable atmosphere – that deserted melancholy that overtakes any place intended for human occupation and left empty. Classrooms when school is dismissed, theatres when the audience has gone, have just that air.

The little man said:

'It was Herr Bruckner's own wish, sir, that the house should remain just as it was and that the picture should stay here. To my grandmother he entrusted the guardianship, and she handed it to my mother. My mother is now dead and the town authorities must make their own arrangements. I cannot, even to please my mother, take on the charge.'

He spoke so definitely that some comment was demanded.

'Oh,' I said, 'I see. You have other plans?'

'No. So long as my mother lived . . . She was old, but in good health, her end was sudden. I have had no time. But now I am cleaning completely; today I do the last small jobs. Then I have done, finished, and I go away from the Franz Bruckner house.'

Something faintly defiant made his words sound as though he were giving *me* notice, but I explained this to myself by remembering how difficult it is to convey nuances of meaning in any but one's native tongue.

'The picture is here, sir,' he said, and opened a door upon a large room, full of sunlight. The floor was bare and highly polished; there was a high porcelain stove of blue and green and yellow tiles. Every piece of furniture was lustrous from years of loving care, bits of brass and copper and some highly coloured pieces of pottery positively winked in the light; after the dimness of the hall it was momentarily dazzling.

The picture was not hung, it stood on an easel, placed slantwise to the windows so that it was turned from the door. I went towards it, thinking that this was the first time I had ever done a thing that Martha Bellamy had said that I simply must do.

I find it hard to describe what I saw. Words like 'awful' and 'appalling' have become the clipped, debased coinage of verbal currency. Also the human eye has become so accustomed to visual representations of the Crucifixion that it has become desensitized. One can crack a joke with a barmaid with a gunmetal crucifix dangling from her neck . . .

What I can, and do, say is that unless a man had the capacity to watch, without flinching, an actual crucifixion, he could not look at that picture without feeling faint with horror.

Large as it was, it was less than life size, yet it seemed larger. And the man on the Cross was not the pale, fair-haired, greatly-suffering-yet-patiently-resigned victim of tradition. He was a young, ebony-skinned, woolly-haired African in the prime of life. He hung on a roughly made cross, and instead of the bearable, because stylized and familiar attitude of pain, he conveyed the real, the beastly immediacy of physical agony. Agony past the limit of human endurance shrieked out from every tortured muscle; but that was not the worst of it. The face was worst of all, because, under the look of torment and despair there was another look, a look of the deepest understanding and forgiveness. The body, wracked past bearing cried 'My God, my God, why hast Thou forsaken me?' but the soul cried, 'Father forgive them, they know not what they do.'

I remember thinking that no human hand could possibly have painted that combination of emotions into a face. I remember stepping back and saying, 'Oh no! No!' in futile protest.

I steadied myself. When you wake from a nightmare you say – This is my bed ... my pillow ... my obedient light ... my table with my book and my spectacles ... it is all right. In some such way I tried to comfort myself. I remembered the date over the door, 1851. This picture was painted just when the Emancipation of the Negro campaign was in full swing. Bruckner had painted this picture as Harriet Beecher Stowe wrote *Uncle Tom's Cabin*, not as a work of art but as a piece of propaganda. He meant it to be symbolic of the suffering Negro race forgiving its oppressors.

Viewed like that it was *just* bearable; just ...

I looked again. And again I recoiled. There was no escaping the truth. A living man hung there awaiting the last mercy of death, and there was nothing to distract the eye or the mind; no weeping women or thieves, penitent or impenitent, no lot-casting Roman legionaries. There was not even the sympathetic darkening of the sky. Behind and above the dark bulk of the cross and its burden was the clear hot blue-white of the African sky, and poised in it, waiting watchfully, a single vulture.

I realized suddenly, and for the first time, that this was a true picture of a scene which must have affronted the light of the sun a thousand times; the cross was a common form of execution with the Romans; all along the Appian way ...

I turned and blundered out of the room, into the hall where the little man was replacing the begonias, yellow, apricot, scarlet, crimson and white, in the iron stand.

'Are you all right, sir?'

I made some effort to speak normally.

'Yes . . . quite all right. It gave me a bit of a shock. You are probably so used to it . . .'

He shuddered.

'I have only looked at it once, sir. Many years ago. I was sick.'

He put down the plant he was holding and opened another door.

'Come in here, sir, and be pleased to sit down. Very infrequently, I believe, a lady tourist has been overcome and my mother always had water handy. But I have something better . . .'

He went to a cupboard and took out a bottle of plum brandy and two glasses. Neatly and quickly he poured two generous measures and handed one to me. I said:

'Thank you. I'm sorry to behave like a lady tourist. I didn't think I was unduly squeamish . . .' The First World War, and the London blitz, I thought. I took a gulp of the pungent liquor. 'There's something about that picture, though. It's a little difficult to believe that it was painted by a human hand.'

'I don't think that it was.' He made this statement with the utmost simplicity and once more I reminded myself that English was not his tongue.

'I said it was difficult to believe, but we know that it *was*,' I said.

'We know nothing,' he spoke firmly. 'Herr Bruckner denied that he painted it – but he was, of course, considered to be mad.'

'To whom did *he* give the credit?'

'Ah,' he said. 'To whom?' He drank, looking at me as he did so, thoughtfully, frowning a little.

'Even my mother, even on her deathbed, forebore to speak her wish, that I should stay and fare for this house. She knew, I am thinking that if I promise I shall break my promise. I cannot live with the picture, show the tourists in and out and listen while they say how wonderful, say what skill, say if Franz Bruckner had lived what great artist he should be.' He reached for my glass, and filled it, not quite so neatly this time, and replenished his own.

'That,' I said, 'at least is true. As a painting it has no equal.'

'From human hand. So you say you find difficult to believe, so I say I *know* it is not. My grandmother was peasant woman, ignorant maybe, but a good Catholic and of great honesty. From her the story is passed to my mother, and from her to me. In the same words. The unlettered are safe keepers for stories, they do not add or take away, they pass on. It would be possible for me to tell you, in the words of my grandmother, the story of that picture.'

'I should like to hear it,' I said.

'I am thinking of the ridicule. To one person only, her daughter, does my grandmother tell his story, and she to me, her son. In the family ridicule is unthinkable; but to you, sir, I am wondering how it will sound. The story is ugly and not fit for mirth.'

'I have already made myself ridiculous,' I reminded him. 'Having to be revived with brandy!'

'That is why perhaps I could tell you. Yes, perhaps I can . . .'

I could tell the story in his own words; but under the influence of emotion and plum brandy his English deteriorated; he halted and fumbled for words, was inclined to repeat himself. So at the risk of putting a story within a story – reckoned bad craftsmanship, I will give his in my own way.

Franz Bruckner was born into comfortable circumstances; his father owned a farm, the only smithy in Adlerwald, and a corn mill. He was an only child and so well-beloved that when, at an early age, he developed abilities and ambitions outside his parents' ken, they did everything to encourage him. He, in turn, was a dutiful son, and so long as his parents lived returned home twice a year, at Christmas and for the feast which marked the end of harvest.

Success came to him early and easily. He was only twenty-four when Queen Victoria bought his 'Sleeping Child' for the embellishment of her own sitting-room at Windsor. A year later the King of the Belgians acquired 'Women Knitting' and 'Old Soldiers taking their Ease', with which he was so much delighted that he conferred a minor honour upon the artist. The old parents lived to rejoice in their son's success and then died, within a few hours of one another during an epidemic in the winter of 1846.

Bruckner came home then, and stayed, sold the farm, the smithy and the corn mill and settled in the house, tended by a woman named Erma. He had, to all appearances, everything to make a man happy, success in his chosen career, comfortable means, good health, youth. But he was not happy. During the months he spent at Adlerwald he was moody and depressed, shunned company, did no painting at all and occasionally spoke with scorn and derision of the work he had already done.

One evening he made a bonfire in the garden and threw on to it every sketch and picture he had; he even took down and burned the picture he had made especially for his mother – the family mill in a red sunset. At that Erma ventured a protest and he told her that his work was all worthless, pretty and nothing more and that if he had his way he would burn everything he had ever painted. He added that he was going, one day, to make a fresh start. After that he seemed more cheerful.

A day or two later he asked Erma if she would be prepared to stay in the house and look after it; it was necessary, he said, that he should go to Africa and stay there for at least three years. Erma replied that she hoped soon to be married, but would stay in the house if her husband could live there too. So it was arranged.

Bruckner was absent for four years. Every quarter a young man from a firm of lawyers in Innsbruck, came up and gave her her wages, and when the roof leaked the same firm attended to the repairs. On his last visit – just before Christmas 1850 – the young man told her that Herr Bruckner was on his way home. He had communicated with the firm and asked that some ready money should await his arrival in Antwerp. 'Travel is so swift these days,' said the young man, 'that you may expect your master at any moment.'

He arrived at the end of January, entering the house with as little commotion as though he had been out for a walk. He carried a small bag containing his night attire, and brought with him a large flat wooden crate. For the season he was oddly dressed in a light ulster and straw hat, but he looked well and seemed in jubilant spirits.

Erma, ever since before Christmas had kept the stove going in the living-room, the bed aired and a chicken in a handy coop. Her young husband went to wring the fowl's neck and get it ready for the oven. Herr Bruckner hung the ulster and the straw hat beside the black coat and stove-pipe hat which he wore for his parents' funeral and then wandered all over the house, saying how pleasant it was to be back, and how well Erma had kept everything. He paused by the rockered cradle where Erma's baby lay and said, 'A bonny child indeed. After supper, Erma, I will show you my first-born. My first *legitimate* off spring.'

'You mean your picture, Herr Bruckner?'

'I mean my picture, Erma. You won't like it. It is not pretty, but it is a great picture.'

'I'm sure it is, if you say so,' said Erma and went to prepare the meal.

Bruckner ate heartily, praising the cooking. 'If you could see some of the things I have eaten in Africa, Erma, you would be astounded.' Always, afterwards, that was what puzzled Erma, that in appearance and manner, in every way, he had seemed so ordinary then.

After the meal he took tools and began to open the crate. Erma, clearing the table, offered her husband's services. 'He's very handy,' she said. But Bruckner said he preferred to do it himself. She left him carefully drawing out the nails.

She was washing up when her husband said, 'He's calling.'

She listened and realized at once that Herr Bruckner was not calling her. He was shouting in a terrible and frightening way.

'Something's amiss with his picture,' she said. She thought herself that it might have got wet, coming all the way from Africa. She ran into the living-room, drying her hands on her apron as she ran.

The picture was propped against the table, and against the wall, as far as he could back from it, was Herr Bruckner, his hands over his face, shouting and moaning and shaking dreadfully.

'What is it?' she asked. 'Oh, Herr Bruckner, what is the matter?'

'The picture,' he gasped. 'Look at it, look at it.'

She picked her way over the wood of the packing case, the straw, the sheet of white linen in which it had been wrapped, stooped slightly, looked, and stepped back. She had never in her life seen a Negro, or a picture of one. She was startled for a second, but her main concern was for the state of the canvas; she had lived long enough in the Bruckner house to know something about pictures, and so far as she could see this one was undamaged.

'The picture is all right, Herr Bruckner.'

Still keeping his hands over his eyes, like a frightened child, he said:

'You look. What colour is he?'

'Black,' she said.

Then Herr Bruckner's madness set in. He began to rave. He said that he had painted the man white, that the transposition of colour was the most difficult thing that any painter had ever attempted, but that he had done it. He intermingled his words with moans and screams and said many other things which Erma did not understand.

Just then her husband, an unhurrying type, opened the door a few inches and shyly inquired if anything was wrong.

'Fetch the doctor, hurry,' Erma said. 'And the priest . . .'

She was practical and downright and completely unaware of the immensity of the problem she had on her hands.

'A good cup of coffee is what you want,' she said.

Bruckner sobbed, 'Don't leave me. Don't leave me alone with *that* . . .' She helped him into the kitchen, poured coffee and held the cup for him, his hand being too unsteady. It didn't steady him at all, but it loosened his tongue and before the doctor – the first to arrive, came panting in, Erma had heard the whole story.

France Bruckner had revolted from his pretty, popular work and after long searching had found his subject – a Crucifixion from life. He had gone to the Belgian Congo and acquired a servant named Joshua whom he had, for three whole years, treated as a pet. 'It was essential that he should have faith in me, know that I should never hurt him, trust me, as Christ trusted God. To the last minute he must trust me, so that his face should show the sense of betrayal.' He made little sketches of Joshua, who was vain and flattered, and who, in the end agreed to be painted tied to a cross. He made it himself and set it in place. Once he was in position Bruckner produced the hammer and the nails and a crown of thorns.

The painting took seven hours of white hot African day. Bruckner was working, as it were, in the negative. 'How else could I do it? I could use only a black man, and even in a masterpiece the world would never have accepted a black

Christ. It was a translation, and I did it perfectly. I was so engrossed that I did not notice the heat, or the flies. If I had known that when *he* died *I* would die too I should have painted on, *gladly*. If only I could be certain that the picture would be brought back and recognized for what it is.'

At that point in his story he jumped up and began to beat his head against the wall; because it was all wasted, some supernatural agency had changed the colour of the man, and the world would never recognize a Negro Christ . . .

Erma was very glad when the doctor arrived, and then, hard on his heels the priest and her husband. The doctor diagnosed delayed sunstroke and administered a strong sedative, the priest said he would come back tomorrow but by that time Herr Bruckner was hopelessly out of his mind, rambling on about his childhood, about pictures and painters and things like ambition. Never once did he mention the story which he had told to Erma, and she, fearing ridicule, never mentioned it either.

Just before he died he had a lucid interval; it was then that he said he wanted his house kept as it was and the picture to stay there and Erma to take care of them both.

'And that,' said the little man, 'is the story of Franz Bruckner, just as I had it from my mother, and she from hers.'

And here we were, back in the present-day, the kitchen solid and ordinary-looking. It could have been the wildest fantasy; but in the room just across the passage there was that picture . . .

'Thank you for telling me,' I said. 'And for the brandy, too.'

He said, with just the faintest air of reproach:

'You do not believe my story, sir.'

'Oh, I believe your story, every word of it. It's Bruckner's own tale about the picture changing colour. That I can't believe. I think he was mad much earlier on; probably when he made that bonfire.'

'Possessed,' he said. 'A man of boundless ambition and with a talent but mediocre. To whom should such a man turn? To God, or to the Devil. And the means he used to attain his ends show us which, do they not? And that the painting should be changed must happen, you see, because otherwise Bruckner has the best of the bargain.'

'The old, old Faust story,' I said.

'Ah, well,' he slightly shrugged a shoulder and then with just a glint of something in his eyes, said, 'Perhaps you would now care to look at the picture again, sir.'

That was a thing I did not wish to do. So thanking him again, I left the house and drove away. I thought, not about magic and madness but about ambition and achievement and it seemed to me that Franz Bruckner had, by whatever means and at whatever cost, attained his end. A negro named Joshua had died untimely and Bruckner had died insane, but the picture was there. And the Martha Bellamys of this world – those upon whom all fame and reputation finally rest – were going around saying, 'You simply must see it.'

You simply must see it. You simply must read it.

Isn't that what we all work for?

A DAY'S JOURNEY

'I DO THINK,' said Mrs. Mallow, almost tearfully, 'that you're being very unkind, Richard. Sulking this way on our last evening.'

'So would you sulk if you'd been made to look an absolute fool.'

'What is there foolish about travelling as far as Paris with Ella?' A little while ago she would have said 'Aunt Ella,' but Richard had had his sixteenth birthday during these holidays and could now dispense with such courtesy titles.

'You practically asked her to travel a day sooner. I heard you. As though I couldn't be trusted to go alone. And I'll tell you this, last time Uncle Tony came with me he was absolutely sozzled. I had to take care of *him*. Now you've gone and landed me with Ella Barrett, of all people!'

'I can never see why you dislike her. She's always been very kind to you.'

'I just don't like her. You can't give a reason for these things.'

He thought of Fiske, who was captain of cricket this coming term. Fiske didn't like *him*, and there was no reason for *that*. Richard had done his best to ingratiate himself, foreseeing Fiske's election and anxious for a place in the team.

'When you're so unreasonable and bad-tempered,' said Mrs. Mallow, even nearer to tears, 'you are just like your father.' That was, from her, a severe rebuke. The faults and failings of Mr. Mallow, divorced twelve years ago, had never been forgotten, had been used, many times, as a warning for his son. Today, for the first time in his life, Richard wondered whether, if all were known, a case couldn't have been made out for his father. The apology which that particular rebuke had hitherto evoked was not forthcoming and Mrs. Mallow did begin to cry.

'It isn't my fault,' she sobbed, 'that I can't make the journey.

I can't help not being strong. I do the best I can to make up for being so useless, and having to live in this place and then you grumble.'

Ordinarily such a speech would have brought instant capitulation. Today Richard merely said:

'But you did go on and on about poor Richard having to travel alone. So now I have a day and a night with that old hen.'

No mean tactician, Mrs. Mallow dried her tears.

'At least, darling, let's have one more nice evening. We'll go to that little place in St. Raphael where they have those lovely prawns. And you can drive . . .'

The one fortunate thing about Mrs. Mallow's formidable assortment of indispositions was that indigestion had no place amongst them.

Next morning, settling down into his place opposite Mrs. Barrett, Richard proceeded to analyse his dislike for her. She was too thin, for one thing; so thin that every time she moved her hands the rings on them slipped about and made a clinking noise. It got on his nerves, like Barrington's sniff. Another thing was that although she was old, almost if not quite as old as his mother, she was got up to look young. His mother, of course, used make-up too, and had her hair 'rinsed' and waved, but for all that she looked her forty years; Ella Barrett did not, at least until you looked closely. And then, her voice was croaky; why the hell, he wondered, couldn't she clear her throat, have a good cough and be done with it?

As soon as the train started she opened her bag, took out a cigarette case, against which her rings clinked again, and a lighter. She held the case towards him:

'I'm sure you do, Richard.'

'Actually, I don't, thank you very much.'

He could have bitten his tongue out. He had a new packet in his pocket and he had intended to take it out, offer it to her, take one himself and defy her to comment. Now, simply because he must snub her, he'd lost his chance to smoke.

'Then you'd like some chocolate. Non-smokers always do,' she said, and from her bag, with more clinking of rings, she produced some.

'Not just now, thank you,' he said. He took up his book and became ostentatiously engrossed. Mrs. Barrett also had a book, she smoked as she read and every time she lifted or lowered her cigarette the rings clinked. The noise disturbed him and the necessity to read somehow took the pleasure out of it. He was glad when it was time for lunch, though, following her along to the dining-car, he was already bristling, ready to resent the slightest encroachment upon his independence.

None was made. When he ordered a half-bottle of his favourite red wine, Mrs. Barrett said:

'I only wish I could drink it, too. Any red wine, for some reason, gives me a stiff neck.'

Her attitude was quite different from his mother's. She was always torn between her continental experience and her ideas of what was suitable for English schoolboys; so she would let him drink wine, but must always remark, 'Just this once can't hurt you,' or some similar deflating words.

Over the meal Mrs. Barrett talked. The husky voice was still irritating, but what she said was sensible. Once she made him laugh. There was a woman in the dining-car who must, he thought as soon as he saw her, be colour blind. She wore a lime green jumper, a leaf green coat, a laurel green hat, a string of jade beads. When she had gone, Mrs. Barrett said:

'Now I understand that old Irish song. "They're hanging men and women too, for the wearing o' the green." '

It was the way she said, 'and women too' that made it funny.

They went back to their seats and resumed their reading. She smoked. Her rings clinked. Once he looked up, impatiently, and she was looking up too. She smiled and laid her book aside.

'I find reading in trains very difficult, really. Do you know any card tricks?'

'No,' he said, untruthfully.

'I know one or two, quite good,' she said; and she dived into her bag and produced a pack of cards.

They were good tricks, far above average; her thin, ring-clinking fingers had a conjurer's dexterity. She was perfectly frank about the trickery, willing to share her mystery and when he was slow and clumsy, she was patient and helpful.

She's really not so bad, he thought, and I *should* like her. But I don't. He could see now why he had never made any headway with Fiske. Ingratiation was no good at all. If you disliked anyone the more they tried to please you the more you added contempt to dislike. The moment he got back to school he'd find Fiske and say, 'Look here, I know you hate my guts, but if you can't see that I'm a better bowler than Orton or Alston, then you're a bloody fool and deserve what you'll get.' He'd say just that. Because now he knew! And it was a useful thing to know. Strange, he thought, that Mrs. Barrett, who must be at least twice his age, had not learned it yet. She went on trying.

Presently he slept for a while, falling asleep and then waking again with the easy transition from one state to another of the healthy young. When he woke the light had changed and their journey had brought them into a countryside where the spring was younger than it was in the south. Young, translucent leaves shone in the declining sunlight, level fields of young corn were ruffled in the wind. He was suddenly and irrationally happy, caught up in the season's magic. He liked the summer term, realized that he was looking forward to it . . . Looking forward not to the coming term only; looking forward, in some new and rather startling way to life itself, to all the time that lay beyond the sunny mornings and golden afternoons and long evenings of the immediate future. The feeling of excitement, of anticipation stirred in his bowels.

He saw that Mrs. Barrett was also looking out at the scene which was streaming past. Her face was sad, stripped of its vivacity as though of a mask. It must, he thought, be awful to be old; to have no future. It would never happen to him because . . . well, there was no reason, of course, only just the certainty. Age was something that happened to other people. And because this thing which could never happen to him had happened to Mrs. Barrett, he would, he thought – generous in his abundant plenty – try to be civil to her at dinner. At lunch he had allowed her to entertain him, and he had laughed, but he made no reciprocal effort. Now he would.

He was immediately, and as time went on, increasingly aware of the paucity of his material. He had almost nothing to say that would entertain a woman. With his mother it was different; she was familiar, by hearsay, with the little self-contained world of school and she was interested, or pretended to be, in anything he chose to tell her – even to details of the food. A similar interest could not be expected of Mrs. Barrett; therefore every remark had to be tried over in his mind before it was uttered, tested for value, as it were and very often discarded. So his efforts to entertain were not very successful, though she came more than half way to meet him, and was very responsive. His failure darkened his mood; how could you expect to talk freely and well to just any old female, forced on you as a travelling companion?

A chance remark of hers saved the situation.

'I see you're reading *Maddon's Rock*. It's a Hammond Innes, isn't it?'

'Yes. An early one. I read *The White South* and since then I've read all his I could get hold of.'

'I like him too,' Mrs. Barrett said, most surprisingly. 'You know how people say, "I hate Dickens, but I like *Pickwick*"; the same with me, I hate adventure stories, but I dote on Hammond Innes. Now why should that be?'

Richard had never thought about it. You liked a book, or a certain author's books, and left it there. But he had, perforce, sat through several sessions organized by a young and enterprising English master, discussions on 'Three Books I Would Take With Me To A Desert Island' and such; and in one of them, Cowper, who was a wizard at English, had pontificated about this particular author's recipe for spellbinding. Richard now brought forward the opinion as his own.

'It has something to do with the illusion of authenticity. They don't read like stories, they read like real experiences. And they say he does go to the places and do all the things that he writes about.'

'Then that explains it,' said Mrs. Barrett in a flattering kind of way. 'Because autobiographies I *can* read.'

After that they talked easily and happily about books throughout the rest of the meal. Not until she lighted a cigarette did the flood of dislike return. He couldn't recant now, and the last hours of his freedom were ticking away. He made up his mind to go to bed early and smoke until he was black in the face. Otherwise he'd hardly get through his supply.

It was dark now; here and there in the night a feeble light showed, glimpsed and lost as the train rushed on. There was something, vague, un-namable, that was sad about night travel. He had never realized that before, but now he did. All these unknown people, closed in their lighted cells, intent upon their own doings, busy with their own lives . . . Why should that be sad? There was no reason, but that didn't alter the fact.

He was glad when a glance at his watch showed him that he could decently say:

'Well, I think I shall turn in.'

Mrs. Barrett said, 'Quite the best thing to do. I shall probably have a drink and then do the same. Good night, Richard.'

His bunk was one of the two worst in the train; one of two in a kind of cupboard, partitioned from the corridor and next to the toilet. But the upper bunk had not been made up and he thought, Thank God, I shall be alone at last. He got into his pyjamas, washed, cleaned his teeth and lay down, pulling the inadequate pillow into the most comfortable position. Then he lighted his cigarette. What an ass he had been, wasting this all-but-last chance. There were rules against smoking at school, but they could easily be circumvented; there was a more powerful tabu, public opinion. Boys honestly believed that smoking stunted your growth and ruined your wind. It was absolute rot. He'd started to smoke when he was thirteen and he was growing fast; a full half inch this holiday; he was now five feet nine; he weighed ten and a half stones and he could run with the best. This year he'd win the mile. He'd be in the First Eleven too, because once he'd had it out, openly, with Fiske, the damn fool would have no choice.

He smoked three cigarettes, slowly, one after the other. He thought about likes and dislikes and all the curious, secret kind of experiences he'd had that day. He thought of Mrs. Barrett. If only she could see him now!

And then, all at once, she was there. The narrow little door into the cupboard opened and she came through. She was wearing a wrap, something soft and dark, very full, so that her skinniness was hidden; and her hair was loose, falling soft and curly on to her shoulders. All the stuff had been washed off her face, leaving a kind of pearly pallor against which her eyes looked enormous.

'I thought I'd just come along and see that you were all right,' she said. 'It's a long time since I had anyone to say good night to.'

He felt as though somebody had caught him a wallop in the stomach. He remembered things he'd heard his mother say, things he hardly noticed at the time . . . a sad life . . . divorce and the other man hadn't married her . . . no children. And it was all mixed up, in the most inexplicable way, with how he had felt about the spring, the coming term, the happy anticipation of the future, and then the sadness of the train going past the little lighted houses. And now it had all ended with Mrs.

Barrett coming, with her washed, unguarded face to say good night to someone who had been beastly to her all day long.

He'd make a real gesture. He'd give her the hearty kiss, the bear's hug as his mother called it, which always seemed to please *her* so much. He had whipped his cigarette out of sight, and now squashed it against the wall of his bunk. He raised himself a little, and feeling superior, generous, penitent, moved his arms into position one of the bear's hug.

Mrs. Barrett leaned towards him. For a moment he felt nothing but sheer surprise. He'd thought anyone so skinny would feel hard, but she was soft, soft and yielding as a kitten. And the kindly innocent kiss which he aimed at her cheek went astray, fell on her mouth and turned into something he had never dreamed of.

He had meant to say, 'Good night; sleep well.' But under the impact of this new thing, the words slipped away, an unspoken farewell to his boyhood.

And he knew why he had never liked her.

The train rushed on through the night.

THE HAPPY CHRISTMAS

WHEN I was a boy we lived in the country, at a place called Priory Farm. It stood at the end of a long lane which ended in an open Green surrounded by cottages. Every cottage had a garden, most of them sedulously tended, and the Green was common land; every cottager had grazing rights which dated straight back to mediaeval times. Most of them took advantage of their rights and there were always ducks and fowls, a goat or two, a fattening pig, occasionally even a cow on the Green. We were a self-contained, and with one exception, an industrious and self-respecting little community.

The exception was a man named Bob Grove who was a drunkard, a poacher and a thief. One would have thought that my father, who was a good Methodist and a staunch teetotaller would have been the last person to employ and tolerate a man like Grove; but in those days there remained something of the old idea of people belonging to places and Bob Grove belonged to Priory Farm, a nuisance to be regretted and grumbled about, like the parlour chimney which smoked, but, in the same way, taken for granted. Also, everyone was sorry for Katie Grove and the seven children.

Katie was tiny, just a thread of a woman, bent forward and slightly to one side from haste and anxiety and overwork. She had perhaps been pretty at one time, she still had a mass of light brown, very crinkly hair, dragged back and pinned in a tight knob. She had enormous grey eyes, rather protuberant, not too steady, a hunted hare's eyes. I think there was almost nothing that she wouldn't have done to earn a shilling and in a more prosperous community she would have been greatly in demand for housework; on the Green, except for my mother who always employed her as much as possible, nobody wanted Katie indoors save in times of sickness and much of her work was done outdoors, hard, manual, man's work. Somehow, in between times, she managed to bear and rear her children.

They were all, from Tom the eldest whose school leaving day was a time to which Katie looked forward eagerly, to the baby, just out of arms, so thin and so pale that they might have served as models for illustrations for Dotheboys Hall; but they were neater and cleaner and better-behaved than the children of some families where the Saturday wages did not go straight into the public house till. They none of them, boy or girl, ever had more than an inch of hair, Katie went round them, basin-and-scissors every month. Their clothes, all handed on to them, were an amazing mass of patches.

It was, in a way, over the matter of clothes that I first came to my senses about Bob Grove. A boy is no sound judge of morals, but he is susceptible to amusement and for a long time, though aware that Bob was 'bad', I rather liked him and derived a great deal of entertainment from his company. In drink he was said to be surly and there were dark stories about his knocking Katie and the children about, but when he was sober he was cheerful and careless; he could whistle like a blackbird and somehow knew all the latest songs. When he was sure of me, he would tell me about his poaching, and he had a knack for telling a story. My reading at that time was carefully supervised, very Methodist. To me, Bob Grove, knocking off a pheasant in Emmerly Wood, under the keeper's very nose, selling it in Shellborough for half a crown, spending two bob on beer and a tanner on a cheap seat at the music hall where he memorized the latest catch tune, stood where Dick Turpin and Jim Hawkins should have stood.

But I learned.

I outgrew my mackintosh, a brown gaberdine lined with Scotch plaid, and it went, as all my clothes did, over the Green to Tom Grove, who though older, was smaller than I. About a fortnight later Mother and I were in Shellborough and happened to pass the shop which served the town in the double capacity of pawnbroker's and secondhand shop. There in the window, under the harsh words, 'Unclaimed Goods and Secondhand Bargains' was my mackintosh. I knew it. I still had affection for it, my new one was nothing near so stylish. Also I could see the three ink spots made when my fountain pen leaked in the pocket.

'Look, Mother,' I exclaimed. 'My mackintosh. The one you gave Tom Grove.'

Mother stopped. Without haste she took out her pince-nez and adjusted them. She peered.

'Yes, it is,' she said. Then, disregarding the fact that no respectable woman would have been seen crossing that dismal threshold, she marched into the shop. I was so terrified that someone might think that she was buying the garment for me – oh shame unconceivable – that I basely fled, ran up the road and waited on the corner. Mother joined me there, carrying the mackintosh. It had cost her two shillings.

On our return Mother halted the trap on the edge of the Green.

'I'm taking this back to Katie,' she said. 'Will you come, or drive on in?'

'I'll come,' I said. So Mother looped the reins and said to the horse, 'Wesley, go home!' He ambled obediently towards the yard gate and his stable. Mother and I crossed the Green.

Katie came to the door and at the sight of the mackintosh in Mother's hands a dark flush ran upwards over her white face.

'That hadn't been in the house an hour afore he took it and sold it,' she said bitterly. 'And I did specially value that mac, ma'am. I looked at it and thought come what might, Tom'd never be wet through no more.'

'Well, here it is, Katie,' said my mother. 'And I shall ask my husband to tell Bob that what I give to you or the children is meant for you, not for him.'

'I'm wholly sorry, ma'am,' Katie said.

'I'm sorry for *you*,' Mother said. 'But . . . well, anyway, that will keep Tom dry. When does he leave school?'

'This very next week. And he got a job, helping in the garden at the Rectory. Three shillings a week.'

'That's splendid,' said Mother. And upon this cheerful note we said good-bye.

Walking back I realized that I had insufficiently valued my own father; with his piety, and his *Christian Herald* and his teetotalism, he might not be such good company as Bob Grove, but in every other way he was better. A way of life must be judged by its results. Remembering the mackintosh I began to avoid Bob.

Late in the November of that year Bob was in real trouble.

He'd stole often enough before, generally from us, and my father had always given him a 'good talking to' and let the matter go, arguing that Katie and the children would suffer from any action taken, but this time Bob had been caught red-handed, stealing fowls from another farm.

'Now he'll get a sharp lesson and maybe that'll bring him to his senses,' said my father. 'We can take care of the family and Tom is working now.'

Magistrates were less sentimental in those days, and although it wasn't actually mentioned, Bob's bad record was well known. He was sent to gaol for two months. The Guardians allowed Katie ten shillings a week, which was more than Bob had ever given her from his wages and everybody let sympathy for her take a practical form. In January, when Bob came home, Katie and the children looked better nourished than ever before.

He was released on a Thursday and on Friday turned up at work, cheerful and unconcerned as ever. Nobody questioned his right to reinstatement; the steady men, who had always looked on him as a bit of a freak, cracked a joke or two, and that was that.

Time moved gently on, marked by one incident. Tom Grove always handed over his three shillings to Katie and one evening Bob tried to take it away from her. Katie tried to hold on to it, and Bob hit her – not for the first time, but Tom was growing up, was a wage-earner now, and he rushed at Bob and grappled with him; Bob knocked him down. Katie then ran screaming to the nearest neighbour, who was our horseman, Peake, Peake ventured to intervene and got a black eye for his pains. Slow to anger, but deadly when roused, he knocked out two of Bob's teeth.

Nobody took much notice of this except that it was understood that Peake and Bob could never share a job again, just as it was understood that we could not have a fire in the parlour when the wind was in the West. (Fifteen years later when Tom Grove married Grace Peake, Peake would not go to the wedding.) Sympathy with Katie became warmer than ever, and one of the favourite topics of chatter among her more fortunate neighbours was what they would do if they were in her shoes. Their plans were varied and interesting, ranging from calling in the police to pushing Bob down the well. Katie did nothing and another year went down the wintry slope to Christmas time.

In those days, though wages were low and hours long and people in general look back on them with distaste, there was much more personal generosity about. My father – and he was far from being unique in this respect – always sent coal and beef to every family whose man he employed; he bought his coal by the truck and on the twentieth of December an old man called Hubble-Bubble delivered to each cottage as much as his donkey-cart could take. Around the same date a bullock went to the butcher's and came back in joints of such beef as is not seen anywhere nowadays. On Christmas Eve, Mother followed up these major offerings with small, personal gifts, tea and tins of toffee, knitted scarves and gloves.

I helped her to carry round the parcels. The Grove's, I remember, was chiefly food with the addition of a few useful, unsaleable things, a pound of candles, a gallon of paraffin oil, a new scrubbing brush. The Grove cottage, as always, compared badly with the rest. In all the others Christmas preparations were in full swing. Bunches of holly were up behind the pictures, there was a smell of puddings cooking, and I had lost count of the mince-pies I had been asked to sample. Everybody seemed happy and my own excitement mounted.

But there was something about the Grove cottage that quenched all joy. The front room of their house, which in ordinary circumstances would have been the parlour, was unfurnished. A sack of potatoes – somebody's Christmas offering I suspect – stood in a corner, and two cabbages lay on top of it. A faint light and a powerful smell of washing came through a half open door at the back. The staircase, uncarpeted, but scrubbed clean, ran up out of the front room.

Katie came in response to Mother's knock and stood there wiping her water-sodden hands on the corner of her sacking apron. Mother said:

'Well, Katie, I've brought you a little offering. And I'm sure I wish you all a very happy Christmas.' Her voice was deceptively hearty. She motioned to me to set the paraffin oil can inside the room and handed to Katie the things she had carried herself.

'And I wish you the same ma'am, and thank you indeed I do,' Katie said. Her eyes, a little wilder, a little less steady than usual, flickered from Mother's face, to mine, to the things we had brought, and then suddenly filled with tears.

'When I think of last year . . .' she said. She spoke exactly like a woman who between the two festive seasons had suffered an irreparable bereavement. Mother understood at once.

'I know, Katie, it is hard for you. But if you *can* bear up . . . things must get better. You've got Tom started now, and Betty's coming along . . . You've got your children, Katie, and a lot to look forward to, I'm sure.' But she didn't sound sure at all.

'Yes, I got my children; and last year we did have a rare happy Christmas; something to remember, that was.'

'You'll have others,' Mother said. 'I only wish there was more we could do for you.'

Katie blinked back the tears and straightened herself, correcting the stoop and lurch of long slavery.

'Don't you fret about us, ma'am. We shall be all right. And thanks again, ever so, for all you hev done.'

We walked back home under a cold clear sky, full of the most amazing stars, a Christmas Eve sky, but the gloom of that empty undecked room, the sinister significance of Katie's words about last year went with us. Inside the house it vanished, for Methodists, distrustful of many pleasures, do allow themselves a joyful celebration of Christ's birth. Over the spiced raisin bread and the mutton-and-apple pie which was our traditional Christmas Eve fare, I soon, and Mother presently, forgot that tragic little family on the other side of the Green.

Peake came, as usual, in the morning to feed the horses at seven. Father was up and about, wearing his overalls over his dark, chapel-going suit. Dora, our maid was cooking an enormous Christmas breakfast and Mother, enveloped in a white apron was putting the turkey into the oven. I heard Father greet Peake, heard Peake's deep, rumbling voice going on in a way more garrulous than ordinary at that hour.

Presently Father looked in at the kitchen door.

'Peake's got some yarn about Grove,' he said. 'An accident last night when he was drunk. Anyway, Tom Grove went to borrow Peake's bike to fetch the doctor. Pop over,' he said to me, 'and see what's the matter. If it's hospital they'll want the trap and I'd better know before chapel time.'

'Don't you start breakfast without me,' I said.

It was a bright, glorious morning with a sky the colour of a hedge-sparrow's egg and the grass all crisp with rime. A knot of women stood talking by the well. Their eyes followed me as I made straight for Groves' cottage. Betty Grove, wrapped in an old shawl and looking very self-important, stood by the gate. She tried to stop me.

'You can't go in. My dad's dead. Fell downstairs and broke his neck. Me brother's gone for the doctor.' She enjoyed every word of that speech.

'I know,' I said, though actually the mention of death was a surprise to me. 'That's why I'm here. I've got a message for my father to your mother.' I walked up the path and reached the front door which stood open.

One glance within and I halted. Bob Grove lay on the floor, not huddled at the foot of the stairs, but stretched out flat on his back, very tidily, his big brown hands lying along his thighs, his face and chest covered by one of Katie's sacking aprons. The cold morning light caught the nails in his heavy boots and made them shine like silver. I had never seen a dead man before and the inevitable emotion took me by the throat. I forgot all his faults and just thought, 'He's dead; and he taught me to whistle.'

I daresay I should have burst into tears but at that moment I became aware of Mrs. Grove. She was on the stairs, rubbing away at one step, the third from the top. I'd seen her work frenziedly at many jobs but I never saw her rub anything with such savage intensity. I swallowed hard on nothing and managed to say:

'Mrs. Grove . . .'

She turned. Her face frightened me. I'd have said that it was always as pale as a human face could be, but now it was bleached, chalk white and as deadly calm as though she, too, had died. But she moved, twisted around on the stairs and came down, pushing into the pocket of her apron the rag she had used for her rubbing. It was, I saw, a piece of an old shirt of my father's.

'Father sent me to see if there was anything he could do,' I said.

'Thank you kindly. No, there's nothing to do now. It's all over. And Tom's gone for the doctor. Thank you all the same.'

We stood face to face and I saw that for the first time in my memory, her eyes were quite steady; steady and – or was it my imagination – less staring.

It seemed to me that something more should be said, but I was still too young to offer easily a sympathy which would sound false even to me. Sentences formed in my head, 'It was the best thing that could have happened' and 'You'll be all right now.' They were true, but they couldn't be spoken either. I fell back on Mother's manner.

'Well, if there's anything we can do, if you want to go anywhere in the trap or anything, you've only to let us know.'

'Yes, I know. Thank you kindly,' she said.

I looked past her and caught another glimpse of Bob lying there stiff and stark with the shining nails in his boots. Then I turned away.

I was no longer hungry for my breakfast, so I walked home quite slowly and as I did so a memory stirred in my mind. Once, in my hearing, somebody, and I couldn't have said which woman it was, had said, 'If I was tied up with that blaggard I'd grease the stairs for him one fine night.'

I stood stock still, wondering should I, ought I, *dare* I go back and say to Katie, 'You must rub his boots as well.' I was so sure of what she had done that I felt it my duty to go back and say it. Then my Methodist conscience set its teeth into me. What about the fourth commandment; if Katie Grove was, as I suspected, guilty of murder, ought I to go hob-nobbing with her? On the other hand Bob was the kind of man who, if he had lived in Old Testament times would surely have come to a bad end, mightn't poor Katie be regarded as the instrument of Jehovah's wrath?

In the end I compromised. I did not go back but I did hope that nobody else, not even the woman who had made it, would remember that remark about greasing the stairs . . .

If she did, if anybody did, they, like me, kept silent about it.

THE WHITE MAN

WHEN the first drum sounded he was actually on his knees, praying for a last-minute miracle. His hands were clenched together on the cane-woven seat of the chair and his head rested on them. The sweat of agony gathered in great drops on his forehead and channelled down between his knuckles and the prominent bones of his hands.

He prayed repetitiously and with the utmost simplicity, as though God were there with him in the room and capable of being persuaded by mere urgency; 'Don't let them do it, God! Dear God, stop it, stop before it is too late! Oh, God, don't let them do it!'

Then he heard the single, vibrant boom and knew that it *was* too late; he raised his head, dropped his haunches on to his heels and so squatted, awaiting the tumult which that single note heralded. It came; the big drum, having made that one crashing claim for attention, set off on a measured chant. 'Boom! Boom! Boom!' it said triumphantly. 'That's the end of that! That's the end of the Reverend Timothy Waters and the United Methodist Mission! That's the end of the white man's God!'

The little drums began their chatter. 'Tap-tap-tap,' they said, 'now let's see. Let's do things our own way, the old way, our own way. Let's see what the old gods can do! Tap-tap-tap!'

Five years' work, Waters thought, all undone, in a moment. The little light, so painfully kindled, so patiently tended, puffed on and extinguished. All dark again. There was nothing in all the world but the darkness and the sound of the drums calling up all the old evil things.

It was, finally, his awareness of the darkness which brought him to his feet. He felt in his pocket and found his matches, but his hands were so damp that several matches failed to ignite; he had to wipe his fingers, and then the matchbox before the flame would spurt. He felt better when the tarnished brass lamp was alight, and as he put the matchbox back into his pocket he touched his pipe, pulled it out and looked at it. Strange, rather sad, he thought; God had abandoned him and here was this toy, symbol of an addiction he secretly regretted, offering its dumb, faithful comfort.

He had just got the pipe going when somebody rapped on the door and flung it open. The thick, bulky figure of Tom Breen, the storekeeper, filled the opening. Waters was conscious first of surprise and then of satisfaction; he was glad that Breen had found him standing upright, his pipe between his teeth and his lamp alight, and not kneeling in the dark.

'Brought your mail,' Breen said curtly, and held out a bundle of letters and periodicals, tied together with a piece of twine.

'That's very kind of you,' Waters said, his precise, clipped enunciation more marked than usual because he was embarrassed. He and Breen were the only white men within a radius of eighty miles, but it was fourteen months since they had spoken to one another, and almost twice as long since they had crossed one another's thresholds. There had been a time when, through loneliness and policy, they had tried to come to terms, but the attempt was doomed from the start and the uneasy association had ended with a really violent quarrel. The resulting situation had its ridiculous side since for many things the missionary was still dependent on the store, but he always sent a native to make his purchases, and Breen, the owner of the only vehicle in the neighbourhood always brought up the mail when he went to the rail-head for supplies, but he never delivered it himself.

Now, answering the surprise in Water's voice, he said:

'Well, mail's mail, when all's said and done, and there was nobody to send. Both my young b—s have miked off. What's going on here? I got back a few minutes back, found the store unlocked and nobody about and all this bloody din going on. What're they up to *now*?'

Waters had just glanced at the top-most letter in the bundle. It was the one he had been awaiting, the one from Headquarters. The name and address of the Mission were printed across the top left-hand corner, and below was his own name and address, neatly typed. It looked so ordinary, so civilized, so much at odds with what was taking place in the nearby clearing; and then suddenly it didn't; there were dark African words in that address, and they made a mock of the 'Reverend' and the 'M.A.' which preceded and followed his name. He raised his eyes, looked into Breen's face and answered the question.

'It's a witch hunt,' he said.

As he spoke he realized that he was announcing his own failure, and prepared himself to bear Breen's mockery. It did not come. With an air both interested and detached Breen said:

'Witch hunt, eh? D'you know, in all my time I never seen one. Thought they was past all that.'

So did I, Waters thought; and something at the back of his mind added the wryly humorous comment – At last Breen and I have found something in common. The noise of the drums which had seemed to recede when they spoke to one another, flowed back into the room.

'Beastly din,' Breen said with some vehemence. 'What's it all about? D'you know?'

'Oh yes, I know. They've been talking about it for months. I've argued and pleaded, urged postponement at least . . .' He looked down again at the top-most letter. 'The irony of it is that if this letter had arrived last week the whole thing might have been avoided.'

'Wasn't even there Thursday,' Breen said. He lodged one thick thigh on the table's edge and lighted a cigarette.

'If you will excuse me one moment,' Waters said punctiliously; he pulled the letter from the bundle and opened it. Before he reached the end of the closely typed page an angry flush coloured his darkly-sallow cheeks; he exclaimed irritably:

'Well! If that's the best they can do!' and without turning the page he crumpled it and thrust it into his pocket.

'I don't get the connection,' Breen said. 'Between your letter and that bloody row out there.'

'It's this sickness. I'm not a medical man, but I did study for a year, and I have books; I've proved that I can recognize most ailments. This I cannot identify. Nor, it seems can anyone else. I've written to several places, finally to Headquarters and they have the . . . the temerity to ask me whether my thermometer is reliable. That's the only explanation they can think of for a man showing every sign of raging fever with a sub-normal temperature. Puerile!'

Breen saw the flash, the steely sparkle of anger in the missionary's grey eyes and thought, with some complacency – I always did hold he was hasty-tempered: fault's not all on my side; here is he, getting his rag out with his own sort! Aloud he said:

'So now, I s'pose they think the sickness is the devil and are busy driving him out.'

'It's much worse than that. I told you. It's a witch hunt. They think someone, or a number of people are to blame. They've met to decide who it is. The whole thing is horrible, obscene.'

'Our poor black brothers,' Breen said musingly, looking, not at the missionary but at the stream of smoke he had blown towards the rafters of the hut. In one of their disputes – over the summary punishment of a native caught pilfering from the store – the missionary had used those words, or some very like them and the temptation to remind him was irresistible.

'Well, that is true,' Waters said. 'They are more to be pitied than blamed. They are frightened, and simple people when they are frightened, do revert to superstition. There is this sickness, which I can't deal with, can't even explain; it's natural enough for them to look about for someone to blame. I've only been here five years you know, and what is five years against centuries? What is one voice against God knows how many? I have tried,' he knew that he was, in a way, humbling himself by this attempt at self-justification, 'this very evening, up to the moment when they put the drums in place I was there, arguing and beseeching ...' he remembered the humiliation of being handled, not roughly, not even disrespectfully, but firmly, turned about and told to go back to his own hut, just as a child, venturing too near a fire might be turned about and sent to a safe place. 'Any mob,' he said, 'even in a civilized country, can get out of control.'

Breen nodded and shifted his position on the table.

'So now what?' he asked with interest. 'What's the drill?'

'This drumming,' Waters said, 'is the summonsing. Everybody within earshot *must* come. To stay away would be a confession of guilt. Presently the drumming will change ...' Oh what was the use, how could you expect Breen to understand words like 'hypnotism' and 'consciousness' and how, without using them, could you explain? In a brusque, dismissing tone, he said, 'They have their appointed hunters who will get up at the right moment and make their accusations. Then those accused will die in a very dreadful way, a very dreadful way indeed.'

'You know a lot about it, don't you,' Breen said, grinding out the end of his cigarette. 'Well, as I said, this is new to me and I been here longer than you. I'll just walk down and give this the once over.'

'I wouldn't,' Waters said earnestly. 'In their present mood they might resent that. And even if they didn't, the end won't be . . . a pretty sight.'

'I've lived here long enough,' Breen said cheerfully, 'not to expect pretty sights. And as you know, I love 'em all *so* much that if they round the thing off with a cannibal feast I'd watch dry-eyed.' He slid off the table and stood upright, scratching at the bush of black hair that showed between the edges of his unbuttoned shirt.

'I really would advise you . . .' Waters began.

'I know. Stay clear. Don't you worry, nothing'll happen to *me*, who else this side of Shegusa'd sell the black bastards good sound gin in soda-water bottles, only me, unregenerate heathen that I am. Good night, Reverend.'

Almost as soon as he had gone the drumming changed. There was a break, a moment's silence, and then, in place of the heavy throbbing and the machine-gun rattle, a level, thrumming monotone. The earlier noise had been like the church bells, calling people in; this was the sinister equivalent of the organ voluntary; the people were now taking their places, squatting down in rows, looking left and right at their neighbours. Presently the noise would take on another character. Soon now the real ceremony would begin.

'You know a lot about it, don't you?' Breen had said that. Now something in the missionary's own mind repeated the statement and the question. You know a lot about it, don't you?

Yes, I know a lot, too much, about it. I know how, as soon as everyone is assembled and quiet the drums will fall silent and then begin again, in quite another rhythm, and seven men, in hideous disguises will stand up, take little forked sticks from their waistcloths and begin to move . . . not dancing exactly, but moving to that terrible rhythm, in and out between the squatting rows. And I know . . . I know . . . down to the last horrid detail, exactly what will happen to those whom they touched with those little forked sticks.

How do I, why do I know so much? I have read about it. There is the answer. I have always been an omnivorous reader and always anything about Africa has been given my avid attention. Heaven knows I was reading about Livingstone and Stanley and Mungo Park when my contemporaries were engrossed with *Treasure Island*. And wasn't that inevitable ... who else had a grandfather who had been the first missionary to cross the Gambia; an intrepid man, with no organization behind him, and without luggage save a Bible, a few simple medicines and – so legend told – four cakes of Brown Windsor soap. Those who saw him leave expected never to see him again, and were proved right; but ten years later an old native, in the last stages of exhaustion walked into an outpost, twenty miles south of Shegusa, carrying a four-year-old child and a mildewed Bible. The child was the son, and the Bible was the book of 'the good man', now dead. Questions seemed only to confuse the old man, so they let him rest and in the morning he had vanished. The Bible was indubitably the property of Samuel Timothy Waters for his mother had written his name in it before presenting it to him on his tenth birthday in the year 1856; she wrote the crabbed painful hand of the just literate. Below her inscription in an easier, flourishing hand, but very shaky were the words:

'November 1886 between the 18th and the 23rd, was born Samuel John, son of Samuel Timothy Waters and Elizabeth his wife. To God be the Glory.'

It was regarded as evidence enough and it was as Samuel John Waters that the infant, after sundry vicissitudes, found harbour in an orphanage where, because it was a Methodist establishment, the Bible and as much of the boy's story as was known, were preserved. Samuel John Waters became a tailor, married, in 1912, the daughter of a Methodist grocer, enlisted in August 1914 and was killed on the Somme, leaving an infant son, Timothy. Samuel John must have told his wife as much as he had been told about his beginnings, and perhaps because in those years and in that class a missionary was regarded as a noble, almost an ideal thing to be, the legend of his grandfather had always loomed large in young Timothy's life; he had decided, at the age of nine, that he too would be a missionary, in West Africa, and he too would go that little bit farther, just as his grandfather had done. Perhaps the proudest moment of his life had been when he landed at Bathurst and learned that the story of the first Waters, setting off into the unknown, so inadequately equipped, had been firmly set in the mosaic of folklore.

The thought of his grandfather had always been a source of strength and inspiration; the mildewed Bible, too precious for ordinary use and carefully preserved in a tin box, was his most cherished possession. There were times when he wished that he knew a little more about his paternal grandmother. Surely no woman was ever summed up, described in so few words, 'Elizabeth his wife'. Where had he found her; who had married them; above all, beyond all, what colour had she been? The name Elizabeth proved nothing, converts so often took another name.

The question had never occurred to him until he was in Africa, even then not immediately, it had not, indeed arisen until he had achieved his ambition and gone that much farther, cut himself off from civilization. Then, very gradually and gently, like the sand running down through an hour-glass the questions and the doubts began to pile up. He found, for example, that the native food, to most white men barely palatable even in times of hunger, was enjoyable. He could sit cross-legged on a bare floor for hours without suffering discomfort. To expose a superstition he had planted some seeds in his garden at the dark of the moon, as the natives invariably did, and had been convinced, against his better judgment that there was something in the theory that growth was more vigorous as the moon waxed. And he had learned the dialect with quite disconcerting ease. His knowledge of witch-hunting procedure might have been taken, *must* have been taken, out of a book, but these other things, little things, negligible things . . .

Not for the first time he put the thought away. What did it matter? In the sight of God all men were equal; and it might well have been part of God's deliberate design to have bred Himself a servant with the ability to live in such a place, such a climate, and remain healthy and sane and sober. The last word reminded him of Breen. Breen had gone down to watch the proceedings and perhaps he was right, a detached anthropological attitude might be the correct one to adopt. Perhaps he should go and stand side-by-side with Breen and be a witness. The final act would be murder, disguise it how you might. Yes, it was his duty to be there.

He was almost at the door when the character of the drumming changed again. The monotonous throbbing ended in one great crashing boom, and then the pattern began, the pattern to which he had, in preparing to speak of it to Breen, chosen the word 'hypnotic'. The word was the right one; the drumming, luring the ear along and then breaking the rhythm, always at the least expected place, made a savage demand upon one's full attention, to more than one's full attention, to one's mind, to one's breathing, to one's pulses. It was impossible to listen to it and retain any individuality, and conscious thought, anything of oneself at all.

Even he could only stand, half-way between the table and door and listen as the noise mounted, straining always for some unattainable note, almost reaching it, falling short and beginning again. All thought of walking down to the clearing deserted him; it was as much as he could do presently, in one of the little breaks of the pattern, to fumble his way back to his chair and drop into it as though someone had caught him a blow at the back of his knees.

The noise continued. You could make a vast mental effort and know that it had been going on for about twenty minutes, but it felt as though it had always been there, and would go on for ever. Waters had often found difficulty in imagining eternity, had sometimes in a wakeful night made himself dizzy with thinking of it. Now he knew that eternity was not an imaginable thing; it had its own existence and you recognized it when you met it. It was here in this noise which was not a mere noise but a shuddering pain in every nerve, a probe at work in the brain, a stranglehold on the throat.

It stopped; so abruptly that it hurt. There was a silence. In it, he knew, the hunters would stalk among the anonymous, paralysed ranks, and they would be the only ones capable of movement. Evil was loose in the clearing, and not only the evil of superstition and paganism; human cruelty and spite moved there too. For who knew who the hunters might be? A neighbour wronged, a lover scorned, a friend turned enemy . . . anyone of these might be among the seven who rose and prowled, paused while the heart stopped, and then perhaps passed on.

In the silence he heard Breen pass on his way back to the store. He moved heavily but swiftly. Even he, brutal, cynical, drunken Breen had seen enough! It said something for his toughness that he could move, that he dared to turn his back and walk away. For this was the moment of fear when all heads were bowed, all faces hidden, all minds silently beseeching – Oh you, this night possessed by spirits and lent the power of dealing horrible death, pass me by! Choose any but me! Husband, wife, child, any but me.

Without knowing it he had slipped from the chair and was squatting back on his heels, his hands clenched together and his head bent. The rigid, shrinking posture, the fear, the wish not to be noticed made him one with all those in the clearing. And it was – as he would remember until the day he died – with an identical relief that he heard at last the cry, first in a single voice and then in a many-throated roar. 'The white man!'

Breen, he thought. They've chosen Breen. Even the quality of his sweat changed from the ammoniac secretion of fear to the bland healing bath that comes with a break in a fever. It was over; he could move again; he could think. He caught himself in the reflection that there was, after all, a kind of rough justice in the choice, Breen with his gin and his wenching . . .

He stood up and drew a deep breath. This mustn't happen, he must save Breen. The store lay a little farther from the clearing, and Breen would not be listening, would not be interested, would never suspect. He must be warned. Thank God, Waters thought, blundering to the door, he has the truck, and I am a good runner.

The emotions of the last hour had weakened him, however, and he was spent, utterly breathless when he reached the store. The door stood open and the lamp was lit but the place was empty. He tried to call, but no sound came from his gasping mouth; forcing himself to one more effort he ran round to the back and there was Breen, blaspheming horribly, swinging away at the starting handle of the old truck. The grating noise it made was swallowed up by the noise of the shouts and screams which announced that everyone in the clearing had just been reprieved from death and turned into a happy witch-hunter.

Breen knew then and realized his danger; there was no need to speak. Waters leaned back against the wall and took great gulps of air. When the engine started it seemed to do so silently, but he could see the truck begin to vibrate. Breen threw the handle in and went round to the driving seat.

'Get in,' he bellowed, 'look alive!'

Waters mouthed at him and made feeble flapping motions with his hands as though he were frightening birds away.

'My Christ,' Breen said, ran round the truck, lifted him as though he was heaving a sack of groundnuts and with a grunt of effort pushed him into the passenger's seat. Then he jumped in himself, released the brake and with a movement strangely careful and unhurried, engaged the gear. Jolting and shuddering, the ancient vehicle moved out on to the track which it had made for itself, and kept open by its regular journeys to Shegusa. Behind it the voice of the mob swelled louder with rage and frustration, and then, second by second, decreased.

The track sloped uphill for a little way; when it flattened out Breen changed gear; they gained speed and he changed again, and the engine ran less noisily. As soon as he could be heard Breen said, with an air of immense satisfaction:

'That's one in the eye for the bloody black bastards! Bloody near squeak though. If you'd waited to be fetched I'd have had to turn and I doubt if we'd have done it.'

'*You* were coming to fetch *me*?'

'What did you think I was doing? Swinging this old crate for exercise?'

'I . . . well, I'm very grateful, very grateful indeed, but I was in no danger. It was you they were after.'

'Me? They got nothing against me! I'm their best friend.'

So Breen believed that he had run for shelter, breathless with terror, so overcome that he had had to be lifted into the truck.

'I'm quite sure it was you they picked on.'

'But, man, I was there; if they'd wanted me . . . I stood there watching, quite a sight it was, bloody funny till I remembered you said something about a horrible death. Then I thought I'd fetch my gun and whichever poor black brother they fixed on I'd let him have clean through the head.' For a fraction of a second he slewed his head round and gave the missionary a mischievous look. 'No credit to me, I always did wonder what it'd feel like to shoot one, I've been tempted many a time! Anyway, I lit my lamp, loaded the gun and was on my way out again when I heard the yelling. Couldn't very well shoot you, Reverend. Methodists wouldn't like it and my motives might be mistook.' He laughed the jiving, belly-shaking laugh that Waters had often found so infuriating. Then he said, in a different voice, 'So you bust your guts running to warn me, eh?'

'Well . . . well, yes. When they said "the white man" I naturally thought of you.'

Breen laughed again, 'What d'you call yourself then? Bloody shining angel or what?'

LA VERGINE CON BAMBINO

MISS MAYHEW and Miss Stanley arrived in Rome towards the end of a lovely day just after Easter. The moment was without excitement for Miss Stanley who had spent an unhappy childhood in that city. In circumstances of poverty and squalor that she would have been glad to forget. Miss Mayhew, however, she was excited enough for both. In all her fifty-four years she had never been out of England, and during the long drive from Calais, with the weather growing warmer every day, and the scenery more exotic, her enthusiasm had mounted, until now, at the sight of the Victor Emmanuel Memorial, shining white in the sun, she uttered a cry of awed admiration.

At this blatant error of taste Miss Stanley smiled a pitying smile, but being tired she postponed her rebuke. She asked, in her fluent Italian, direction of a passer-by and then steered a swift determined course towards the little house which was the cause, as it was the destination, of their journey.

The house was rented by Jonathan Mayhew, Miss Mayhew's nephew: he had been engaged, for the last three years, on one of his immensely erudite studies of classical Roman life. Just before Easter he had written to his aunt, telling her that he found it necessary to visit Constantinople and suggesting that she should come and occupy the house during his absence. He did not wish, he wrote, to relinquish his tenancy because small, pleasant houses for hire were not easily found in Rome just now; nor did he wish to leave his books and collection of pottery in charge of unsupervised servants. He added – and Miss Mayhew could not blind herself to the obviousness of the after-thought – that it would be pleasant for her to see something of Rome.

Exactly how pleasant it would be for an inexperienced, congenitally timid, middle-aged woman to become caretaker of a house in a city where she did not understand a word of the language, he had not paused to consider: Miss Mayhew, who did not lack imagination, could guess, and would have sent back a gentle refusal, but for Miss Stanley.

For twenty-three years Miss Mayhew had been doing exactly what Miss Stanley ordered, or advised. Miss Stanley had come to teach History in the fashionable girls' school where Miss Mayhew was under-Matron; it was the chance discovery of the latter's relationship to Dr. Jonathan Mayhew which had bridged the slight social gap and caused Miss Stanley to cultivate Miss Mayhew's acquaintance. The friendship was three years old when Miss Mayhew received a legacy, not large, but sufficient for independence. Miss Stanley advised retirement, and that was welcome advice.

'But I dread the thought of living alone,' Miss Mayhew said.

'Buy a house within reasonable distance, and I will come and live with you,' said Miss Stanley, crisply. 'And don't think I'm doing you a favour, Kate. Non-resident staff always have the best of it.'

So it was arranged; and it worked splendidly. Miss Stanley was sensible, practical, self-assured, Miss Mayhew meek and amenable. Every morning, before she drove off to the school, Miss Stanley told Miss Mayhew what to do and Miss Mayhew carried out her orders. After all this time obedience and dependence upon Miss Stanley's judgment was so much a habit that when, after the receipt of Jonathan's letter, Miss Stanley said:

'But of course you must go, Kate. Jonathan's work is of the *utmost* importance; it is a privilege to help him, however indirectly. Creative work can only be successful if the mind is relieved of all petty matters. I will drive you to the door, stay as long as I can, and if you are still there at the end of term, I'll come straight out to you again.'

It had not escaped Miss Mayhew's notice that all through the years Miss Stanley had yearned for a meeting with Jonathan. She visualized it with some dismay. Unless his character had undergone a remarkable change, poor Laura was in for a disappointment, and the effect of Laura's manner upon Jonathan if it resembled the effect it had upon other men was something Miss Mayhew would rather not think about.

II

She need not have worried. Jonathan had left Rome on the morning of their arrival. They were admitted to the house by an extremely good-looking young Italian girl who at once drew Miss Mayhew's attention to an envelope on the table in the hall.

Jonathan wrote that he was sorry to miss his aunt and her friend, but somebody had offered him a lift as far as Belgrade. His housekeeper, he said, had given notice, but he had been lucky enough to replace her at once. The girl knew the house, having been called in for odd jobs from time to time; she had a fair grasp of English and could make tea. Her name was Benita.

'There you are, Kate,' said Miss Stanley, to whom Miss Mayhew had handed the note. 'Once you face things, difficulties just melt away. With a maid who speaks English you'll be quite at home.'

Only then, by the measure of her relief, did Miss Mayhew realize how frightened, and how very rash, she had been.

There followed some delightful, if exhausting, days of sight-seeing. Sometimes in a picture gallery, looking at a painting in which an artist had immortalized his mistress, or his patron's wife, Miss Mayhew would think – Nothing like as pretty as Benita. Once she spoke the thought aloud, and Miss Stanley gave a snort of disgust.

'Don't let that pretty face take you in, Kate. The girl's a sloven. Unless you keep her up to the mark, and pretty sharply too, you'll have food poison. I'm going to put the fear of God into her before I leave, and the rest is up to you.'

Before she left Miss Stanley not only spoke strictly to Benita: she inspected every light switch, every tap and every lock in the house; she made a table for the easy conversion of pounds and shillings into lire and a list of shops deserving of patronage. When she drove away to face the new term everything was in order.

III

It had been arranged that Benita should be free every Saturday afternoon from two until ten, 'and not one moment later, mind that,' Miss Stanley had said.

On the first Saturday, when the girl came to clear the lunch table something in her manner informed Miss Mayhew that she was about to be asked for something. She feared it might be an advance of wages, a thing Miss Stanley had expressly forbidden.

'She'll try it. I know Italians through and through, Kate. Once give her money in advance and you'll never see her again.' The fear of being left alone made Miss Mayhew determine to be firm.

'It is,' Benita said, 'very great favour I ask. Not for myself, for the baby.'

Jonathan had credited Benita with a fair grasp of English; Miss Stanley had said that she understood exactly as much as she wanted to and no more; Miss Mayhew found her painstaking speech not the least of her many charms. It combined an almost mediaeval stateliness and the crudest Americanisms; as now, when asked, 'What baby?' she described him as 'the son of my poor mother' and 'my kid brother'. Benita's mother, it was explained, was very sick, hospital sick and there was no one at home to care for the baby; it would be a favour past all gratitude if he could come here for one week, two week and be looked after by Benita.

'How old is he?'

He was just six months; just so small; and so good, you would astonish yourself how good.

'But of course,' said Miss Mayhew, delighted at having been confronted by so small a problem. 'It will mean more work for you, Benita, but I can help you. I'm . . . very fond of babies. I could push him out.'

Benita's smooth ivory brow wrinkled. The Signora had said 'of course' which meant 'yes' and then spoke of pushing out which meant the opposite.

'Push out?'

'In a perambulator,' said Miss Mayhew, miming.

Benita smiled.

'I bring him then? Oh, thank you, Signora. Thanks a million. And then some.'

IV

Miss Mayhew was in the kitchen, making herself the last cup of tea of the day, when Benita returned. It was easy to see why the girl had looked blank at the mention of pushing out a baby. He had no perambulator. Benita came in, carrying a shawled cocoon in one arm and on the other a flat vegetable basket holding the baby's few belongings. She walked with an unusually heavy step and looked dispirited.

Miss Mayhew's sentimental mind immediately thought that just like that, weary, weighed down with responsibility, might Mary have looked arriving in Egypt. And no older, no more beautiful, surely.

'You're tired,' she said kindly. She reached for another cup and filled it, forgetting that Benita did not care for tea. 'There, sit down and drink that. And give me . . . May I take him?'

Benita dropped the baby into Miss Mayhew's arms, and the vegetable basket on to the table, performing both actions in exactly the same manner. Then she sat down and kicked off her shoes. Very gently, conscious of a tremulous excitement, Miss Mayhew began to loosen the shawl. She had always longed to hold a baby in her arms, and this was the first time she had ever done so. She expected to find a thin, dark-skinned, probably dirty baby like some she had seen in the poorer parts of the city; instead, inside the shawl she found the most beautiful baby she had ever seen. And she did know about babies, her frustrated maternal feelings had made her an avid gazer into perambulators, a ready purchaser for any magazine with a baby on its cover, a student of all advertisements for baby foods and appurtenances. The child in her arms with his plump, just-sun-touched limbs, his pink, petal-smooth cheeks, silver-gilt hair was a match for them all; and he gave off that warm-wool, fresh-milk, fragrant-powder odour which she recognized as being just right.

'But he's beautiful,' she said.

Benita said nothing. Miss Mayhew wondered whether her remark had conveyed surprise and thus sounded tactless, or whether in Italy, as in India, it was regarded as unlucky to praise a child's looks. She asked quickly:

'What is his name?'

'Angelo.'

'What a lovely, suitable name.'

'It's a lulu!'

Now what did that mean? An Italian expression perhaps.

At that moment the baby woke, opened his blue-grey eyes between golden lashes, studied the strange face gazing down at him, and began to cry.

Benita jumped up.

'Give him to me, Signora. I beg you, do not trouble yourself. Your tea, it grows cold. He shall not be noisy, I promise you.' She snatched the child and gave him something very near a shake. He cried louder.

'I think he is hungry,' said Miss Mayhew. 'What does he eat?'

'Tonight he will eat the minestrone.'

'Oh.' Miss Mayhew's voice was dubious. Italian minestrone, vouched for by Miss Stanley as being the *real* thing, was quite unlike the soup served by that name in English restaurants; it was as thick as porridge, dark brown in colour, and highly seasoned. Still, this was an Italian baby and Benita was his sister. One mustn't interfere. Miss Mayhew carried her tea into the sitting-room and thought about a perambulator with a fringed linen canopy, a crib with a blue cover, woolly toys . . .

V

Sunday was rather a strange day. Naturally Benita did not realize how pleased Miss Mayhew was to have a baby in the house, or that she had already fallen deeply in love with Angelo. She seemed to wish to pretend that he was not in the house at all, and any mention of him put her on the defensive. And it wasn't due to jealousy; she took no joy in the child at all. Miss Mayhew could see that; and she could also see that though the mother of Benita and Angelo was plainly a woman with all the right ideas about raising babies, Benita was woefully ignorant. Miss Mayhew had made her own bed and dusted the sitting-room to give Benita time to bath Angelo and perform his essential laundry, but her last sight of him on that Sunday evening informed her that more minestrone had caked on his face and his clothing than had entered his stomach, and that he had not been 'changed'. Moreover Benita had managed to convey that her visits to the kitchen, her interest in the baby were alike unwelcome. Miss Mayhew went to bed very worried, because tomorrow, unless things altered very much she would be obliged to take action, a thing she always found very difficult indeed.

Actually – just as Laura had said – the difficulty melted away. Miss Mayhew stayed away from the kitchen until after breakfast, and when she entered it she carried that universal solvent, ready money.

'I want you,' she said, 'to leave everything, Benita, and go out and buy a perambulator – with a canopy. You understand? Linen, to shade the baby from the sun. And buy also a crib, a cot . . . a small bed for a baby, you know what I mean?'

'I know, Signora.'

'And here is a list of foods for babies. In England they are to be bought at any chemist's . . . apothecary's . . . drug stores. Of course, I don't know whether the names, here, would be the same . . .' She forced herself, for the first time in many years, to assume that air of authority which had sometimes been necessary to make a girl to swallow a distasteful dose.

'You *know* what I want, Benita; proper food for a baby of six months. I don't think Angelo likes the minestrone, and even if he did he should have something more.'

Benita said, 'I understand, Signora. I get you.' She went off willingly and Miss Mayhew turned her attention to Angelo. It was really alarming, she thought, how rapidly a neglected baby could deteriorate in less than twenty-four hours. She made some bread-and-milk, very sweet, and fed him. Then she bathed him and dressed him in the fresh clothes which his mother had sent in the vegetable basket. He accepted her ministrations with the utmost amiability. She talked to him, saying idiot things, 'Aren't you the lovely boy then, aren't you? Boofuls boy! Precious boy!' And being talked to in English didn't upset him at all. He cooed and gurgled and once gave her a heart-catching, toothless smile.

Benita came back. She seemed pleased with her purchases and spoke of 'bargains', but Miss Mayhew was disappointed. Consulting the exchange table which Laura had provided, she had given Benita money for articles not of the luxury class, but good and solid. Everything the girl had bought was of the cheapest quality, not at all what Miss Mayhew had visualized. The perambulator was almost springless and had no brake, the crib flimsy and already splintering. But it was to Benita's credit rather than otherwise, Miss Mayhew felt, that she had not spent lavishly; there would be a good deal of change. When it appeared that there was none, Miss Mayhew reflected that in Rome prices were outrageous. She then forgot all about money in the joy of putting the clean sweet-smelling baby into the perambulator and wheeling him out into the shade cast by the one tree – a magnolia – in the garden. It was pleasant there, as warm as most English summer days, and she stayed beside the baby, coming in only to prepare his food, making Benita watch the procedure, and to fetch clean nappies. Benita washed the soiled ones and did the housework. It was dawning upon her that the Signora *liked* looking after the baby. When Miss Mayhew prepared more food though Angelo had not made a sound to indicate that he was hungry, and then, at six o'clock, carried him indoors and said it was bedtime, Benita was sure. To this English lady a baby was a plaything, a toy. And who had provided it? Some reward was in order.

Serving the modest meal called 'dinner' at seven o'clock, Benita said:

'Signora, if it was agreeable to you, I could visit my mother on the hospital for a little while this evening.'

'But of course, Benita.'

'She will be happy to hear of your goodness to Angelo.'

Miss Mayhew was so touched by this, knowing that all she did was for her own pleasure, that she consulted Miss Stanley's table again and gave Benita the equivalent of ten shillings, telling her to buy her mother some fruit, or flowers.

VI

After that the days assumed a kind of pattern. Benita went out every evening, not always to the hospital; sometimes, she explained, she hurried all the way across the city to her home to do a little cooking and cleaning. It was sometimes as late as eleven before she returned, but there was always an excuse, and once, when she had been very late indeed, so late that Miss Mayhew had stayed awake, worrying, and in the morning said:

'You did not come home alone, Benita,' Benita opened her lovely dark eyes which always made Miss Mayhew think of pansy flowers and said:

'But no, Signora. Not so late, alone. My brother accompanied me.'

Miss Mayhew never failed to inquire how Benita's mother was progressing, and the report was always favourable.

'A little, a very little better, Signora,' Benita would say, measuring off the improvement between her thumb and forefinger.

Miss Mayhew would then give a few instructions about meals or things needed from the shops, and turn her full attention to Angelo. As the days grew warmer and the shade of the one tree more narrow, she began to take him out in the perambulator, choosing streets with one shady side. One day she found, quite by chance, a public garden, thick with massed trees, and with a fountain playing. During the day it was almost deserted, and she spent hours there, spreading a rug upon which the baby could crawl and stretch himself. Very occasionally a woman would pass and look at Angelo just as Miss Mayhew had, all her life, looked at babies; then her pride in his condition and her feeling of possessiveness would swell to the point of pain.

Though vague and sentimental, she was not a fool, and fully realized that all this joy had its price. Already she could taste the bitterness of the inevitable parting. She savoured it every time she had a letter from Laura, who was a faithful correspondent, and who said, only fifty-six, only forty-nine, only forty days before I see you again. (Miss Stanley was missing Miss Mayhew's housekeeping more than she had anticipated.) The baby would certainly have to be out of the house before Laura arrived. There was a threat, too, from another direction. The tiny measures of improvement in Benita's mother's condition were mounting up; one day she would go home and very soon after that, surely, she would want her baby back. Whenever these thoughts assailed her Miss Mayhew recognized them and then pushed them aside; it was like dying; one knew one must, but one enjoyed being alive meanwhile.

Miss Mayhew had, all through her life, been the victim of migraine and halfway through June she had an attack which kept her in bed for two days. Benita looked after her well, and seemed puzzled that a mere headache should lead to such complete lack of appetite. Several times during those two days she brought up trays of food, carefully cooked and temptingly displayed, and each time, after refusing them, Miss Mayhew would mention Angelo. Each time Benita gave a reassuring reply. On the morning of the third day Miss Mayhew woke to that cessation of misery, that resurgence of life that is the migraine's victim's compensation; she wasn't just better, she was positively restored. She thought of all the trips that Benita had made up the stairs; she thought of the joy of seeing Angelo again and she thought, as always after these days of fasting of *cheese*. She would go down at once, not waiting for Benita to bring the tea-tray, she'd look at Angelo, cut herself a hunk of cheese and carry her tea into the garden.

The kitchen was brilliant with sunlight. The kettle was boiling on the stove, the tea-tray stood ready at one end of the hopelessly cluttered table. Angelo lay on the wide-seated basket chair. He was wailing. Ordinarily the noise he made was a healthy, arrogant demand for attention, this morning it was a peevish, rather hopeless protest against things that had gone wrong. And how wrong! From the door Miss Mayhew could smell the stench which told her that he hadn't been changed since she did it last. Benita stood by a square of looking-glass, pushing her hair back and studying the effect of some earrings.

All this Miss Mayhew took in at a glance. She saw Benita turn her head left and right, and then, letting her hair fall back into place, reach out and give Angelo a smart slap on the upper part of his leg, at the same time spitting out an Italian word which plainly meant 'Shut up'.

With no hesitation at all, no diffidence, Miss Mayhew cried, 'Don't do that!' and swooped down on the now violently yelling baby. He was once again encrusted with dried minestrone, a saliva-slimed crust was stuck in the fold of his soft neck and he stank to high heaven, but she said, 'Who's a booful boy then? Who's a precious?' and the yelling stopped.

Later on, when Angelo had been fed and cleaned and lay in his perambulator, trying to cram his foot into his mouth, Miss Mayhew had what she called a 'good straight talk' with Benita. She wished Laura could have heard her saying:

'You're really not fit to have charge of a baby, Benita. I only hope that I shall be able to look after him until he is handed back to your mother. There's really no excuse for you, for you must have *seen* how to deal with babies. What on earth will you do when you have a baby of your own?'

Benita gave her what Miss Mayhew called 'a funny look', but the frank speaking did have some effect. It was very humbly and ingratiatingly that Benita, that evening, asked leave to go to the hospital.

'My mother, I think, is to be dismissed today, Signora. I would like very much to take her clothes and help her dress and bring her home.'

That was, Miss Mayhew thought, the maddening part. Towards her baby brother Benita had been callous; towards her employer, smitten down with migraine, she had been most attentive, and towards her mother she had been, and was, extremely kind. Some kind of national inconsistency ... something no foreigner could ever understand. Like fox-hunting in England ...

'You may go, Benita,' Miss Mayhew said.

VII

So that evening she was alone when the bell rang. Miss Mayhew halted in the hall to make sure that the noise had not awakened Angelo, and then went to the door. A very neat, indeed spruce, middle-aged woman stood on the step.

'Would you,' she asked, 'be Miss Mayhew? I thought so. My name's Shafton, Mrs. Glenda Shafton. I'm from Atlantic Bridge.'

She spoke the last words as though they would, to anyone, be self-explanatory. Something to do with Jonathan, Miss Mayhew thought.

'Will you come in?'

'I do apologize for coming at this hour, and for not coming before,' Mrs. Shafton said. 'I've been on vacation and everything's got a bit behindhand. We aren't generally this careless. But Miss Slade, my assistant, would have checked up, only, this being a respectable address, and you being English she let it slide. Somebody this afternoon came across with the news that Benita was back on her beat so I reckoned I'd best come along right away.'

'I'm afraid I haven't the slightest notion what you are talking about, Mrs. Shafton.'

'Atlantic Bridge,' said Mrs. Shafton. Suspicion narrowed her eyes. 'Don't tell me he isn't *here*?'

'My nephew, Dr. Jonathan Mayhew, has gone to Constantinople ... Istanbul ... I'm just keeping house.'

'I'm not talking about *him*! I'm checking up on the Bianco baby.'

'The baby? You mean Angelo.'

'That's the one. Is he here?'

'Oh, he's here. Very well and sound asleep. You are from the hospital?'

'I told you. I'm from Atlantic Bridge. Did you never hear of that organization?'

They had reached the sitting-room. Miss Mayhew, much bemused, was able to say:

'Do sit down. No. I'm afraid I never have. What is it?'

'An organization for taking care of unmarried girls and their babies. You see, during the war, all our fellows didn't behave just as they should, and we back home felt a certain responsibility. And since then, though we're short of funds and workers, there never has been a time when we could shut down. Take Benita Bianco for an example, well advanced in labour when she arrived. Most of them are. You can't shut the door in their faces.'

You'd have thought, Mrs. Shafton said to herself, that anybody of the age of the woman now confronting her, even if English and old-fashioned, would have understood the Facts of Life. But this Miss ... Miss Mayhew looked more shocked than anybody she'd ever seen.

'Are you telling me,' Miss Mayhew said, moving her dry lips with difficulty, 'that Angelo ... is ... Benita's ... That Benita is his *mother*?'

Always, behind the thought of the inevitable parting, there had been the substantial, sensible figure. 'The Mother', the one who had reared Angelo, smooth-limbed, full-fleshed, clean, confident, powdered. She had, in an emergency, handed Angelo to Miss Mayhew, and Miss Mayhew was prepared, any day now, to hand Angelo back to her, smooth-limbed, full-fleshed, clean, confident and powdered.

But she didn't exist, at least she didn't exist if what this extremely reliable-looking woman was saying was so.

'But of course Benita is his mother,' Mrs. Shafton said. 'What tale did she tell you?'

Miss Mayhew explained, ending with the words, 'I thought he had been amazingly well looked after.'

'We do our best,' Mrs. Shafton said modestly.

'Then why did she bring him away? She didn't want him.'

Mrs. Shafton said the reason was only too obvious. Atlantic Bridge dealt with confinements, and kept babies for the first two months without charge.

'That gives the girls a chance to get back on their feet. After that we reckon they can handle a job, so we make a small charge for keeping the babies. Let's see . . .' she put lire into dollars and dollars into English money, 'it'd be about half a crown a week.'

'And that she would well have afforded.'

'But why should she?' asked Mrs. Shafton, 'when you were there, willing to do it for free?'

It was there that Miss Mayhew began to cry. That was one of the most shaming things about migraine; you suffered, you knew a strange uplift of spirit and then there was the decline. Very often, at about this point Miss Mayhew had wept over a piece of burnt toast or some similar triviality. But now she was weeping for Angelo, and for herself.

'I thought . . .' she sobbed, '. . . good mother . . . given him back . . . Benita . . . nothing but minestrone, with proper food there to hand . . . never changed . . . terribly chafed, almost raw . . . and she slapped him . . .'

'See here,' said Mrs. Shafton, 'you mustn't upset yourself like this. We do check up. Right here, this minute, I'm checking up.'

'But in the end, what happens to the babies?'

'Well,' Mrs. Shafton hesitated. 'It varies. Quite often the mother's family, sometimes the father's, can be persuaded to take them. But Benita has no folks; she says she's an orphan and I guess we have to believe that. Then we do arrange a lot of adoptions. Of course there Angelo's colour is a disadvantage. You see, an Italian couple prefer an Italian looking baby, and Angelo couldn't be called that, could he? Still, I must admit – and I was reared Congregationalist – we have found the Catholic Orphanages most co-operative.'

At that Miss Mayhew sobbed harder. 'One of the books I brought out to read . . . *Little Boy Lost* . . . I just couldn't bear *that* for Angelo. No love . . . and chilblains . . . Oh dear, if only I could adopt him myself.'

'Well,' said Mrs. Shafton, 'what's stopping you?'

VIII

From that moment on Miss Mayhew found herself in the hands of another master. Glenda, though physically less imposing than Laura, was, if anything, more ruthless and direct. And in her hands, torn by desire, Miss Mayhew was more than ordinarily feeble and helpless. She knew, from the first moment, that she had only to say, 'I share a house with a friend who would utterly disapprove of this idea.' But she never said that. She said every other thing.

She said, 'Benita knows how fond I am of the baby. She'd find some way of twisting this to her own advantage. She'd make me pay.'

Glenda Shafton said, 'Of course she would. But she is not to know. From the first she put this baby down for adoption. I shall inform her that I have found a prospective adopter and call the baby in.'

Miss Mayhew said, 'But aren't there all sorts of formalities? You can't just take an Italian baby into England, can you?'

Glenda Shafton said, 'You leave all that to me. I've handled cases far more awkward.'

Miss Mayhew said, 'I do feel that I'm rather *old* to go about adopting babies.'

'You're what? Fifty-four. My dear girl, I'm sixty in November and the way things look I shall be coping with babies for the next fifteen years! Old! In five years time you'll be playing ball with that young man.'

Miss Mayhew said, wringing her hands, 'I don't seem to have any *choice*. I can't leave him to Benita. She doesn't *care*.'

'Would you expect her to?' Mrs. Shafton asked. 'She's just a common little prostitute; she hasn't a clue as to who the father was. To her Angelo was a stroke of sheer bad luck. That conditions her attitude, of course. To give them their due, most Italian women, though not so hot on hygiene, are very *fond* of their children.'

Once again Miss Mayhew thought of that non-existent motherly figure to whom she could have handed Angelo. She thought of Benita, busy with the ear-rings, slapping Angelo for crying when he had every reason to cry.

'I don't know what to say, and that is the truth,' she cried.

'Well, you don't have to decide right here this minute. Of course the thing will take a bit of arranging. When would you be going home?'

'Oh, not before, certainly not before the first week in August.' And that called up the vision of Laura arriving, of having to be told. Sweat broke out all over Miss Mayhew's face.

'Then there's not all that hurry. You think it over and give me a ring. Here's the address and the number. And if you come down on the baby's side, I'll tell Miss Benita we've found a home for him and call him in.'

She stood up briskly. Miss Mayhew rose and said, timidly:

'I suppose you wouldn't care to take a peep at him.' To the end of her days she could never decide what made her say that; was it pride? The wish to send Mrs. Shafton away thinking well of her despite the tears and the indecisiveness? Sheer fate?

'I sure would,' said Mrs. Shafton; and Miss Mayhew led the way to Jonathan's bedroom, where she had placed the crib after finding that nothing could make Benita keep her own room from being a pig-sty.

Angelo lay there, more beautiful than any of the babies in any of the pictures, flushed with sleep.

'Ah,' said Mrs. Shafton, 'you've certainly done a beautiful job on him!'

Then madness entered into Miss Mayhew and she said in a high, shaky, defiant voice.

'And I intend to go on doing it. Nothing, nobody shall stop me.'

IX

Benita came in while Miss Mayhew was reading Jonathan's letter.

'Signora, my mother is now restored to health. Quite Oh Kay. And she wishes back her baby.'

'Naturally, Benita. When will you take him?'

'Afternoon would be best. Signora, the perambulator and the crib, would you wish I should dispose of them for you?'

'You may give them to your mother, Benita, with my compliments.'

Benita's lovely soulful eyes sparkled. She pressed home the advantage.

'One thing I am thinking, Signora. Angelo is now spoilt for the minestrone. He will be missing the Ov-al-tine.' Crafty, avaricious little wretch!

'He'll soon become accustomed to what your mother can provide, Benita.'

'Thank you, Signora,' said Benita, exactly as an under-tipped waiter would use the words.

And, Oh, thought Miss Mayhew, if I didn't know that he was on his way to Atlantic Bridge to wait for me, I could not have borne this moment. I did right; no matter what Laura says, I am right!

She returned to Jonathan's letters, which, like all his communications, was short and to the point. He had hit on the trail of something that made it necessary for him to go to Tripoli and it wasn't likely that he would be returning to Rome. So would she please have his books and pottery crated and sent to a depository. The lease on the house ended on 1st August and he had written to say he would not be renewing it. He gave her the name and address of the firm with whom to leave the keys. In another obvious afterthought he hoped she had enjoyed her stay in Rome.

So, she thought, it was all a waste; he might just as well have given up the house at Easter, and I need never have come. And then she had a flash of enlightenment; there had been need, Angelo's need. For one happy, dizzying moment she had an absolute faith in destiny.

On the last day of June she gave Benita her month's wages and told her that she could begin looking for other employment. Benita staged a touching little scene.

'Never,' she said, 'never shall I find another lady of so good a heart to set me free each evening to help my poor mother. To myself I said, when I opened the door to you – There is one with a heart of kindness. Until the last moment, Signora, I shall stay with you.'

Miss Mayhew believed that; in few households would Benita have been able to pursue both her occupations. During July her return to the house was often very late indeed – she had been searching the city for work, she said, and had missed several excellent posts because of her determination to stay with Miss Mayhew until the end. Miss Mayhew seemed less impressed than Benita had hoped. Miss Mayhew had other things to think about. The school broke up on the 18th July and Laura would be in Rome on the 24th.

X

Miss Mayhew waited until Benita had gone out – searching for work. Then she said:

'Laura, I have something very important to tell you, but first you must promise me not to say a word to Benita about it, or to mention the matter in her hearing.'

'I think you can trust me to use discretion in my relationships with servants, Kate dear.'

('Kate dear' was new. Indeed Miss Mayhew had been surprised and somewhat discomfited by the warmth of their reunion. It made what she had to say more difficult.)

She told the whole story and Laura, though her face was eloquent, did not interrupt her. When Miss Mayhew fell silent, Miss Stanley lighted a cigarette, drew on it and blew out a cloud of smoke before she spoke.

'My poor darling,' she said, 'it's easy enough to see what has happened to you. You've been victimized all round. This Mrs. Shafton, how *dare* she talk you into such a crazy scheme? I'll deal with her! What's the number?'

'I haven't been victimized, Laura. Of my own free will I did it. I *want* that baby. I want him more than I ever wanted anything in my life. I love him. And I intend to have him.'

She had never spoken so firmly and positively about anything.

'But Kate, have you thought about how a baby will fit into our lives, into our home? Here I suppose you never wanted to go out in the evening, or if you did, Benita could stay in. What will happen at home? What about the Music Lovers' Circle for instance.'

She had chosen badly.

'I've always been very bored at the concerts, Laura. I only went to please you.'

'Our little trips to London, then. The theatre. The ballet. How can they be managed?'

'I can do without them, Laura, I shall have Angelo.'

'I should like to point out that you are taking an entirely egoistic view of this affair, Kate. What about *me*? I dislike young children. How am I to be expected to work in the evenings, for instance, with a noisy baby in the house and wet ... washing everywhere?'

Miss Mayhew had thought of that, and with her face reddening in an unbecoming way and even seeming to swell slightly, she said:

'I would do everything that I could to see that you were not incommoded, Laura; but if the idea is really so distasteful to you, you're under no obligation to live with us, you know.'

Miss Stanley ground out her cigarette.

'Fine independent talk! I don't think you realize how much I look after you. How would you set about getting back to England on your own? Tell me that.'

'Angelo and I would fly. It's quite easy; and it would be better for him than the train.'

Miss Stanley could feel herself becoming angry. She wanted to say – So you throw over an old, tried friend for any little bastard! She wanted to say – I hope Angelo will look after you well when you have your beastly migraine. But she restrained herself and in a cold, quiet voice said:

'Perhaps that is what you had better do.'

She expected Kate to break then, waited for a moment, and then walked out of the room. Now, she thought, she'll cry all night.

Miss Mayhew did cry a little before she slept, but Miss Stanley had the worse night; it was she who would be uprooted, homeless, thrown out. She knew no one with whom she could bear to share a house; to take one on her own she would need a housekeeper. Even in this past term, the easiest and pleasantest of the year, she had seriously missed Kate's unobtrusive attentions.

It was Miss Stanley who, in the morning, went to find Miss Mayhew and say:

'I think we were both over-wrought last evening and said hasty things, Kate. A friendship as old as ours mustn't be jettisoned so lightly. If you're really set on this crazy scheme . . .'

'Oh, I am, Laura,' cried Miss Mayhew, tears springing to her eyes. 'And I'm sure that when you see Angelo . . .'

She proceeded to outline, with a wealth of detail which showed how much thought she had given the matter, exactly how she proposed to organize things at home so that Angelo would give Laura no cause for complaint.

'. . . so you see he won't disturb you at all. And I'm sure Mrs. Lomax would come and sit in the evenings, so we could still have our little outings.'

There was a drawn-out silence, then Miss Stanley said:

'Well . . . since you are so set on it; it's your house, after all. Mind, I think you're taking a terrible risk. Breeding will out, you know. I can see trouble ahead.'

Miss Mayhew said, with great simplicity, 'Whatever he has it in him to be, Laura, surely in the end he'll be the better for having been cared for and loved. Left here I see no chance for him at all.'

Even Miss Stanley could not refute that. She turned away and went to see how much progress Benita had made with cleaning the kitchen, which had been in a shocking state, just as she had expected, when she arrived.

Benita stood at the sink, so that the harsh morning light streamed over her perfect face. There was something so beautiful, so even virginal about her that Miss Stanley was moved to anger. Why should she think she had so successfully deceived Kate? She'd go away and say, 'Silly old English cow; she'd believe anything!' Besides, it was all her fault, if she'd never had the wretched baby, or, having it, if she had looked after it properly ... Now the one thing certain was that life in the comfortable Oxfordshire house would never, could never, be the same again!

Using the gutter-Italian of her childhood, words whose English equivalents had never crossed her lips, Miss Stanley allowed Benita to understand that nobody had been deceived by her. Benita blinked under the suddenness and the ferocity of the attack, but even as she blinked, her agile mind was seeking, and finding some way of twisting this development to her own advantage. Turning from the sink she put her hands on her hips and spat out a statement which made the colour drain from Miss Stanley's face.

'Go straight upstairs,' she said. 'Collect what belongs to you and leave this house.'

'This month,' said Benita, 'I am to be paid.'

'I shall have the money for you when you come down. Be quick!' She followed the girl into the hall and watched her up the stairs. On no account must she be allowed to come into contact with Kate again.

Benita's few clothes and trinkets were easily contained in the flat vegetable basket; she came downstairs, took her money from Miss Stanley's hand and departed, jauntily, by the front door. The last throw had been a failure but on the whole, out of the shopping, especially the perambulator and the crib – profitable both in their buying and their re-sale – she had not done at all badly. Her one regret was that she had not known that the good-hearted one knew her secret; had she known she could have perfected her tale and extorted who knew what enormous sums.

Miss Stanley went back into the sitting-room.

'Kate,' she said, 'would they let you have that baby today?'

'Oh yes. Everything is signed and settled. He's just waiting to be collected.' Her face took on a vivacity which Miss Stanley had never seen before. 'You mean have him here, today?'

'I should like to leave today. There's nothing left here to do, is there? We could get to Grossetto before it was too hot; and anyway you're as cool in a moving car as anywhere.'

'But you've only just arrived. You were driving all yesterday.'

'I'm prepared to drive all day today. I want to get out of this vile, stinking place.' Her voice took on a shrillness, almost a hysterical note. 'There's something evil about the very air. Look at the Roman Emperors! Look at the Popes! Even decent people, if they're here long enough, go the same way. My own father . . .' But there the long habit of secrecy checked her. And then, remembering her own closely held secret, she wondered about Kate. Was it possible that she knew, that the whole thing, the visit, the adoption was all a put up job.

'By the way,' she said, casually, but with a watchful eye on Kate's face, 'I sent that little slut packing. I let her know that she hadn't utterly fooled us; that I knew she'd had her baby here.'

'But you didn't mention . . .' Not that it mattered now with everything arranged, and their departure so imminent.

'Of course not. What we *should* have found out, Kate, is who the father was.'

Miss Mayhew's candid, periwinkle-blue gaze met her friend's without flinching.

'Nobody knows; not even Benita.'

No, Kate did not know. And the girl had probably said the first hurtful thing that came into her head; or had her eye on extortion . . . It would be interesting to see whether any of the intellectual brilliance had been passed on . . .

XI

Back home the ménage à trois worked out better than Miss Mayhew had hoped or Miss Stanley had feared. Miss Mayhew was not in the least surprised to find that even Laura could not remain impervious to Angelo's charm. (Looking ahead, prudently, to school days, they had renamed him, plain Robert.)

What did somewhat surprise Miss Mayhew was that Miss Stanley suddenly became extremely critical of Jonathan's work. Several of his theories, she said, had been proved quite fallacious; and when his latest book appeared she said it was absolute tripe.

BUT I'VE HAD EVERYTHING!

YESTERDAY I heard my sister-in-law say to her daughter, 'I don't want you to end up a cranky old spinster like your Aunt Jean.' I almost called out, 'But I've had everything!' However, I restrained myself; had she known that I had overheard she would have been upset, for she is a kind woman. I just tip-toed away, thinking how strange that she should speak, should think of me with such contemptuous pity. And why, I wondered, *cranky*? Could it be because I am happy in spite of being fifty and unmarried? If she only knew. I thought: and I spent the day re-living in my memory that summer which changed, and made, my life . . .

The year was 1926 and I was nineteen. My mother and I and my brother – when he was home from the University – were living in a rather nasty little flat in Ealing. My father had died young and left what would, for one woman, have been adequate means but was not enough for a family. The money there was must be spent on the boy, the first-born, so I had left school at sixteen, taken a course in typing and shorthand and got myself a job. Nowadays even incompetent typists are in short supply, but in those days we were ten a penny and to get a job at fifty shillings a week you had to offer a language. At school I had been rather good at French and after I left I kept it up: I also began to put aside a small sum, sometimes no more than a shilling, each week, so that one day I might go to France, hear the language spoken by native tongues and perhaps be able to come back and find a better job.

At the moment I was one of six shorthand typists employed by a big engineering firm with an office on Victoria Embankment. There were three partners, Mr. Hardistone, Mr. Lacey and Mr. Gunning. Each had his own private secretary, very superior and enviable, and we six formed a pool upon which heads of departments and various specialists could draw as occasion arose. The work was dull and impersonal.

That year I was to have my holiday in June and two days before it was to begin Mr. Hardistone's secretary telephoned down to the typists' room and asked me to go to his office immediately. I had never known Mr. Hardistone to draw on the typists' pool and had he done so he would have asked for Rose – much my superior in our little hierarchy. And it couldn't be the sack; Mr. Hardistone would never deal with such a trivial detail. Puzzled, yet in a way stimulated – perhaps this was my great chance! – I took pad and pencil and hurried into the presence.

Mr. Hardistone said, 'Sit down, Miss er – er – Benson.' He glanced at a paper to make sure of the name. I sat down and adopted the attitude of an eager, competent girl awaiting dictation.

'You're due to begin your holiday on Saturday, I believe,' he said.

My heart and my stomach took the swift lift down. I had my twenty pounds saved at last; my ticket was bought and I had booked a room in an unbelievably cheap pension which someone had recommended to me. That twenty pounds represented three years of lunching on a bun and a cup of tea, of walking to save a bus fare, of digging out enough lipstick for one more make-up on the end of a nail file, of endlessly mending stockings – sordid little economies which no one dreams of nowadays. And it hadn't been easy to convince my mother that any girl of nineteen, however plain of face and dedicated of purpose, would be safe in Paris, alone. Still I had managed it, and now, by the tone of Mr. Hardistone's voice I knew that my plan was threatened.

'Would it,' he asked, 'be asking too much to suggest a postponement?'

I wanted to say – Yes, it would. But I knew how easily jobs were lost, how hardly found. I said, and I could feel my lower lip tremble as I spoke:

'It would be rather *awkward*. I was going to France, you see.'

He looked at me with a faint interest and surprise; holidays abroad were less a matter of course in those days.

'And you had made your reservations?'

I nodded. 'At such short notice,' I said, 'they might not give me back my . . .'

'All that,' he spoke briskly, 'could be taken care of. Let me explain the situation, Mr. Lacey, as you know, has been in hospital.'

I did just know that because some busybody had made a collection to send him some flowers. I had given sixpence, bitterly grudged.

'He's better now, and convalescing at home. We've filled in for him as much as possible, but there are some matters with which only he can deal. Also he has this paper to prepare for the Canadian Conference, so he needs a typist for about a fortnight.'

But why *me*? Why not his own stuck-up Miss Dredger? I suppose my face showed what I was thinking.

'It means staying down in Norfolk – during the week, at least, and Miss Dredger's invalid mother cannot be left at night,' Mr. Hardistone explained.

Miss Dredger can't be bullied and put-upon, I thought sourly.

'You, in any case, would be absent from the office, so you seemed the obvious choice. It wouldn't be hard work, I don't suppose Tom . . . Mr. Lacey will be capable of much sustained effort. You'd be in the country . . .'

Doing myself no good. Once deferred, my plan might never come off; Mother might change her mind; something might crop up to reduce my capital; *anything* might happen.

'Well, if you can't, you can't,' said Mr. Hardistone, becoming impatient with me. 'One of the others must go . . .'

And that would be held against me ever after; unco-operative, in an emergency; disobliging. That would do me no good either.

'I'll go,' I said, ungraciously.

He said that I might take that afternoon and the next day to make my arrangements. He said that his secretary would look after my cancellations. He said there'd be my fare down and both ways for the intervening week-end; ten pounds out of petty cash he said. Just like that. Ten pounds – half of what I'd saved so painfully. For a moment the idea of going to Swan and Edgar's and buying one of those pretty cotton dresses – prohibitive at thirty-five shillings – shot through my head. Then I thought, how silly! What was going to be good enough for Paris would be good enough for Norfolk, surely. And anything I could save out of that ten pounds was going into my holiday fund . . . Heavens, I thought, I may even yet get to Versailles and see the Petit Trianon!

Mother, who had been quite indifferent as to how I was clad in Paris, began to concern herself with my wardrobe as soon as I explained my change of programme.

'They'll dress for dinner,' she said. 'You must have a dinner dress.'

'I'm going there to *work*,' I protested. 'I shall probably be given a tray on the typing table.'

'All the same . . .' she said; and went away, and I heard her rummaging about in her bedroom. Presently she came back carrying a dress, pretty material, green silk with a raised stripe of deeper green, but positively Edwardian in style, full and long in the skirt, low-necked and with tight, wrist-long sleeves. A museum piece.

'I am not,' I said firmly, 'going to wear that!'

'It's a fashion that is coming in again,' she said. 'I saw one exactly like it in a magazine only the other day. They called it a Picture Dress. It'd need a bit of taking in, you're so skinny. But with a few tucks and my cameo brooch and ear-rings . . .'

That broke me down. She had had a few bits of good jewellery but one by one they had been sold, even her engagement ring. The cameos were left because they had no value. I could see myself working away in the evenings, wearing my cotton dress if it were warm, my jersey and skirt if it were chilly, but if Mother wished to visualize me peacocking about in green silk, well, that didn't cost anything.

I stood still while she pinned the tucks, and almost unwillingly I saw that the colour, the silkiness, the fullness did suit me. I looked rather nice and it was a pity that I should never wear that dress where there was anyone to see . . .

The train reached my destination soon after seven in the evening and the sun was still shining. The station's name, 'Stemmington' was laid out in flowers on the sloping bank, the letters white against a background of purplish pink; the fence at the back of the platform was thickly hung with climbing roses, pink and white and crimson. Looking back I can think now that there and then the keynote of my experience was struck – that even the railway station should be so pretty.

A nice old man, rather lame, hobbled up and offered to carry my suitcase; mindful of my sixpence I said that I could manage. I rather regretted that when I found that Mr. Lacey had sent his car and chauffeur to meet me. I had often seen that car outside the office. Little had I ever thought to ride in it.

We drove through the village where all the cottage gardens were ablaze with flowers, sweet-williams, stocks and snapdragons, and after that the hedges closed in, wearing the last of the hawthorn and the first wild-roses. I thought – with the unknowing, pleasant melancholy of the young – of the Drinkwater poem about the people, now long dead, grieving, as the living do, over the passing of youth, of a summer season, of happiness.

> 'Theirs was the bitterness we know;
> Because the clouds of hawthorn keep
> So short a state and kisses go
> To tombs immeasurably deep.'

With me it was an entirely literary feeling; I was too young then to value youth, or to believe that it could ever pass; the summer ahead seemed endless, and except for Mother and Jim long ago – nobody had ever kissed me. I was just an ignorant, romantic girl who had done a bit of reading because reading was the cheapest form of entertainment.

My thoughts changed as we turned into a gateway and came in sight of the house. Its real garden, I was to learn, lay to the rear; in front there was nothing but a superbly kept lawn and a huge, darkly-spreading cedar tree. The front of the house was impressive, Georgian, exactly symmetrical, with many evenly spaced windows. It looked uninhabited, rather gloomy, and the tree was sinister with age. Nervousness assailed me, and I wondered again, as I had wondered in the train, what Mr. Lacey would be like to work for. In my three years with the firm I had only seen him once at really close quarters. I had happened one day to be in the publicity department when he rang through for a file and I was sent with it. He'd said 'Thanks' without looking up and I had merely noticed that close to he looked older than he did from a distance. He was slightly built and had a boyish head of hair. From across the desk I could see that some silver hairs contributed to that effect of shining fairness. Now, entering his house I wondered whether he would dictate fast or slow, expect his typist to be familiar with esoteric technical terms or not, whether, in short, I could satisfy him.

A stout, cheerful-looking woman in a white overall admitted me; the chauffeur brought in my case and carried it away through a door beyond the staircase. Immediately Mr. Lacey came through a doorway at the far side of the hall. I hardly recognized him; he'd acquired a deep tan, and was wearing a blue shirt, short-sleeved and open at the neck, and a pair of pinkish-brown linen slacks. He looked young again, and the shirt made his eyes seem very blue.

He said, in a voice that sounded warm and sincere, how *good* it was of me to come, and how much obliged he was. I asked after his health and he said, 'Absolutely splendid.' Then he said:

'Let Mrs. Parker show you your room. Throw off your hat and come down and have some sherry. We're on the terrace.' He pointed to the open doorway and I could see that on that side was a garden all gilded in the sunshine.

My room lay on that side of the house, too, and a rosebush climbed up so that the roses nodded by the windowsill. It was like a room in a film; all in two colours, deep rose and white, and it was an unoccupied room, waiting for me. It is difficult for anyone who has had a room of her own to realize how much that meant to me. In the flat there were two bedrooms; the larger was Mother's the smaller I used when Jim was away, but it had been his room originally and every vacation staked his claim anew, so that it was always his room, not mine, his school photographs, his books, his holiday clothes, the relics of his various hobbies. This lovely room, for the duration of my stay, would be all mine. I would put out the little travelling clock which I had won at a school sports, and the old silver hairbrush and comb which had been my grandmother's – the cherubs polished almost out of existence – and then this room would be mine as the one in the flat had never been and would never be. When I opened the door in a little alcove I found that I also had a bathroom of my own. It was octagonal, and had panelled walls and a little high-hobbed fireplace . . . plainly once on a time a powdering closet. Wonderful!

I took off my hat, ran a comb through my hair, washed my hands and put a little powder on my nose and went down. The staircaise curved like a half-opened fan and the slender mahogany banister rail was like cool smooth silk under my hand.

The terrace ran the whole length of the back of the house,

and what looked to me like a formidable gathering of people were at the far end where a plane tree, out on the lawn, cast some shade. I felt my legs go stiff with shyness, so that I began to move jerkily. Mr. Lacey, however, was looking out for me. He came and took me by the elbow and led me into the group, making introductions which were largely wasted upon me because I was in such a state of confusion that I was incapable of associating the name I heard with the face confronting me. But there I was at last, in a chair, a glass of sherry in my hand and Mr. Lacey beside me, asking me questions about the office, questions which I could answer and which gave me a kind of standing.

'You must excuse us a moment,' he said. He asked after everyone in the office even the man on the door: he found, or pretended to find, some entertainment in my replies, so that he laughed every now and then in a whole-hearted, boyish manner. I was, all at once, not just the tuppenny typist, robbed of her holiday, come down to oblige, but a person with wit and social value who had dropped in on the party. A man said, 'I *do* think, Tom, that you might let us in on this!' A woman said with mock, exaggerated despair, 'Now you see why men adore going to their offices!'

I was not for a moment deceived; it was all his doing not mine. I was duly grateful.

The one person I had noticed was Mrs. Lacey, and she would have been noticeable in any company. To begin with she wasn't English. Whether she were Greek or Italian or Spanish I never knew, and did not like to ask; but it was Latin blood which had given her that black, black hair, those great dark eyes and that creamy only just-not-greasy skin. She had an unfashionable figure for that period, curved, definitely feminine, and tiny hands and feet. Her English was fluent, even colloquial, but full of oddities. She would ask, 'What we shall do now?' and say, 'Let's we go to dinner at the Club, eh?' or 'How you are pretty in that dress!' Divorced from the lilting voice, the flashing eyes, the weaving, red-tipped hands the words convey nothing of the fascination of her talk, but it was there, just as it is with little children whose unpredictable use of words renders their constant chatter more endurable than it would otherwise be. Actually Mrs. Lacey was anything but childlike, there was nothing of Dora Copperfield about *her*, nevertheless her manner of speaking, and her gaiety gave her a kind of authorized irresponsibility; you felt you could never blame her, or rely on her, or expect her to be anything except enchanting. That she most certainly was, and if other men than her husband found her attractive who can wonder? Or judge? People who have never driven a high-powered car don't know the temptation to speed, and people who have never had any charm are spared the temptation to exploit it.

The party broke up; all the guests save one married couple who were staying in the house, went away, and we separated until dinner-time which was at half past eight. I had a quick bath and put on my 'best' dress, a flowered voile, sober enough to be next summer's office wear. My sartorial unorthodoxy worried no one least of all me. I had come here on a job; I didn't move in circles where people 'dressed' for dinner, so why think about it?

The food was such I had never known; the conversation was of a kind equally new to me, light, amusing, trivial perhaps, but all informed by a kind of wit and grace and tolerance as delightful as they are rare in most people's experience. Afterwards Mr. Lacey – it still comes natural to me to think of him that way – took me and showed me the library where we were to work, the typewriter and the table which he hoped would be the right height. Then he walked with me to a pool where there were some water lilies which opened when the sun went down. They were fragrant, I remember, in a rather nasty way, like stale scent on clothes that have been shut in a cupboard for a long time. When we got back to the house a table for Bridge was set in the drawing-room. Mrs. Lacey asked if I played, because she would be delighted not to have to, she said; but she was plainly relieved when I said that I did not and that I was tired from the journey and would go to bed early. I did so, after another, gloating, more leisurely bath. At home our geyser went on a meter, sixpence a time and a shilling a week was honestly all I could spare in the interests of cleanliness.

The days that followed merge into one another in my memory. There was a good deal of correspondence to deal with and the Conference paper to prepare; then Mrs. Lacey asked me to help her send out a lot of notices about a Red Cross garden party she was giving in July. When I wasn't working I lolled about in the garden; the weather stayed lovely, June at its very best.

On the Friday morning Mr. Lacey said to me, 'Now Miss Benson, about the week-end. I want you to do exactly what you like. I don't suppose there'll be much opportunity for work, we shall have several people staying. On the other hand, if you do stay we might fit in an hour or two. Just as you like.'

I hadn't the slightest intention of going home unless I had to. Admittedly Mr. Hardistone had provided the fare – but he had also provided for taxis, to stay where I was and save the fare seemed to me as guiltless as heaving my suit case on a bus.

Also I knew that Jim would be home, so I should be sleeping with Mother and that had several disadvantages. The bedside lamp was on her side and she never read in bed, so I couldn't very well do so; she had too many blankets for my liking, and she snored. I said, very truly, that I should be glad to stay.

The new guests arrived on Friday afternoon and on the Saturday morning Mrs. Lacey took me by the arm and said, 'This evening, by miracle, we go out. We dine and dance at the Club, first time since Tom, poor man, is ill. And you must come, Miss Benson, because you will enjoy yourself, and to keep even numbers. We are having one man too much, you understand . . . But . . . here is difficulty. Is formal, the Club, on Saturdays. For men the black tie, for us . . .' she sketched an evening dress about her body. 'Is understandable, your formal stay home. You permit I should lend you a dress? Please! You are more tall but also more slim. Here and here . . .' she slapped her bosom and her bottom, 'you do not fill her out, so she falls to here.' She touched her knee. 'Also a hem it will not take me a minute to let down. With the needle I am like you with typewriter, much at home.'

I said, 'Actually I did bring an evening dress, at least a dinner dress, but it is my mother's and very unfashionable. I didn't mean to wear it unless I had to. Would you like to see it?'

'Is *good* idea,' she said. 'One thing I much enjoy is to see other women's dresses.' She took my arm again and came tripping along to my room. I brought out the dress and it looked very comic.

'Put her on,' she said. 'Is no good to hang a dress over the arm and say "Here is dress." Best dress in the world is nothing not having the body inside.' So I put it on and that is when she said, 'Oh, how you are pretty in that dress.' She also said, 'Is very latest style. All our eyes you knock out, eh?'

'If you are sure it will do . . .' I said.

'Do? Is beautiful. Is just like in a picture the name of which I forget.'

I could only hope to myself that it wasn't *Whistler's Mother*.

The Club was a large Tudor house with a beamed hall as large as a barn. There was a dance floor in the middle and tables with seductively shaded lamps on them all along the sides. The band was up in what had been the Minstrels' Gallery. It was all rather romantic. The place was crowded and the dinner seemed to go on for hours because we danced between the courses. Mr. Lacey declared that he did not intend to dance, thus reminding everyone of what they tended to forget – that he was still convalescent, and making me feel that I need not, really, have come at all; but I was glad that he hadn't said so before because I was enjoying it all so much. I was fond of dancing, and did it pretty well. Jim practised on me and taught me all the latest steps. Sometimes in his vacations we slipped away to the local Palais de Danse, where, if the clothes were informal and the manners unpolished, the band was excellent and the standard of dancing very high indeed. These excursions were kept secret from Mother, who, if she had known of them, would, I think, have had a fit.

Presently it was again my turn to sit out with Mr. Lacey. He gave me some champagne from the bottle in the ice-bucket and lit my cigarette and said:

'I do hope you're enjoying yourself, Miss Benson. I still feel a bit guilty about your week-end.'

I found myself, all at once, becoming garrulous and confidential. I began to tell him exactly how *much* I was enjoying all my stay, and how little missing the week-end meant to me. Perhaps fortunately for my self-respect this confession had not gone very far before I realized that his attention had left me. His eyes were following his wife around the room.

She was dancing with the man who had come unaccompanied. His name was Kingston, and during the war he had been in the Flying Corps and won a D.F.C. After the Russian Revolution he had fought on the 'White' side against the Bolsheviki, and when he got back to England he had written a short, angry book called *Ordered Home* in which he asserted that if his little group had not been recalled they could have turned the tide and altered world history. It had no literary merit but it said precisely what he wanted to say and it was very famous for a little while. He was handsome in a rugged, masculine way, and when, some years later, in his middle forties he suddenly went in for film work and became a star it didn't surprise me at all.

I stopped my silly chatter and began to watch too. They swung around at the corner and came towards us. Seconds before it happened I could see it coming and I began to plead, silently, in my mind— Don't *do* it! Not here! Wait, at least until you're round at the other side, out of his sight! But of course it happened. I saw his hand move between her shoulder-blades: his head came down, hers lifted, their arms tightened, and there they were, dancing in what I recognized as the real old Palais de Danse style, cheek to cheek, breast to breast, thigh to thigh.

I remember thinking to myself that the Puritans, in their dislike for dancing *had* a case, of a sort . . . it was a form of sexual stimulation . . . the music's excitement . . . the body's proximity. African drums, I thought. But it was nothing really; and I badly wanted to say something that would make it seem like nothing. But, of course, it just had to be ignored; in fact I pretended that I had spilt a drop of champagne on my skirt, and scrubbed away diligently with my handkerchief. I had, however, caught a glimpse of Mr. Lacey's face; down each side of his nose and around his lips it looked as though it had been brushed by a chalky finger. The sight hurt me, low down in my stomach where I had not known you could have a pain.

I was still hunting for something gay and careless to say when he stirred.

'I think I've sat here long enough,' he said. 'I feel like taking a turn. Miss Benson, may I have the pleasure of a dance with you?'

'Do you think you should?' I asked. 'After all you are . . .'

'*Malade imaginaire*. Come on, up you get . . .' He reached out a hand and pulled me to my feet. I realized then that he wasn't too steady; he'd been sitting there, drinking with each of us women in turn for quite a long time.

Then his arm went round me and I had to admit to myself something that I'd known for the last three or four days at least and refused for every reason in the world, to accept as knowledge. I loved him. I was hopelessly, helplessly, everlastingly in love. It had started when he took me by the elbow and led me along the terrace, trying to make everything easy for me, and it had gone on growing ever since. Everything he'd said or done since then had just added to my infatuation, added another shining layer to the tower of my dream. I was happily, I say *happily,* aware of the futility of this feeling; I knew that short of some cataclysmic event which would leave him the only man alive in the world and me the only woman, there was nothing that would make him see me as anything but an efficient typist with ginger hair and a long horse face. If I hadn't realized that Heaven knows what would have happened to me, frustration, misery, madness. As it was, I could accept the situation, and at the same time accept . . . well, all I was given.

Here we were, for instance, in one another's arms. I had *longed* to touch him, never dreamed of being able to do so, now here it was. All mine. I knew that I meant no more to him than I had to Mr. Hardistone that morning in the office; somebody to do some typing . . . somebody to dance with . . . no difference at all. I knew that Mr. Lacey had asked me to dance and was holding me a little closer than necessary because he was jealous of Mr. Kingston; he'd thought – I'll show her! And I just happened to be the nearest woman. Knowing all this made no difference to me; it didn't matter in the least. This was my moment, and I knew then that it would last me for ever.

He said, close to my ear, 'You know, you're very sweet.' And I tightened my fingers on his hand and said, 'So are you.' All the time some part of me stood away, detached from the rest and regarded him pityingly. You poor man, you poor, dear, nice man! She's got somebody famous and glamorous and desirable, and you have to take it out on your typist, plain Jean Benson, in her mother's dress. What a shame!

The music changed to a dreamy waltz and the lights began to vary, sweeping waves of different colours across the crowded floor; sometimes, between colours, it was almost dark. In one such interval he kissed me, and that was almost too much; I turned faint with adoration. Everything is a matter of comparison – what we put in a dustbin would be a feast to some starving Chinese. So it was with me. His kiss was idle, without real feeling, I knew that; but it gave me an opportunity to kiss him back with my whole heart on my lips.

Immediately after that I heard his breathing change and I said – I thought tactfully:

'I'm rather tired. I've danced a lot and I'm out of practice.'

He said, 'Now you're angry with me. Should I apologize?'

'Oh,' I said, 'never. Never. It's all been so perfect . . . so wonderful . . . But I do think we should stop now.'

So we sat down, not looking at one another for a moment. Then somebody joined us and it was all right.

And that, really, is all. Nothing else happened and nothing at all was said. During the next week he seemed to recover his wonderful energy and we worked very hard. It was understood that I was to leave on the Friday morning because Mr. and Mrs. Lacey were going away that week-end. On Thursday they went into Norwich and bought me a handbag which is still my best. It is made of crocodile leather, and has a matching purse and wallet, a silver compact and lipstick case and pencil. I expect she chose it.

On the Friday morning I got up early and went into the garden before breakfast as usual. That was always the most wonderful time, with the dew on everything, so fresh, so sparkling, so unbelievably lovely. I crossed the lawn and went down the grass path which ran between wide herbaceous borders, full of lupins, blue and pink, deep rose and salmon colour, and of sweet scented peonies. Behind them towered the tall delphiniums which would bloom when I was far away. It was a little like dying – this knowing that beauty would be there, unseen by you. I thought of Drinkwater again. Not sadly though; we all must die . . .

I came to my favourite spot of all, a rose garden enclosed by a close-clipped, dark green hedge. It had a sundial in the middle and stone paths radiating out, flanked by standard roses so old that they were taller than I was. Set between them, and in beds in the grass were bush roses. I walked about, feasting my eyes on dark velvety roses, pale shell-pink ones, waxen white and some coloured like apricots, all with their leaves washed clean and with drops of dew resting in the curves of their petals. Soon I should be on my way back to the dark, cramped flat, to the arid pavements, the tired, petrol-tainted air. But I didn't mind.

I looked at the sundial and thought about time. It's like a policeman, always moving us on. However much we have, and however long we have it, in the end we lose it. There is nothing permanent in this world except the impermanence. The thing is to have had some happiness, just once, and to have enjoyed it to the full, without reserve, or grudging, or regret. And I had done just that. I stood there and looked about me and I knew that all this beauty and my moment of love – better than years of marriage because *nobody* could go on feeling faint with joy on account of a kiss – was enough to last me for ever.

I was right, too. Nothing particularly pleasant has happened to me since. I never did get to France. Almost as soon as I got home Mother had to have a little operation and my twenty pounds saved her from the public ward that she dreaded; and later on I found that the driving force, the itch for self-advancement had gone out of me. So here I am, getting old, unmarried and perhaps – for self judgment in such matters is quite impossible – a bit cranky. The one thing I am *not* is pitiable. I've had everything!

FATHER FRANCISCO'S OINTMENT

SUNRISE, like sunset, was in these latitudes a sudden, almost momentary affair, and he who would take advantage of a comparatively cool hour must be up betimes. The earliest cock had hardly finished his first call when Father Francisco opened his door and stepped out into the light, now grey and rose flushed, soon to be brazen and pitiless.

His adobe hut was exactly like those of the villagers, but it boasted a better-tended, more conscientiously-watered garden, devoted entirely to vegetables and herbs. The little church was almost as humble as the hut, but larger and with its leaf-thatched roof surmounted by a wooden cross, disproportionately tall, so that often, in the windy season, it would blow over, bringing a portion of the roof with it. It was always replaced exactly as before, for it pleased the old man to think that the cross was a landmark, dominating the valley and easily visible from the higher ground.

Between the hut and the church lay the graveyard, many-mounded now, by the gathering in, over almost fifty-five years, of the dead from a wide area in a land where few people lived to be old. Father Francisco's eyes, still keen-sighted for all their seventy-nine years, surveyed his little world in the rapidly brightening light and were about to assure him that all was well when suddenly they narrowed. The wrinkles at their corners tightened, something like a frown marred the placidity of his brow. He began to walk, almost hurriedly, along the narrow dusty path which ran alongside the graveyard. Yes, it was true, his eyes had not deceived, nor the light tricked him; the fence had been moved; instead of running straight it now bulged so that the most recent grave, that of a man named Simon Pombo, which had lain on one side of it, now lay on the other. When he reached the spot Father Francisco could see the holes where the stakes had originally been, and a touch on the fence informed him that they were very insecure in their new places. The obvious explanation flowed into his mind; Simon had been buried only two days before, and his grave was very near the fence; the pressure of bodies had loosed the stakes and old Tomas, who was growing very blind, had made a bad job of replacing them. It was the work of a moment to uproot them and press them back into the proper position, and once that was done the graveyard lay as it had done for forty-three years, neatly divided into three portions, the one in which a grave cost two goats or the equivalent, the one in which one goat or its worth could buy you a place, and the one in which your bones could rest without any payment at all.

The division of the graveyard into three sections was a device upon which Father Francisco had often congratulated himself. When he had come, as a young man, to bring the Faith to this remote village everyone there had been bitterly poor, so poor that every year there were deaths from hunger. He had been poor too, had suffered with his neighbours; there had been years when he had subsisted on bread and what vegetables he could grow. Then, in the year 1910 things had changed; there was a rubber hunger in the world, and there were rubber trees in the forest; a collecting centre for the raw stuff was set up at what was then a mere fishing village forty miles down river. The local trees were not good, even then, so Father Francisco's Indians were spared the exploitation which happened in other places, but any man who could bother to go into the forest, bring out rubber and get it down to Majos could sell it, sell it for real coined money, the first that many of them had ever seen.

The young priest had tried to take advantage of changed circumstances and had begun to preach the virtues of charity. It was not understood; here where until lately everyone had been so poor, there was no habit, no tradition of charity. He had been obliged to stand by and see those able-bodied men who could go rubber hunting return to their village after a visit to Majos loaded with useless rubbish, tin watches without works, their hands painted at one unchanging hour, brass lamps which burned oil of which they had none, sleazy satin cushion-covers painted with gaudy flowers. One man had come back wearing a horse's collar as though it were a necklace. Infuriated that those who could not were still starving as before, Father Francisco put his wits to work. He had noticed that even those who were most callous towards the living could be tender towards the dead; a man might let his parents starve and then feast the whole village when one of them was buried, and that observation gave birth to his scheme. He divided the graveyard and fixed his scale of charges and his plan still worked though the poor rubber trees had long since been bled to death. The income thus raised was piteously small, but reasonably steady; a kind of snobbery made everyone anxious to bury their dead in the two-goat-or-its-equivalent enclosure. Father Francisco devoted every bit of the money to the welfare of his flock, buying flour for the old or widowed, condensed milk for undernourished babies, tools for anyone likely to make a little use of them and occasionally a pair of shoes for a boy who was set on going down-river to Majos to try his luck. He had also, over the years, spent considerable sums on the raw material required for his famous ointment.

It was of the ointment that he was thinking as he pushed home the last stake and straightened himself. It was time he made a new batch of it; the big vat was empty, cleaned out and awaiting replenishment and only one small jar was left on the shelf. He should have faced the task some days ago; he knew that, and knew also that his reluctance to do so was a sign of old age. He sighed, and then with a little self-admonitory shake of the head, proceeded with his morning's routine.

In the afternoon he set out to visit the widow, Maria Pombo. He carried a basket containing a scrawny fowl which had been given him during the morning, some vegetables from his garden and the last pot of ointment. Manuela, Maria's daughter was suffering from an unsightly rash, and although he hoped and believed that his last gift of oinment had already worked a cure it was as well to be prepared; also, with the last pot out of his house he would be compelled to get to work that evening.

Manuela herself met him at her mother's doorway and as soon as she had greeted him, pointed to her unblemished cheeks and forehead, her sad-expressioned Indian face lighting up with an amazingly bright smile. He thought once more that a smile on these dark melancholy faces was like the concentrated sunshine that sometimes breaks from the edge of a thunder cloud.

'That is good, very good,' he said. 'And your mother, how is she?'

'She is sad.'

'Naturally.'

'She is lame, also. Very lame of one foot.'

'Dear me. We must see what can be done about that.'

Maria was sitting on a stool and excused herself from rising which led him to believe that she was indeed much incapacitated. He noticed that she seemed nervous as well as miserable. Her eyes refused to meet his. He set down the basket and said:

'Now, show me the foot that hurts you.'

In all the years of his mission Father Francisco had never met an Indian who did not display with pleasurable pride any wound or sign of sickness. They bore pain with admirable fortitude but of its cause they made the greatest possible show. Yet now Maria, invited to give evidence of lameness, drew both her feet farther back under her skirt and seemed to shrink. When he insisted she hesitated again, as though not quite certain which foot to bring forward, and then, slowly, advanced the left one.

It had the straight, prehensile toes of a foot that has never known the confinement of shoes, the arch was firm, the skin unbroken and she did not flinch under his probing fingers. So far as he could see and feel there was nothing wrong with her foot at all.

The old man was wise. In civilized places doctors might be astonishing themselves by the discovery that distress of mind could lead to physical ills; Father Francisco in his backwater had known that for half a century. Setting the foot gently on the ground he said:

'Manuela must rub it with ointment, twice a day. It will soon be better.' Then he said, 'I wrote to Miguel, Maria. He should be on his way by now. He will look after you. At heart Miguel is a good boy.'

'Simon was a good man,' Maria said, and there was something almost aggressive, a challenge in her voice.

'Indubitably. A very good man,' the old priest said. Shiftless and slothful, like so many of them; but then one had to make allowances for the climate, for their ill-nourished bodies, their ignorance . . .

'Then why . . .' Maria began and broke off, pressing her hands to her mouth.

Father Francisco could complete that sentence without taking thought. *Then why did he have to die?* That was the agonized question he had been asked so often and he knew all the well-tried answers. He spent the next quarter of an hour repeating them for Maria's benefit and then, with a final cheerful mention of Miguel he took his leave.

He had not gone twenty paces before he remembered his basket and turned back. It did not surprise him to find Maria on her feet, moving with ease, with briskness even, as she put away his gifts; what did surprise him was that, at the sight of him she cried out and dropped the chicken. Then, wringing her hands and wailing loudly she ran towards him and went down at his feet.

Mingled with the wails and sobs were some words; at first a meaningless jumble about her wickedness and need for forgiveness and then something more coherent. She was not lame, she said, not lame at all, she had just pretended that in case he should guess.

He had always found visits to the bereaved the most exhausting of his duties and he had thought this one safely concluded, so it was with a sinking of the heart that he set about dealing with this fresh outbreak of emotion. He was very gentle, however.

'What was I not to guess, Maria? What are you hiding from me? Nothing very bad, I am sure.'

She checked her sobbing and raised her head; tears shone on her face and the wetness emphasized the flatness of its planes, its faintly simian look. 'Father, I moved the fence.'

Surprised again, mildly curious, he asked:

'And why did you do that?'

'He was a good man. I could not let him lie in Hell! On the night of his burying he came to me with reproaches. What, he asked, did I ever do to you that you should let me lie in Hell. So I did the one thing that I could do, Father. I moved the fence.'

He was still blind to the implication. Her words made no sense and it was possible that her grief had crazed her a little. He was again aware of an inward weariness.

'Get up, Maria,' he said, 'and sit on your stool. I will sit also. Now, try to tell me calmly what is troubling you. Simon was, as you say, a good man. And I have told you many times that Hell is for the wicked who are finally unrepentant. Why should you think that he is in Hell?'

For the first time she looked him full in the face and said with a deadly simplicity:

'Because I lacked the price of the goat.'

Like the first faint twinge of a pain that will grow and develop into agony by-and-by, suspicion began to stir in him. But this was incredible! How could he, even for a moment, entertain such an idea?

He said patiently, 'You lacked the price of a goat, Maria; the cost of a burial place on one side of the fence. Is that what you mean?' He could see by her face that this was what she did mean. 'Are you telling me that you believe that where a man's bones are laid has any effect upon the destination of his soul?'

'It is well known. That is why we wish to lay our dead in the part where the price is high, so that they may go straight to Heaven; or at the worst beyond the first fence, since there is hope in Purgatory.'

Father Francisco put up his veined old hand and held it for a second before his face as though some shocking sight confronted him. God help me, he thought; this is heresy . . . and I had regarded it as snobbery! He dropped his hand and said in an attempt at repudiation:

'Maria, you say "well-known", you say "we", but this is something that *you* yourself have imagined. Is that not so?'

'Everyone knows it,' she said. 'For two goats or their worth, Heaven; for one goat, Purgatory; no goat, Hell. Why else, Father, do the bereaved rob themselves? Why else do not all the dead lie where my Simon lay?'

Now he was certain, and the shock brought on one of the little dizzy spells which ordinarily only assailed him after long stooping over his plants. He was far more shocked than he would have been in the early days. Then every kind of superstition was rife; the old beliefs so often thrusting through to tangle with his new teaching that sometimes even he had despaired of ever separating them. But this woman, Maria Pombo, was a second-generation Christian whom he had baptized, to whom he had administered her first Communion, at whose wedding he had officiated and whose children he had, in their turn, baptized. He looked at her as though seeing her for the first time and noted the coarse lustreless hair, the dirty hands with their broken nails, the bare feet. He was aware too of the smell of her, compounded of sweat and wood smoke and a kind of animal femininity. A physical repulsion, once frequent and troublesome, long ago outgrown, seized him. He almost hated her, and understood for the first time the feelings of ancient potentates who, brought bad tidings, struck down the messenger. In a few words Maria Pombo had made nonsense of his life's work.

Years of self-discipline stood him in good stead and after a moment he was able to ask, gently:

'Maria, has anything that I have ever *said* led you to believe such a thing?'

'Your heart is too kind for such a saying. Also there is no need to say what is so well known to everyone.'

'But it is not true, Maria. There is no word of truth in it. When a man dies his soul falls into the hands of God and only God can judge him. To believe otherwise is wrong, wicked.'

'The fences . . .' she began. He interrupted her, and in short, simple words, explained why he had reared the fences in the first place, and how the whole village had benefited from the system. 'Even your Miguel,' he concluded, 'but for the burial price would have gone down to Majos barefoot and half naked like a boy from the jungle. Now do you understand?'

That question she did not answer. Instead she said, not argumentatively, but as a flat statement:

'So it may be. But it is taught that Our Blessed Lord, who was without sin, descended into Hell, and He was buried in a garden which is not the right place for burying.'

It was too much. A fresh wave of dizziness swept over him. The stink of her seemed to increase and thicken; he must get into the air or be sick. He rose unsteadily, and mumbling about none of it being true and that he would explain everything later, made his way out of the hut. Outside, despite the heat and the glare he felt some physical relief, though a new misery of spirit came to gnaw at him; in the crisis he had proved inadequate; he had run away! Blind, deaf and complacent, and now a deserter!

II

He moved more swiftly, more clumsily than usual, kicking up little clouds of dust which rose and settled on his hat and his worn old soutane. A few young children, playing in a narrow strip of shade rose as he approached and waited for his greeting. So strong is habit that he slowed down, and then, with a dismissive wave of the hand shot forward again. He had caught sight of little Juanita, standing lop-sidedly because for the last year her left leg had not kept pace with the growth of her right. He would now never be able to send her down the river to the hospital; in future cripples must remain crippled and the hungry must live with their hunger. His little income had been the price of heresy, and heresy must be rooted out.

He was tempted to go straight into the church, where it was cooler and where some comfort might await him, but he put that temptation aside. He went into the graveyard, to the first stake of the first fence and pulled it up, and then next, and the next. It was hard work, the stakes had been firmly driven in the first place and many seasons of rain and baking sunshine had cemented them into their holes. Sweat streamed from him as he worked and his breath came in little shallow gasps. Now and again he turned dizzy and was obliged to rest for a moment, but by sunset every stake had been uprooted and the fences lay flat on the dusty ground. Old Thomas could break them up and collect them in the morning; they would make good firewood. Moving slowly and stiffly, Father Francisco entered the church.

It was dark when he emerged. His face had the drained, exhausted calm of convalescence; the worst was over now. He had reached for and found the comfort he sought. He had faced his failure squarely and recognized his fault; he had given too much attention to material things, to trivialities like condensed milk, and footwear, and flour. The world had got the upper hand with him and he was grateful that Maria Pombo had pointed out the danger before it was too late. He was ready to begin again.

The first task to hand was the making of the fresh batch of ointment. That in itself might be classed as a material concern, but there was no profit attached to it, he always gave it away and the labour of its making would serve two purposes, it would distract his mind, and, since he was so near exhaustion, serve as a discipline. He rolled up his sleeves, pinned a ragged towel about his waist, set his big wooden tub on the table, found his smooth-worn beating stick, and collected his materials, the twice-refined fat, the two-year-old honey, the dried powdered mandrake and meillot.

The finished product was known for miles up and down both sides of the river simply as Father Francisco's Ointment. In many other places, made by other hands, it had other names.

Everywhere it was recognized as a panacea for everything except mortal illness or broken bones. Father Franscico had learned how to make it in his seminary, in far-away Pamplona where the recipe had been cherished and handed down through many generations. The secret lay in the making and like many trade secrets consisted largely of sheer hard work. The mixture had to be beaten continuously for two hours, no light work, since in an early stage it became as sticky as putty. After the beating it was set aside and the honey hardened again to lend the whole a firm consistency.

In his early days Father Francisco had seen with concern a tendency amongst his patients to eat the concoction; fat and honey he knew to be harmless, more nourishing and tasty than many things the Indians ate, about the mandrake and meillot he was not sure, but he consulted a Herbal and learned that mandrake was an efficient stimulant for the bowel and meillot not listed as poisonous, so the ointment was used internally as well as externally and many wonderful cures were claimed for it.

He tried to think about the cures as he beat the sticky mass; they at least were something positive, though it was humiliating – no, not humiliating, *sad* – to think that a life's work, fifty-five years of lonely exile should result in . . . No, that was no way to think. This was a new beginning; it must be made cheerfully. Think of something heartening! He changed the stick from his right to his left hand; at least he still could beat ointment; he was old, but he was active. And look what he had survived; a broken leg when a mule dropped dead under him; a snakebite; uncountable bouts of fever, four near escapes from drowning. But all to what end? That Maria Pombo should say . . .

He changed hands again and ventured to look at the cheap tin clock. It must be wrong! Only twenty minutes, and he seemed to have been beating for hours. He remembered that in the seminary, though the Infirmarian was old, there were always young strong arms to do the beating . . . how he wished . . .

Someone knocked on the door. Father Francisco called 'Come in,' and when the door opened stared for a moment, not recognizing his visitor. Then he dropped the stick and stretched out both hands.

'Miguel, my boy! I knew you would come. Oh, how ever so glad I am to see you!'

'I came as soon as I could,' the young Indian said.

'I was sorry to send such sad news. But your father made a good end, Miguel, and is now safe with God.'

The boy said nothing; he just stood, mid-way between the table and the door, his dark face inscrutable. Father Francisco glanced at the clock.

'If I had known you would come tonight I would not have started this, but having begun I must go on without pause. Sit down Miguel. Tell me all your news and speak loudly because with this some noise is unavoidable.'

There had been a time when Miguel Pombo had been delighted to help with anything; he had often beaten the ointment, straining his puny strength, proud to be entrusted. Father Franscisco would not have been surprised if he had now said, 'Let me,' and taken the stick. But he did not; nor did he sit down.

Over the tub the old man regarded him. Just like all the boys who went down to Majos he had wasted a good deal of money. He wore a suit of mauvish colour, too wide in the shoulder, too pinched in at the waist, a pink shirt, silk? yes, a pink silk shirt, a painted tie, yellow shoes with pointed toes, a wrist-watch on a wide metal band, a tie-pin with a red stone, a ring that matched it; and he had a fountain pen clipped to his breast pocket. It's like a uniform, the old man thought; but one shouldn't criticize, they are young, inexperienced, very ignorant . . .

'There is food in the cupboard, Miguel.'

'I have eaten, thank you.'

The stiff restraint, the unfriendliness of his manner could no longer be ignored.

'Well, don't just stand there, Miguel,' said Father Francisco in a voice made tetchy by the aching of his arms and shoulders. 'Sit down. Or, if you want to be useful, blow up the fire and make some coffee. You know where to find things. Everything *here* is just the same.' He heard his own sharp tone, regretted it and added in a more genial voice, 'Yes, make coffee. It will be like old times, you and I, drinking coffee together, eh?'

The hoped for response did not come, but the boy moved, laid a handful of sticks on the dormant charcoal of the little stove and plied the bellows. He set the smoke-blackened, long-spouted pot on the brightening fire, watched it for a moment and then straightened up, placed one hand in his pocket and came nearer, so that he stood on the opposite side of the table.

'Father,' he said, and the old man realized that it was the

first time he had addressed him in that way; and even now there was a faint challenge in the word.

'Yes, Miguel, I am listening.'

'I wish you to know,' the boy said in a wooden voice, as though saying aloud something often rehearsed in silence, 'that I speak now for my mother, not for myself. I know that a dead man is a dead man and that where his bones lie is without consequence. Indeed in Majos I have heard tell of men blown to small pieces who have no grave at all. But my mother is an ignorant woman and she believes as they all believe that for lack of the price of a goat a man's soul can go to damnation. Her heart is sore and to all explanations her ears are deaf. Therefore,' he drew his hand out of his pocket and held it forward, full of silver coins, 'will you take this and allow the fence to remain where my mother moved it, so that she may think that my father is in Purgatory?'

For the second time that day Father Francisco knew near-hatred; this time it took a dangerous form. He longed to lift the stick and strike Miguel Pombo. Hit him on the padded shoulders of that ridiculous suit, spatter the mauve stuff with sticky ointment. He longed to cry – This is what I have had to contend with! If you had done your duty and sent money home instead of decking yourself out like a popinjay this situation would never have arisen; your mother could have paid the price and Juanita could have gone to the hospital!

Ah, but then he would never have known the false beliefs stalking the village. Was he resenting enlightenment? God forgive me, he prayed, and stuck the stick upright in the ointment.

'Put away your money,' he said, 'your mother will need all the help you can give her. And you may tell her that the fences are down. I have had many painful experiences, Miguel, but never one to equal this afternoon's when your mother told me what she believed. Even had it been a harmless thing it would still have seemed dreadful to me that a belief, any belief, should have been held and I not be aware of it. Your mother said that everyone believed that the divisions had significance and in my first despair I believed her, but I am now recovered and hope that it is not true.'

Without knowing it he looked at the boy hopefully. The reassurance he sought was not forthcoming.

'I do not know one person who does not so believe – in the village, in all the villages. I also . . . until I went to Majos and found no fences in the graveyard. I have spoken to men from other places who knew of no fences. And it has seemed to me a strange thing that you, so gentle with the living should be so harsh towards the dead.'

The coffee boiled. Miguel poured the black bitter brew into two thick white cups and held one towards the priest who took it and sat down. The batch of ointment would be ruined, but what did that matter?

'If I seemed so,' he began, 'it is because you, all of you, are so much the other way. Did you, Miguel Pombo, care whether your parents had bread for their mouths? How much have you spent on yourself, needlessly, wastefully. *Now* you come home and pull out your silver and take on yourself to rebuke me for harshness.' He saw Miguel's dark face take on the sullen look which all Indians assumed when rebuked. Modifying his tone, the old man repeated what he had told Maria that afternoon, the reason for his making the divisions, the good that had resulted. He ended with what was, in spite of everything, still uppermost in his mind, 'For no other boy can I do what I did for you, Miguel; Juanita will limp all her life . . .' a new and horrible thought struck him, 'even my ointment; the fat costs money nowadays, the honey too . . .' He broke off and stared with stricken eyes at the big tub. This might be the last batch of ointment that he would ever make.

Miguel said, 'In Majos, Father, one must work hard for little money, and a good appearance is essential. My father could have worked harder than he did; why should I support him? My mother, of course, I shall care for.'

The old man seemed not to be listening. He sat, holding the coffee cup between his thin hands and staring at the tub of ointment.

'Manuela tells me that lately the spots on her face were so thick that she was ashamed to be seen,' Miguel said in a different tone.

'They were unsightly.'

'And your ointment cured them.'

'So it would seem.' He looked at the boy. In Indians, he had discovered, the feeling of sympathy with the sufferings of others was rudimentary, almost non-existent, but in Miguel's last words he seemed to detect a desire to cheer, to direct attention to that one of his activities for which success could be claimed.

'A thought has come to me,' Miguel said. 'In Majos there are many women, many with spots on their faces, and many more, who though their faces are smooth are always looking for means to improve them. I think that an ointment which could do what yours has done for Manuela would sell very readily in the town.'

'That is possible; but it is a long journey. I have no time to peddle ointment in Majos, Miguel.'

'That would be my part. I would sell it.'

'How could you do that? Relinquish a certain, profitable employment, spend two thirds of your time going up and down the river? That is foolishness.'

'When I came home this time,' Miguel said, 'it was for the last time in the old way. Next week the motor boat arrives. The journey will then be nothing. Already I have promised my mother that every Saturday I shall sleep at home. Every Sunday when I return I could take the ointment with me.' Enthusiasm lightened his face. 'I know where to begin. There is a girl who sells the tickets for the cinema show; a pretty girl but much disfigured by spots. To her I shall *give* the ointment and she will be cured and everyone will ask how and she will say – It is a secret known only to Miguel Pombo. Ha! And that shall be its name when I begin to sell it. Secret. A short name, Father, is best, easy to remember and to pass on. In one week I could make you more money than the fences gave you in a year!'

'A rash promise. How much then do you think you could sell?'

'Twice that amount in a week, at the beginning. Later more, much more.'

'This for me is a month's supply,' said Father Francisco.

'But it is many years now since you were in Majos. Every day there are more people, they are thicker than fleas on a dog. Every day I shall sit in the café near the cinema and sell Secret.'

'You must not neglect your own work, Miguel.'

'In the evening I will do it.' At least to start with, he thought; but already the dream was forming. At its heart sat Miguel Pombo in a cool shady office, smoking a large cigar and checking over thousands of orders for Secret. He saw it packed in small pink pots with the name in bright blue letters across the lid.

'I suppose we could try it,' Father Francisco said. He thought that Miguel over-rated his abilities as a salesman and naturally enough, being a country boy, the population of the town. Still, if he sold a *little*, just enough to pay for the raw materials of the next batch.

'We will try it,' he said in a more positive voice.

Miguel rose.

'I will return now and make my mother happy. I must go back to work tomorrow and I will take the ointment with me.' Words of the new language of commerce rang in his mind, words like 'costs', 'profits', 'commission' and 'percentage', but it was not, he decided, a language that Father Francisco would understand. The old man would make the ointment and have, for his labour, enough money for his simple charities; the rest would go to Miguel Pombo who had had the idea, who would sell, and advertise and organize ... He took his leave with all the old affectionate respect and went away.

When he had gone Father Francisco looked at the clock. Two hours' continuous beating had been the rule he had been taught and to which he had adhered. The best thing to do now, he decided, was to ignore that wasted twenty minutes and begin again. Hc braced himself, rolled back a sleeve which had loosened, and took up the stick. Soon his shoulders were aching, his fingers cramped about the stick; he sought relief in his thoughts. His mind had never taken easily to mysticism but tonight it seemed to him that it was possible that it was for this that he had first noticed Miguel Pombo, cultivated his intelligence, taught him a little and helped him down to Majos. It was possible that when God shut one door He opened another. It would be wonderful if this new venture succeeded; it would be ... He realized suddenly that if it did succeed he had engaged himself to perform, twice a week, a task which lately he had found exhausting to perform once a month. Sweat made his hands so wet that the one holding the stick slipped. He looked into a future that consisted solely of beating ointment, beating, beating; twice a week for two hours on end without pause. Then he saw, beyond the labour, the fruits of it; bags of flour, tins of condensed milk, little Juanita able to run and jump like the rest. God give me strength for this new task, he prayed, wiped his free hand on the towel, transferred the stick to it and went on beating with renewed vigour.

THE GOOD MEMORY

THE gentleman from England was not expected until eleven o'clock, but Gertrud began her preparations in good time. The very old, like the very young, were capable of putting up considerable opposition to any change in their routine. Fortunately the old woman had wakened in a good mood and eaten her breakfast with enjoyment.

Trouble started when Gertrud entered the room carrying an armful of fresh linen for the bed.

'And what are you about *now*?' the great-grandmother demanded in a surprisingly vigorous voice. 'Am I to die today that you bring out the best linen? Even so, one is not laid out beforehand. Put it back.'

The pinched patient look which in the last year had begun to mark Gertrud's ordinarily amiable face, deepened.

'But this is the day when the gentleman from England who is staying in Anna's gasthaus is coming to visit you, Great-grandmamma.'

'I know that. It is news to me that he comes to inspect my bed-linen. And you would do better to kill a goose and cook it. Any poor man who eats at Anna's table will be hungry. She never could cook.'

Ordinarily – and the old woman knew it – Gertrud could be easily provoked into taking up arms on Anna's behalf. She waited for the swift retort that all Anna's guests were appreciative of the food served at the guesthouse, and that many of them wrote letters which said so. And she had the answer to that, all ready on the tip of her tongue.

This morning, however, Gertrud did not take up the challenge.

'Anna has provided the gentleman with a picnic lunch. She did not wish to make me more work, she said.'

'Then he may eat his lunch, and he may make his visit; but

the linen my grandmother wove with her own hands goes back in the chest. You understand me?'

Gertrud, knowing that a more vital issue would shortly be at stake, replaced the linen and brought out other, fresh and white, but of inferior quality and remade the bed. That done she fetched brush and comb.

Despite her great age – she would be a hundred if she lived two months more – the old woman still had hair, glitteringly silver, thanks to Gertrud's care, and growing back in pretty waves from her forehead and over her ears. Anxious now to smooth down a temper ruffled by the dispute over the bed-linen, Gertrud said:

'Your hair is still lovely.'

'And why? Because it was never cut. You will live to see, Gertrud, that all these women who cut their hair will go bald, just as men do. I observed when Anna made her last visit – which is longer ago than is right – her hair was growing thin. To be sure she does her best to hide it, frizzing it out in waves and curls, but I could see. My sight is good.'

'Your sight is excellent.' It was fact that she often regretted, but she stated it heartily now; anything to promote good temper.

'And I can hear. And my memory is good. But for my fall – and that could have happened to anyone – I should now be as active as my grandmother. I have spoken to you of her. She could remember the Battle of Austerlitz and she once walked many miles to see Napoleon. To the end of her day she could describe him; ill-favoured, she said, small and pale and pot-bellied. She was a wonderful woman.'

Memories of her grandmother carried her happily through the hairdressing. Gertrud took away the brush and comb and came back to the bed, holding in her hands the shawl which Anna had knitted and given to the great-grandmother as a Christmas present last year. It was a beautiful shawl, made of white wool, knitted in a lacy pattern but with a plain, more solid border all embroidered with tiny flowers in bright colours. When it was presented the old woman had pretended to be pleased with it, though expressing surprise that Anna *could* knit; but she had stubbornly refused to wear it. It was, she said, a silly colour. It would soil easily and then Gertrud would wash it, and the colours would certainly run. She had two good shawls, one brown and one grey, so this could be laid away – but carefully, mind, with plenty of lavender and rosemary to keep away the moths.

Now, watching Gertrud fold it into a double triangle, she was about to protest, to order it back into the chest, when the worn machinery of her mind slipped a cog. Eighty-three years slid away. Dressing up to compete with Amalia . . . It was silly, but one always did it. Amalia was invariably decorated like a shrine at Eastertide, and no man could keep his eyes off her. They didn't marry her, oh no! Men had their weak moments, but they managed to keep their wits about them, and in the end they married sensible girls who could cook and sew and do a day's work in the fields. But . . . there had been a time when even Franz had been dazzled by Amalia. Oh, the tears I shed in secret; and oh, how sweetly I revenged myself. I dressed up and took from her the one man who *might* have married her. Karl didn't care what he ate, or what he wore and he had no field, he would have married Amalia, but for me. So, when I married Franz, as I always intended to do, he went away. And years later, when all the songs and verses he made were gathered into a book, it was not to Amalia that he sent it. It was to me. And I was so sick, as a woman should be if her child is to be healthy, that I couldn't see to read . . . but it was to me he sent it . . .

Gertrud had finished arranging the shawl, and stepping back, admired the effect. Her great-grandmother looked well cared for, did her great credit. It was natural, after all, to desire something to show for a year's work and self-sacrifice. Gertrud had been very happy working in a kindergarten in Innsbruck when confronted by an uncompromisable choice – other people's children or your own great-grandmother who had broken her thigh slipping on an ice-covered path and whose bones were too old to knit properly. A year, stuck away here in a mountain village had seemed very long, the work she did unrewarding. But now, by a curious chance, the light of public notice had fallen upon the old woman, and would reflect upon Gertrud. The gentleman from England would surely, in mere justice, put into his book that the woman, the one woman who remembered Karl Hertzog, was well-tended by her great-granddaughter.

'I want my book,' the old woman said.

'But you gave it to Anna,' Gertrud said. 'You remember.

When Anna started her gasthaus you said she could take anything she liked out of the parlour. It was nothing to do with me; it was all years ago.'

'It is not very likely that I should ask you how I should dispose of my own belongings, Gertrud. Anna, silly as she is with her frizzled hair and her airs and graces is your elder sister. I gave her my parlour furniture – which I never used – to help her earn an honest living. It is not for you to reproach me. When I die you will have everything else. But Anna shouldn't have taken the book. I set great store by that.'

It wasn't true. Anna had given Gertrud an account of the episode and Anna had never, to Gertrud's knowledge, told a lie. Anna's husband had been killed in the war, and she had started a guesthouse to support herself and her three children, and the great-grandmother had said, 'To help with the furnishing you may have everything in my parlour. I never sit there nowadays.' So Anna had come up the mountain with a cart and the furniture had been loaded on to it. The book, a china figure and a glass bell had laid together on the top of a painted cupboard, and Anna had said, 'What about the book?' and the old woman had said, 'If it helps to furnish your house take it. It was written by a very foolish young man and is connected with something I would rather forget than remember.' So Anna had taken it.

And now, years later, along had come this Englishman, and had picked up the book and read the inscription, and mentioned it to Anna, who had said that the book had belonged to her great-grandmother who, in her youth, had known Karl Hertzog. And the Englishman had become very much excited, because nowadays Karl Hertzog was extremely famous, and nothing, absolutely nothing was known about his early life. He'd lived in a Hamburg slum, drunk, dissolute, published this one small book of poems and died. Anna said that at the mention of a living person who remembered Karl Hertzog the Englishman had acted as though he had discovered a gold-mine.

Gertrud said, 'I dare say that when the Englishman comes he will bring the book. It's about the book that he is coming to talk to you. You remember? About the book, and about Karl, when he was a young man.'

'I remember. And I can tell him enough to fill his ears. The book, Gertrud, must remain here. If Anna can afford to have her hair waved and curled she can afford to buy a book for her own parlour.'

Gertrud nodded agreement, looking at the shrivelled little body in the big bed, with its neatly arranged hair, and pretty shawl. It was difficult to believe that great-grandmamma had ever been the central figure of a romance, should have broken a young man's heart, and yet inspired him to write poetry. But that was what Anna had written:

'My English gentleman seemed astonished that I had never read the verses. I made time to do so, of course, as soon as he explained that they were all written to, or about, our great-grandmamma. I understood at once what she meant by saying the book was concerned with something she did not wish to remember. She, who always appears so straitlaced and speaks so censoriously. If half of what these verses hint at is true she was anything but straitlaced when young; and if they are not true, how dare he send her the book?'

Like most of Anna's comments, that was shrewd and down-to-earth. One of the reasons why Gertrud was so fond of Anna was that Anna saw things clearly and spoke frankly. Anna was the one member of the family who saw Gertrud's sacrifice for what it was, and admitted that tending an old, old woman, however venerable, however admirable, could be heavy, thankless work.

Gertrud said, 'Now I will go down and make everything tidy, and get ready the coffee. Even though Anna has packed food for the gentleman, I thought he would welcome some coffee.'

'If it is made properly,' said the old woman, dryly. 'I have said before, and I say again, there is no body to your coffee, Gertrud. To make good coffee one must *use* coffee!'

Gertrud might have retorted that she had said before and could now say again, that the price of coffee had risen fantastically. Four times, in this one year, the price had increased.

'I will try to make the coffee to your liking,' she said meekly. 'And you . . .' she hesitated, because the next words might be taken amiss, 'you will try to remember everything about Karl Hertzog, to tell the gentleman.'

'I do not have to try. I remember everything about Karl. My memory is good.'

When one is old and bedridden what other escape is there save through the door of memory? She slipped through it with ease; and her hair was black and thick and shining, her foot light in the flowery meadows. She was seventeen years old and after harvest she was going to marry Franz, the only son of the most well-to-do farmer in the village. When spring came in that year, bringing the first flowers her future had stretched out, sunny, flawless, ordinary. Then the innkeeper's wife had fallen ill and her niece, Amalia, had come from somewhere on the other side of the mountain, to help with the work. Amalia wasn't even very pretty, but there was something about her, about the way she walked, and laughed and spoke and looked at you; in less than a week every woman in the village knew that Amalia was 'bad', and every man knew that she was irresistible. Even steady Franz ... During that month there were more bitter words spoken, more tears shed in the village than ever before in a year. The weather grew fine and the mud that followed the melting of the snow, dried out, and a gang of tree-fellers came to camp and work in the forest above the meadows. One of them, a young giant with red hair seemed to be exactly Amalia's match; they were a pair, alike in their recklessness, their disregard for the opinion of others and in their attractiveness ...

Even now, after all these years something stirred within the frame of the old woman on the bed as she remembered Karl ... She had taken him from Amalia to avenge herself because Franz's allegiance had wavered. Reason enough, was it not? A good reason? Yes. But not the whole. No, not the whole. There had been mad moments during that summer, moments when Karl with his foot-loose talk had made life in the village, all the years of the future going on in their predictable fashion, seem unbearably dull; moments when Karl's kisses – taken in secret, for she was always very careful – had made marriage with good steady Franz seem impossible. That summer revealed to her a wild streak in her nature, something she had never suspected.

Good sense conquered in the end. The tree-felling was finished. Karl had no notion where he would go, what he would do next. He said, 'I'll find something, I always do.' He said, 'Come with me.' He said, 'I love you as I never expected to love any girl.' But she thought of the winter coming, of the snug farmhouse. One day there would be children, and children needed a settled home, security.

I chose rightly, the old woman thought to herself, just as she had thought for thousands of nights, settling herself for sleep in the soft goose-feather bed, close by snoring Franz. And, as on those thousands of nights the thought was soothing. Her chin fell forward on to the folds of the white shawl; her eyelids drooped.

She woke when Gertrud and the gentleman from England came into the room. Gertrud carried the coffee tray and the gentleman had a book in his hand. He looked and moved as though he were in church. He was in fact awed; this was only a degree less wonderful than coming face to face with the Dark Lady of the Sonnets. At the back of his mind something said teasingly and repeatedly, 'And did you once see Shelley plain?'

He walked in that reverent way towards the bed, told her his name, said how honoured he was to be received by her. Her faded blue eyes met his with complete incomprehension and then turned towards Gertrud. She would have something to say to *her* later on! At least once a day the girl did something quite infuriating but never before had she dared to bring a complete stranger upstairs, into her very bedroom.

Gertrud saw the glance and understood it in part.

'You remember, Great-grandmamma. Mr. Ransome is the gentleman from England who has come to hear all that you remember about Karl Hertzog.'

'Of course I remember,' the old woman said sharply. It would never do to admit that her memory was failing; that sometimes – as now – the fog came down, blotting out everything except immediate things. 'I have a good memory.'

'That is what I have been saying,' said Gertrud.

'Anything that you can recall about him as a young man,' said the gentleman, 'would be so very welcome. You see, it was not until many years after his death that his work was recognized. Virtually nothing is known of him.'

'You said Karl?'

The gentleman nodded, smiling.

She made an effort. Once again the worn cogs of her mind were set in motion, almost engaged, failed. Karl. Karl. One of her own sons had born that name, and one of *his*. It was a common name. Which Karl did they mean? And what did they want to know about him? What was there to say about somebody called Karl? The blankness of her own mind filled her with terror; for the first time in many years she had a desire to cry. She wanted to cry and say – I am a very old woman, I can't remember anything. You shouldn't bother me! But if she said that, in Gertrud's hearing, she would lose all power for ever.

She groped in the fog of senility baffled, lost, but not yet entirely defeated. Karl, they said. That would be a man then. And there was one thing you could safely say about any man. She said it, looking from one face to another with an air of triumph.

'He was very fond of Sauerkraut,' she said.

THE SPELL BINDERS

I HAD known Walter Barnwell for seven or eight years and we were, in a curious, negative kind of way, friends, though neither of us could have said why. I thought he was dull and pompous, spoiled by always having had things too easy; and he thought I was flippant and cynical and deserved to end where I had – teaching classics at a small and undistinguished prep. school.

It seemed strange that any kind of friendship should have developed and been maintained between us, but propinquity, as has been observed before, is a powerful thing. Walter came into my orbit when one of his aunts – a sour old besom who lived in a house on the edge of the school grounds, and who wrote regular letters complaining of the noise the boys made – died and left him her house. He came down to dispose of her effects, fell in love with the house, which was a gem of the Queen Anne period, and decided to come and live in it, with his collections of china and glass.

Once installed, he found himself stranded. He hadn't been there long before he bought – in a London sale which was reported in the papers, a Bow clock, quite indescribably beautiful. He showed it to Mrs. Hannet-Stokes – the social leader of the neighbourhood and she spoke for all her set when she said:

'But Mr. Barnwell, for that money you could have bought a really good hunter!'

I chanced to meet the poor little man when he was feeling lonely and discouraged. I displayed – and it was unfeigned – an interest in, an admiration for, all the beautiful things he had gathered together. So, though disapproving, he clung to me as to a rock in a weary land. I, for my part, was damned glad to go, two or three times a month, and eat one of his superb dinners, drink his good wines and his brandy, bask in the warmth of his heaped log fires, and look at all his treasures. My inevitable envy was pleasantly mitigated by a kind of contempt. He was so dull; nothing amused him. My life was hard, disgusting, frustrating, sometimes intolerable, but I could, almost always, amuse myself.

Walter's house, though it gave an illusion of spaciousness, was not, in fact, over-large, and he had, wisely, before moving in, spent a great deal of money upon central heating and having it well modernized, so it was easy to run. He had an outside man who did the garden, cleaned the car and carried in fuel; he had a housekeeper named Mrs. Missell, a grim-faced old Tartar, but a wonderful cook, and he had also, for a number of years, a house-parlourmaid named Annie. Quite a bit of the mild kind of prejudice which built up against him was due, to tell the truth, to his managing to *keep* an indoor staff of two. Nobody else, for miles around, could do that. He didn't hunt, he wasn't married, and he collected china, ivory, jade, he had *two* women servants. There *must* be something wrong somewhere.

Nothing was wrong with Walter in fact things were too good with him until Easter of the year 1955 when Annie received a most unexpected proposal from the milkman. They were married three weeks later and public opinion was outraged by the ease with which Annie was replaced by another girl named Florence. What was even more shocking was that in July Walter actually sacked Florence; she had been insolent to Mrs. Missell; (she should have had a George Medal at least), and she had broken, by careless dusting, the delicate fingers of a Dresden figure. Florence was followed by Ada, Rosa, a German named Erma, an Italian named Maria, a Swede named Margarita and two more English girls. They in turn qualified for George Medals, and worked havoc with the Dresden, the Chelsea, the Lowestoft, not to mention the Bristol glass.

'But what is really serious,' Walter said to me when I dined with him one evening late in November of 1955 on the eve of yet another departure, 'is that Mrs. Missell is becoming unsettled by all these comings and goings. She actually said to me this morning – and I have never been so taken aback in all my life – she said that unless we soon found some steady and reliable girl she would find this all too much for her. Fred, I am becoming desperate.'

'There just aren't girls to be found,' I said. I brought him up to date with the labour situation. I described the shifts and straits to which we at the school had been reduced, the Head's wife's evening efforts with what should have been, what might so easily have been, the last supper, the boys' bed-making and washing up.

'But that,' said Walter, 'is where you are wrong. There are plenty of girls about. I have had eight since April and it is now November. No, Fred, the fault lies in the girls; in their *attitude.*'

He had a genius for stating the obvious.

'All right then,' I agreed, 'it's their attitude. It comes to the same thing in the end.'

He brooded for a moment and then gave me the first surprise our long acquaintanceship had ever afforded.

'What is Pedlar's Plaster?'

'It might mean anything,' I said. 'I've only read about it in one sense – the common dock leaf. Pedlars, you see, suffered from an occupational disease, sore feet, and a nice cool dock leaf put over a blister or a raw spot would afford some relief.'

'You are sure about that?'

'About the relief? No, I never had occasion to try it.'

'About the name?'

'Oh yes,' I said. 'I can remember two references off-hand. In Balmain's *Herbal* and a book called *Pedlars and Packmen.* The dock leaf was known by, and for all I know, still may be called, by that name.'

'Then I'll show you something.' He got up and went to his bookshelves. 'I was, on one occasion, driving through Halesworth in Suffolk,' he said. 'And there was a sale, so I looked in, and there, shoved aside with the rubbish, was a Bible box – you've seen my Bible box? I got it for five shillings. The auctioneer didn't know his job at all. He hadn't even looked inside. There were several little things, none of them valuable, but curious and interesting. And there was *this.*'

He held out to me a very small book, bound in leather which had cracked and peeled. A shabby thing, quite unlike the rest of his treasures. I would have taken it, but he drew it back, sat down in his chair and turned the pages.

'Look at that,' he said.

It had a musty reek. The pages were yellowed, spotted with brown. The print was thick, uneven and badly aligned. A very old book indeed. Instinctively I looked at the front pages. It was undated. I turned back to the page which Walter had indicated and read:

'How to Catch a Virgin and Bend Her to Your Service.'

I glanced through the instructions and then I laughed.

'What fun this sounds! So simple, too. Do try it, Walter; one day when I have some time off. I would love to see you come home followed by a virgin "amenable and meek". Like Mary's little lamb.'

'I intend to,' he said solemnly. 'I was merely waiting to identify Pedlar's Plaster.'

I flicked over a page.

'And when you've brought this one off, here's another. A beauty. "How to Raise a Crop of Warts upon the Countenance of an Enemy." *I'm* tempted to try that on the Head.'

'You are, as usual, flippant.'

'Nonsense amuses me.'

'How do you know it is nonsense?'

I had the perfect answer to that. 'If there were anything in it,' I said, 'the institution of Holy Matrimony would have died out within a fortnight of this book's publication.'

He was not amused; he took the book from me, rather crossly, I thought.

'Mind you,' I said teasingly, 'you'll have to go carefully about this dabbing ointment on girls. You might find yourself up for assault!'

'But you'll be with me. You just said so.'

'You regard my company as a guarantee of respectability? Thank you, Walter. Just let me know when you finish your brew.'

I went back to school and gave the joke no more thought until, about ten days later, the Head played his recurrent trick of shoving an extra evening's duty on me. How nice it would be, I reflected, to raise a crop of warts on that smug countenance. I'm afraid that the thought made me accept the imposition with something less than my usual rancour. He looked quite surprised.

A day or two after that Walter telephoned me. He suggested picking me up at half past six and taking me to dine at a club to which he belonged in Talbridgeworth. He'd made his magic ointment – he showed it to me, a greenish paste; he carried it in one of those delightful little silver and enamel snuff-boxes.

He'd picked the girl, too; she was a waitress at the club. As we entered I said, rather aptly, I thought, 'Lay on, Macduff!'

We went into the bar, and Walter, who ordinarily drank sherry before dinner and was fussy about it, chose whisky, to my delight; and he drank three, so I guessed he was bracing himself. In the dining-room he refused a table near the fire, and chose another in a less favoured place. I soon saw the point of that. We had no sooner seated ourselves than up came the waitress, and my respect for Walter's acumen rose. It wasn't only about china that he was knowledgeable. This girl, whose name was Muriel, *could*, I thought, only have been a success in Wells' Country of the Blind, or the Polar winter when it is dark for twenty-four hours a day. She was fat and shapeless, she had a squint and no forehead, a receding chin and prominent teeth.

She said amiably:

'Good evening, Mr. Barnwell,' and proffered the menu.

Walter said, 'Good evening Muriel,' and drawing his hand from his pocket, took the menu. I watched carefully and saw that the 'touch' had been successful. While we decided what to eat Muriel studied the base of her thumb, thoughtfully licked it and rubbed it on her apron. When she went towards the service door I said:

'Well done, Walter!'

Nothing happened however. All through the meal I amused myself by imagining improbable situations, always assuming that the spell had worked. How embarrassed Walter would be! We lingered over the meal, and then over coffee and brandy, allowing time for the magic to 'take'. But there was no reaction at all.

'I would hardly have believed it, would you?' Walter said solemnly, as we walked, unaccompanied, unfollowed, to the car park.

'I still don't,' I said. 'Either you didn't make it right, or it's a phony recipe.'

'No. I have noticed that almost every girl, in her middle teens, has some attractiveness, however plain she is going to be later. Just a blush of youth as it were.'

'Then you must try a younger subject.'

'I intend to,' he said. 'Incidentally Mrs. Missell mentioned leaving again today. I have no time to waste.' He looked at his watch. 'It's too late to see a film, but I have an excuse . . .' He started the car and steered for the cinema.

The main film was well under way and the usherettes were standing gossiping softly at the back of the foyer. Recently an attempt to brighten up the place had been made and had included dressing the girls in page-boy uniforms, very natty; tight straight trousers, tight braided jackets and little pill box hats. It is a juvenile style; all the same, the girl for whom Walter made a bee-line couldn't have been more than sixteen. An older girl, who was on the outside of the group, turned and looked at us inquiringly, but Walter showed his mettle.

'It's this young lady I want to have a word with,' he said, indicating the girl of his choice. To her he said, 'I think you showed me into my seat last Thursday evening. I wonder if you noticed that I dropped a glove?'

She said in a prim, automatic way. 'All lost property is collected by the cleaners and taken to the manager's office where it can be reclaimed.'

All the other girls nodded a confirmation of that.

'Thank you so much,' Walter said heartily. 'And where is the office?'

'Up the stairs, first landing, second door.'

'Thank you,' he said again; and taking his hand from his pocket he pressed half a crown into hers.

'You're welcome,' she said, and turned back to her friends.

We mounted the stairs and Walter looked, slowly, seriously, through a box of curious objects which the manager obligingly produced. There were at least two dozen gloves, paired or single, there was a mass of worthless trinkets, strings of beads, rings, bracelets; and three cigarette lighters, one of them a good one.

'People are very careless,' said the manager.

'Gosh,' I said, 'there's my lighter! I've hunted everywhere. I never thought of asking here.'

'Which one?' he asked, without interest.

'That,' I said, indicating the good one. He handed it to me and I cuddled it in my hand.

'Dear old friend,' I said, 'how I have missed you!'

'No,' said Walter, regretfully, 'I don't see my glove here.'

We slowly descended the stairs. Within the cinema the story, judging by the noise, was reaching its climax. The usherettes, though still gossiping, were alerted. Walter gave his intended prey a wistful look and received a stony stare.

Outside he said, 'Perfectly scandalous! A girl of that age!'

'Anyway,' I said. 'I've got a . . . my lighter back.'

It would be tedious to tell in detail every move in this campaign, which, even to me, soon ceased to be even mildly amusing and became a bore. There was one bright spot. Walter, under pressure from Mrs. Missell became desperate and bold enough to venture forth alone in his search. He boarded a bus one day, and touched a likely looking subject who dealt him a backhander which broke his upper denture. None of his other attempts met with any response at all. The autumn term ended, Christmas came and went.

It was January and school had started again when Walter invited me to dinner.

'It'll be the last time that I can offer you any entertainment I'm afraid. Mrs. Missell has given notice.'

'I am sorry to hear that,' I said, and there was genuine regret in my voice. Goodbye to those snug little dinners.

Walter's failure had depressed him so much that I hadn't the heart to say 'I told you so,' when he said, dolefully:

'Well, so much for magic. And so much for the womanhood of England. Would you believe that my own niece, my sister Hilda's child . . . still at school . . . I tried her in the holidays. It really is disgraceful.'

I said, in an attempt to be just:

'You can't blame both, Walter. It seems to me just another proof that magic and spell-binding are all nonsense.'

'I've tried, in all, thirty-two.' He took the little snuff-box and dropped it into the waste-paper basket.

'Hi,' I said, 'don't throw out the baby with the bath water. It's a pleasant little box, valuable, too.'

'I never want to see it again.'

'Then if I may,' I said, retrieving it. 'It will make an elegant container for my aspirin.' In my job the aspirin consumption is above average. I put the box in my pocket.

At the school all doors were locked, promptly, at ten o'clock; the Head, or the master on duty saw to that. Inside the side door was a board, with several hooks, and on those hooks were three spare keys to the Yale lock of that door. If a master, or the Matron, was off duty and expected to be later than ten, he or she took a key and stuck on its hook a piece of card bearing his or her name. When the key was replaced the piece of card was put in an old nib box on the window-sill.

On the evening of this dismal dinner with Walter I walked back to school, arriving just as the clock struck eleven. Matron had been out and had returned just before me and was standing by the door, wrestling with her key. As soon as she saw me she voiced a complaint which I had heard before.

'This key is faulty. Nine times out of ten it gives me trouble.'

'It's Freudian,' I explained. 'Your subconscious shirks the idea of returning to this place of wrath and tears.'

She gave me the sniff and the look, so eloquent of disapproval.

'You try it, then,' she said, and stood back.

I gave the key the little extra push it needed, and turned it. The door opened and she walked in ahead of me. I gave her her key, by which she could reclaim her piece of cardboard, and then hung up my own.

'Good night, Matron,' I said civilly. I was almost at the foot of the stairs when she called me, keeping her voice low.

'Mr. Summers, it's such a cold night. I'm going to make myself a cup of cocoa. Would you like some?'

I was, actually, in no need of cocoa, but I make it a practice never to refuse anything. So I turned and followed her into the kitchen, and smoked a cigarette while she made the cocoa, using, I noticed with approval, all milk and no water. We sat down on opposite sides of the big scrubbed table, and I looked at her, consciously, for the first time. In her uniform she was simply 'Matron', solid, well starched and corseted, level-headed, hygienic, slightly awe-inspiring. Out of uniform she much resembled a policewoman in plain clothes. She had reddish hair and the raw-looking complexion which so often accompanies it, her eyes were a hard pale blue and her eyelashes almost white.

As we drank our innocuous but illicit nightcap she leaned forward so that her solid bosom touched the table.

'You've got a button loose on that coat,' she said. 'If you give it to me in the morning I'll sew it on for you.'

'That's very kind,' I said. It was also surprising. She was prone to pointing out the self-evident fact that she had only one pair of hands, that little boys couldn't be expected to do things for themselves but that adult males must expect no coddling.

'I've often wondered about you, you know, Mr. Summers,' she went on. 'You seem to me far too good and clever to be stuck in a place like this. You should have a school of your own.'

'Then for once we are of the same opinion.'

'Why don't you start one, or buy one?'

'For the same reason, I imagine, that you don't buy a mink coat.'

I expected anger; but she laughed, looking down at the rubbed, lustreless fur of her beaver lamb.

'I could have a mink coat if I wanted one,' she said. 'But mink would be wasted on me. I intend to do something sensible and constructive with my money.'

'You have money?'

'A nest egg,' she said modestly.

'Nice for you. Well, thanks for the cocoa.'

'And don't forget that button,' she said.

I swear, by all that I hold holy – though what that might be I should find hard to say – that I had no suspicion as to what had happened. I even forgot to take advantage of the offer to fix my button, but next day, when I went to my room I found it sewn on, and what is more, my suit had been sponged and pressed. At bedtime I threw myself into bed as usual, and practically bounced out again; my sagging, springless mattress, worn hollow by the pressure of many weary bodies, had been replaced by a brand new Sleep-Tite, very buoyant. I might have been more startled by this replacement had it not been so long overdue, a quarter of a century to put it charitably. I hoped that some poor slob, master or boy, was feeling similarly pleased with my old one, for mine had been far from the worst in the establishment.

Two days later I had a mild sniffle. It was a bitterly cold day, and I was due for duty on the football field. I was viewing this prospect with distaste, but with fortitude when Matron announced:

'Mr. Summers is incubating a really nasty cold. A couple of days in bed for him *now* will save a heap of trouble later on.' I was, again, somewhat surprised, but the surprise was swallowed up in relief. I retired to my comfortable Sleep-Tite and watched, with great pleasure, a few snowflakes drift idly down.

Truth, as they say, is great and cannot be hid. Truth began to dawn on me when, at the end of my second day in bed, Matron herself brought up my supper tray. In one corner of it was a tiny glass vase of sweet dark violets. There was clear soup in a covered cup, and in one of those double plates, kept heated by hot water (where had she found that Victorian relic?) some breast of chicken in white sauce, new potatoes well-buttered, and fresh, defrosted peas.

She laid this oblation on my knees and said:

'And you don't have the Head or his wife to thank for that! I went into town – this is my free day, you know – and did the shopping myself.'

Then I knew. Nothing but magic could account for this. At some time during his thirty-two experiments Walter had smeared some of the paste on the outside of the box, I had touched it, and in handing Matron her key I had, all unwittingly, worked the spell. Dreamily sipping the soup I looked into a future not lacking in comfort; good matrons are as rare as good parlourmaids and wield great power. Sheltered under Matron's banner who dared touched me, criticize or impose upon me? No one can say that my expectations were anything but modest . . .

'I've been thinking,' she said, 'about our conversation the other evening. You remember? About your having a school of your own. I cut this out of the paper . . .'

I took the clipping. While I read it she watched me with the intent, pathetically earnest expression of a well-meaning dog which has done its best and hopes for a word of praise. The clipping concerned a prep. school, for sale 'on account of ill-health', as they invariably are, and no wonder. It sounded stylish and prosperous, and was expensive; but half the price could remain on mortage.

'Would it do?' Matron asked.

'Do for what?'

'Us.' She blushed furiously. 'You see . . . I thought, you and I, between us . . . You're wasted here, really, and my money is just waiting. I mean, I'd like a place of my own but I'm not clever enough alone. With you . . .'

'It needs careful thinking over,' I said. 'Tell me, why pick on me? Bates is younger and handles boys well, Thomas has a better degree. Why me?'

She looked confused.

'Instinct, I suppose. At least partly. And then you're so clever. It came over me the other evening when you mentioned Freud and my not wanting, in my subconscious, to come back here. You see it was so *true*; but I hadn't realized it. Then it struck me, just like lightning.'

'Well,' I said, 'that seems a slender reason for taking such a risk. But I'll think it over, if that's what you really want.'

'Oh, I do. That's all I want in the world, Mr. Summers – to do something for you.'

'Now look,' I said sternly, 'let's start off on the right foot. You're doing nothing for me. Let that be understood. I'm taking on, to please you, a great deal more work and responsibility; I'm not taking on any obligation as well.'

'Oh no, no. Of course not.' She sounded horrified. 'I didn't mean it that way at all. I only meant that if we went into partnership I should be able to look after you, see that you didn't work too hard, and had decent food, and so on. As for obligation, why, you know very well, Mr. Summers, it would be the other way round. I should be indebted to you all my life.'

That sounded more like it. I glanced at the cutting again.

'Broadstairs – very nice. You'd like me to investigate this?'

'If only you would.'

I do not usually indulge in day-dreams, but I did, for a second or two, visualize the scene in which I told the Head that I was going to have a school of my own. That would move him little, chaps like me are ten a penny. It would be when I said that Matron was coming with me . . . Much worse than a crop of warts! That brought my mind back to poor old Walter.

'Give me my dressing-gown,' I said. 'I want to make a telephone call.'

'You can do that from my room. I have an extension in case of illness, you know.'

She helped me into my dressing-gown, found my slippers, and then, supporting me tenderly, but stoutly, led me to her room. I dismissed her and gave Walter's number. When he answered me, in a very dispirited voice, I said:

'Make a new batch, old man, and try again. They're hard to come by, but my word, when it works, it's wonderful!'

'It's too late. You see, I remembered what you said about Holy Matrimony, Fred. I've just asked Mrs. Missell to marry me.'

'Ah well,' I said, 'that's nearly as good. Best of luck. Walter.'

Laughing heartily I went back to bed.

A GIFT FOR A QUEEN

THE girls had gone joyfully and noisily about the task entrusted to them by their schoolmaster, and as hut after hut bloomed into gaiety under their hands their excitement had increased until it was like intoxication, but when they approached the hut that stood a little apart from the rest they ceased their chattering and began to move quietly.

The afternoon sun cast a small shadow in front of the hut, and there, in his doorway, the old man had fallen asleep, the bone from which he had been grubbing the last succulent crumbs of marrow still clasped in his skinny hands. His head, which nowadays seemed so much too big for his body lolled forward as though the thin, stringy neck had at last given up the task of holding it upright.

All the girls were relieved to find him thus for the old man's fearsome reputation had outlived his activities by several decades; one of them – his great-grand-daughter – was delighted as well as relieved. It was one of her duties to visit him every day, bringing food and fetching water for him, and she knew exactly how difficult he could be. He was deaf, more than a little blind and slightly astray in his wits, but none of his infirmities could be relied upon. Every now and then, when one least expected it, he could hear well enough to be angered by what was said, see well enough to aim a blow with precision, and think with enough clarity to phrase a hurtful remark. Earlier in the day, when she paid her routine visit she had tried to prepare him for this one, but he had been very deaf just then, understanding nothing, muttering angrily and reaching for his stick. Back in the village she had tried to dissuade the girls from coming at all, but the schoolmaster had said, 'every hut'; and then she had tried to excuse herself from being one of the party, whereupon her mother had called her undutiful and threatened to box her ears.

Now she saw that if they were swift and careful, and lucky,

they might get away before he woke to ask awkward questions, slash about with his stick if the answers displeased him and address her in front of her companions by the many-syllabled African name which she detested – with good reason – and which no one but he used nowadays.

Moving quietly, now and again suppressing the giggles which the very secrecy of their doings evoked, the girls decorated the hut. They hung a string of small triangular pennants, red, white and blue, along the edge of the thatch. The great-grand-daughter climbed upon the petrol can which served the old man for a water pot, and poised there, planted a small Union Jack. That done, the girls drew away a little, admiring their work and whispering together. The great favour, the very special thing, had not yet been put in place. Only six of the pretty pictures had been included in the parcel and for five of them priority of claim had been easily established; the sixth had been a matter of some dispute which the schoolmaster had settled, with arbitrary tact by saying that it should go to the oldest man in the village.

Nobody knew the age of the old man, his life reached back to a time when no one heeded such reckonings; sometimes when his mind was clear he claimed to remember conditions and events so strange that they sounded as though they had been part of a completely different world. The schoolmaster – combining arithmetic with history – had one day said that if the old man were speaking the truth when he said that he remembered the coming of the white man, he must be ninety-three years old. A great age, indeed. But, said the schoolmaster, ever careful of detail, it might not be true; some old people recounted as their own memories things they had heard from their elders. Of one thing there was no doubt, this was the oldest man in the village and the sixth picture was his due. The great-grand-daughter considered it a sorry waste.

Carefully avoiding contact with the old man they fixed the picture just above his doorway; and that disturbed him; he woke and was apparently in full possession of his senses. He recognized his great-grand-daughter and demanded to know what was afoot. She told him exactly what she had tried to tell him earlier in the day.

'Show me,' he said, and reached out his hands so that they could pull him to his feet. He turned and regarded their handiwork and the great-grand-daughter held her breath. One of two things would happen now; he would become angry and order them to remove all that rubbish, or he would begin to ramble on about another Queen, the one that only old people remembered and they must stand, first on one foot, then on the other, and hear out the tedious tale, since to do otherwise would be disrespectful to elders.

The old man cupped his hands about his eyes, glanced at the flag and the bunting and then stared at the picture.

'She is very young,' he said at last.

'And beautiful,' one of the girls ventured.

'*I* am speaking,' he said crushingly. 'She is very young; but the other was young too, as I remember. Young enough to take the advice of her old men, which is the only way of wisdom for the young. It is to be hoped that this one has wise old men about her.' He dropped his hands and turned to them suddenly:

'Show me the gift.'

The great-grand-daughter sighed and fidgeted. Of course, it was too much to expect that he should remain sensible for more than a minute. A girl more bold and less experienced said:

'The picture is the gift. There were six only and you have one because ...'

'Stupid child of stupid parents,' he said. 'I mean the gift to the Queen for her Crowning. What do we send? What gift do the people of this village send to the young Queen? Answer me!'

'There is no gift.'

The great-grand-daughter took a hasty backward step. Now he would be angry. But again he surprised her. In their hollow sockets his eyes slid about in a crafty, knowing way. They were lying, of course; naturally there was a gift, and he had not been asked to contribute, either because they had forgotten, or because they considered him too poor. That was the kind of thing that happened when you were too old to ply your trade and too feeble to mix with your fellows. It was shameful.

'Go away,' he said; and the girls went willingly, breaking into squeals of laughter as soon as they were at a safe distance.

The old man sat down just where he was and stared at his decorated hut. Old memories moved in him powerfully; the dim twilight of senility lifted and lightened. He could remember three Crownings, best of all he could remember something rarer, Jubilee. They had sent a gift then, a stool all made of native woods, cunningly laid together and richly carved, a stool upon which the great Queen, Victoria, could sit while she dealt out justice or listened to the advice of her old wise men. He had been a rich man then, a man of great substance and importance, he had contributed two cows to the cost of the stool, two good cows. Now, because he was poor and old . . . it was shameful!

He sat there while the shadows of his hut grew and stretched out until it engulfed him. The little sunset breeze sprang up and ruffled the pennants and the flag. He could remember the first of its kind he had ever seen; it had had great significance then, for where that flag flew the slave-traders never came. He remembered another thing, too – the flag was never left out all night; that was a rule. Nobody in those days would have planted the flag on the roof of a hut, out of an old man's reach and gone away and left it there. Ignorant, they were all ignorant nowadays, despite the schoolmaster. Well, about the flag he could do nothing; but about the gift, he could. They'd see! He would give her such a present, that pretty young Queen, that beside it all other presents would look like rubbish, like nothing.

Next morning, when his great-grand-daughter came to bring him his daily dole of food and to fill his water-pot she found him busy with something in the corner of his hut; he was muttering away to himself and she hoped to escape his notice. But he said, sharply:

'Little-Wind-Before-The-Thunder, stay where you are.' He turned, keeping his body between her and whatever it was that he had been messing about with. 'Never mind the water; there is enough for today; I have other work for you. I need a new gourd, one that has never been used for any purpose; I need four white stones; I need a forked stick, freshly broken and peeled; also seven hairs from a black goat and a chicken, alive.'

She stood still, a little astonished, a little worried, running the list off on her fingers, very far from denying his requests, but not as instantly acquiescent as he thought she should be.

'You will bring me what I need, Little-Wind-Before-The-Thunder and you will bring it secretly. Otherwise I shall put a curse on you and every hair on your head, every tooth in your mouth will drop out. That I swear. Who, then, will marry you?'

'But a *chicken,*' she protested. Everything else was easy, though her father's black goat would probably butt her.

'A chicken, alive,' the old man said firmly. 'Can you no longer run as fast as a fowl, sitting all day on a bench in the school? Your hair and your teeth shall be the price. Say over to me what it is I have asked you.'

Already her scalp felt uneasy, she ran her tongue around her teeth. She repeated the list of his requirements.

'Within an hour, Little-Wind-Before-The-Thunder,' he said, bringing out the name with malice.

'Within an hour,' she said meekly, wondering what the schoolmaster would say, wondering about the goat's temper, wondering whose chicken . . .

But she was back, within the hour. The old man met her at the door and took the things from her without thanks. He stood there until she had gone and then stepped outside and looked up at the picture of the young Queen.

'All will be well,' he told her. 'I will make you a gift. I am old and I am poor and they laugh nowadays when I say what I can do. I have no cow, but my mind has its skill and my hand its cunning. It will be a good gift.'

With the slow movement of the old, the brittle-boned, he went back into his hut and hung a mat over the door. He set to work, doing for love the things he had done in bygone years for heavy payment, ah, the high-rumped cows, the goats, the good knives, the blocks of salt he earned . . .

Outside the sun mounted; the white hot light poured down on the baked earth, the dwindling river, the water-hungry land of Africa. Inside the hut, in the stifling semi-darkness the old witch-doctor worked away, making for Elizabeth the Second the best gift it was in his power to give.

Presently, in far-away London the rain came down and the waiting people put up their umbrellas.